The Parting Gift

Other books by Robert Mendelsohn
published by Prion

The Long Journey Back
The Red Pagoda
The Hibiscus Trail
Clash of Honour
Footsteps on a Drum

The Parting Gift

Robert Mendelsohn

First published 2000 by
Prion Books Limited,
Imperial Works, Perren Street,
London NW5 3ED
www.prionbooks.com

A catalogue record for this book is available from the British
Library

ISBN 1-85375-377-7

Cover design by Bob Eames
Printed in Great Britain by
Creative Print & Design, Wales

For David

Chapter One

The last time I saw him was two days before he disappeared.

By then I had got to know him well. Well enough to recognize the foot-dragging sound of his walk long before anyone knew he was coming. I'd imagine the curt yet quiet growl of his voice. It would ring in my ears well ahead of his arrival and linger hours after he was gone. Perhaps it was fear or that itch of apprehension you get under your collar when you deal with the unknown. I did not look forward to his visits but I needed him.

He was not a rude man exactly, but he had the knack of upsetting people. Other than asking for me he never greeted anyone and made no small-talk. He never made an appointment and always demanded to see me as soon as he turned up. He had become a kind of out-of-favour fixture in my office, like an old filing cabinet or a disused lamp. Behind my back no one paid him any attention. He seemed a cheerless, pitiful figure, way beyond any help or redemption. The kind of man people keep away from. Yet from the first I knew he was going to make me a fortune so I stuck it out.

Not all lawyers are greedy, but I was in the throes of a particularly heavy separation that was fast leading to divorce, and I needed the money. I would have done anything to have avoided this, because I love my estranged wife more than life. I have to admit it was all my fault. I had made a terrible mistake that had hurt her. She kicked me out and served an injunction on me. I could not even leave the country, and as this man's case required the services of a detective rather than those of a legal mind I was in trouble. That was just one complication this new client had thrown on my table. There were more.

To start with, he did not talk much, and when he did he

spoke only Spanish. I used to have a good command of that language. I had learned it in my youth when my English father took me with him on his holidays to the island of Mallorca. I had forgotten most of it, and at the beginning I suggested employing an interpreter, but he wouldn't have anyone listening to him but me. Secrecy, he insisted, was the key to his trust. If any of it was to come out, he would drop me immediately. He said that quietly, without a hint of a threat, and then he started talking. He spoke slowly, with an even voice that gave nothing away except clues for which I was expected to find the answers. It was, all of it, hugely mystifying. I became obsessed with trying to understand each and every remark he made, as though my life depended on it. I dug deep and managed to scoop those Spanish words out of my past and soon I was able to converse with him. I caught myself making great efforts and wasn't quite sure why. Perhaps it was the eerie fascination I found in the complicated saga this drab-looking man was unfolding for me. Perhaps it was just curiosity. Whatever it was, I got myself thoroughly involved with what he said and failed to anticipate the emotional trap he was setting for me.

He was a strange man and had incredible problems, yet he was the most patient individual I have ever met. Whenever I was busy he'd sit in the waiting-room for hours. If there were too many people there he'd wait in the corridor, outside the office. He was a painfully shy man, and even though he stood out there for ever he never asked for anything. Not even a glass of water. He did not read or smoke or talk to anyone, and I cannot imagine what he did with all that time. I suppose he learned patience during the long years he had spent in jail.

There was something about him that made you feel uncomfortable. I am not sure whether it was the way he looked or the secretive pitch of his speech; it could have been the way he had of looking over his shoulder when we spoke, or the threatening tone of his voice whenever he was lying. He was an emaciated, tall man who walked with a stoop. There was none of that happy-go-lucky, open manner you'd expect in people from his part of the world. No exotic rhythm in his gestures. He had coal-black hair, strong black eyes, and the whitest skin you ever saw. It seemed as if he had never seen the sun although he had lived in the tropics all his life. You were never sure what he was thinking; his sombre expression scarcely altered. Maybe it was because he never looked you in the eye.

Superficially he was harmless, but my secretary was frightened of him. She said he had the demeanour of a third world police torturer. I could well understand the way she felt. Often, when he was asking questions, I had the feeling he knew the answers better than me. Sometimes it was more than a feeling. Sometimes I was certain he knew much more than he let on. I must admit I felt almost touched by evil after every session, and yet I could never have enough of him. There was no logic in this at all. Not then, at the beginning, when he came to see me almost daily. On the contrary. I would often try to keep him in my office longer than necessary without knowing what the attraction was.

Maybe it was pity. Maybe I kept trying to please him because nothing seemed to make him happy. His clear dissatisfaction with my efforts kept me going. Maybe I hated him to start with, but not for long. There are few mysteries in life, and by the time I understood the reason for my growing affection for him, it was all too late.

* * *

Cuba. That was where he had come from. I had not realized there were any Jews left on the island after Castro came to power. He did not want to live in Israel and did not like us or our way of life, but he had nowhere else to go. Immigrants to this country are encouraged to learn Hebrew and are usually consigned a place in which to live, and if they are qualified they are given a job. If not, they are offered training. I pointed all this out to him but he was not interested and his lethargy whenever I broached the subject made this very clear. He did not make any effort to settle. Perhaps he did not intend to stay alive long enough.

It became obvious that he hated capitalism and business and despised money, yet it was money that had brought him to me in the first place. You did not need to be a great psychologist to see that he carried an unbearable weight on his shoulders. There was a heaviness, a darkness born of some deep-seated injury in the way he looked, the way he moved and behind every word he spoke. But he did not open up and I did not prod. He talked incessantly about his father, although he clearly detested him. He said very little about himself.

His name was Alex Moreno. He made it clear there was no need for me to know much about him or his former life. It had nothing to do with our business. What really mattered was his father's bizarre past. It promised to bring me close to fulfilling the greatest dream a man ever had, and I wasn't going to let that out of my grasp. No one throws a winning lottery ticket away.

He'd spend hours with me. Sometimes he'd be quiet and I'd stare into his enigmatic eyes and wait for words that never came. Sometimes he'd pour the story out non-stop, like a waterfall. He always ended our talks abruptly. Usually in mid-sentence, mine or his, he'd get up and leave without a word. Not a single thank you or goodbye or I'll see you again. I had to be nice to him if I wanted to achieve my ambitions, and I suspect he knew this. He used my greed and that shamed me. Perhaps this was the source of the bad taste in my mouth each time he left the office.

He never told me where he was staying or how to contact him, even though we both knew he would always be back. Always, until that last time. By then my suspicions and trepidation had turned into love because I had solved the puzzle of the man and understood my own part in his life. A part that was going to shock me into forgetting where we had begun and change the way I looked at life for ever.

To start with I did not have to go far. To verify whether or not some of what he had told me was true only required a three-hour drive north, to the ancient village of Rosh Pina in the upper Galilee. Not to the place itself, but the old cemetery.

Chapter Two

There is something peaceful about a cemetery when there is no funeral in progress. I saw serene cypress trees, soaring in silence over proud squads of black granite. I saw rows of flower beds and sniffed freshly cut grass, and the air was still. Yet the calm harmony of this resting place did not last. The old man who stood by the iron gate accosted me as soon as I walked inside. He was broad-shouldered and strong and had a full head of silvery hair. He smelled of cheap soap and his clothes were simple but in good repair. His wise face was creased by years in the sun although his green eyes had the inquisitive, energetic gaze of a youth. I must have been confused for I put my hand in my pocket to look for small change, but he shook his head.

'I was not looking for charity,' he said.

'I am sorry. I thought...'

'You thought...What did you think? You thought I was a beggar?'

'No. I don't know what I thought. Maybe...'

'Do I know you?'

'I don't think so... no.'

'You look familiar.'

'I have never been here before.'

'Well, there's no harm in asking, is there? Did you come to visit someone?'

'Just looking.'

He regarded me carefully and said:

'You are from a city... Haifa perhaps?'

'No. Tel Aviv. How did you know?'

'You have soft hands. I can see you are not a farmer. We worked hard here fifty years ago… clearing rocks and planting. No one works any more. They have machines… or they hire outside labour. People who come in the morning and work and get paid and then at night they go. A man must sleep near his earth to have roots. No. No one works now... my son had soft hands too. He was an air force pilot. He is here. I can show you where he lies.'

'I am sorry.'

'At my age a man knows more people under the ground than over it.'

'Have you lived here long?'

'I was born in the village,' he said with pride. 'My father and mother and my wife are up here too. My brother died in America. My sister lives down the road in Tiberias, with my daughter, but we don't meet much.'

'I am sorry.'

'You keep saying you are sorry. Is it because of where we are? There is nothing sad about this place. It's nice to come here. You can walk among the stones and read about people who once lived and worked and talked and married and made love. Of course, I know every one of them, but even if you don't it can be an interesting day out. You walk around and you read what it says on the stone and you try and guess what they were like…'

'You really know everybody here?'

'Oh, sure. My people were among the first families to settle on this hill. Sure I know the people up here. If not in person I would have known the family. At least those who lived here when I was a boy. It was a small place when I was young. What is your name?'

I told him.

'My name is Daniel Katz. People call me Danny.'

It was too young a nickname for a senior citizen. I gave him my hand and he shook it. His grip was warm and strong.

'Did you know Abraham Moreno?'

'Moreno? There is no Moreno here.'

'I'd say he lived here in the twenties... just after the First World War.'

'No Moreno. You won't find a Moreno here...'

'No. He's not buried here. I thought maybe someone else... maybe his family...'

'You will not find anyone called Moreno up here.'

'He may have changed his name...'

'What was it before?'

'I don't know. Could have been anything. Moreno means obscure... dark... it can mean black. Yes... Black is Schwartz in German. Was there a Schwartz in the village? He would have emigrated. Late twenties. Maybe 1928 or 1929...'

A glint of recognition flashed across the old man's eyes.

'Yes,' he said, 'I know the one. Abraham Schwartz. Went to Brazil to look for gold.'

'What happened to him?'

'I don't know. Wait... No, that wasn't why Schwartz left... He had to go because of something he'd done. I don't remember what it was. Some scandal. Something bad. Or even worse... someone died I think. I don't remember. It'll come back to me. You know how it is. When you get old, you don't lose your memory, you lose control over it.'

'I know what you mean.'

'You couldn't possibly know what I mean. Not at your age.'

'Did you know Abraham Schwartz?'

'Sure I did. He was maybe four or five years older than me. Of course, five years is a long time when you're a child but I knew him. I knew him well.'

'What was he like?'

'Was? Is he dead?'

'I think he is.'

'Ah, well. What was he like? He was a strong boy... muscular. He had a full, unruly head of black hair and soft, beautiful blue eyes. He was a good talker and he was brave.

All the women loved him. What was he like? He was tall too. As tall as you, I would say. He even looked a bit like you. He was very good-looking and wild, almost savage… And he could talk and when he did people listened to him. He didn't like school but he liked the girls. Those were different times, you know. You didn't go around with women the way you youngsters do today. I mean, there were morals, religion. There was a tradition of chastity and people waited until they got married. But after they were married, well, things changed for some…if you were that way inclined. Most women were too busy working the fields and cooking and cleaning and bearing children. In that way women were equal to men. This was a hard country in those days and the life we led treated women the same as men. No …perhaps they were not just equal. Women were perhaps... yes, women were more than men. If anything, they had more tenacity…more depth…more staying power. All in all they worked harder, in the fields and in the house, and when they had babies they didn't linger in bed for weeks. They would take the infants out to the yard with them. They too died of malaria and carried guns and…'

'What was Abraham Schwartz like? Was he…'

'I'm trying to tell you. He was restless. The village was too small for him. The Galilee was too small for him. I think the country was too small for him. He would have left anyway, even if 1929 and the hard times had passed us by. The crisis was only an excuse. You know, Schwartz was a sort of legend in his own lifetime. After he'd left there were rumours. The kind of rumours you'd expect in a small place like this. People saw him… oh they saw him all over the place. They said he'd become rich and powerful. He was seen in Cairo, Beirut…I remember someone saying they saw him in Spain... years later, during the Civil War. I don't believe that at all, personally, but this was what was said. You see, I knew he couldn't have been there because I was in Spain myself then, between 1936 and 1937, and I didn't see him.'

'What did you go to Spain for?'

'To fight for the Republic... I went there with a group of German students I met while I was living in Paris. I hung around with one in particular, an art student called Hans. We were best friends. He gave me a few of his canvases but they were destroyed. Yes, Hans. We went everywhere together. We joined the Thaeleman Battalion and the other Germans who had gone out there to fight for freedom. They were special, and not only because they had come to fight. They were brave because once they had gone to Spain they could not go back to Germany. Not as long as it was run by the Nazis. And in 1936 it looked like the Nazis were going to run Germany for ever.

'The battalion fought very fiercely and suffered a lot of casualties. Those men who did not die went to Russia and some of them became big shots in East Germany after the war. But not Hans. He and I joined up with a company of Spanish men and women and we spent almost a year with them. That was where I learned to speak Spanish like a native. Our fighting days ended at the Battle of Teruel when the Republicans lost the war. After the Fascists came to power Hans got together with one of our comrades, a girl from Catalonia who took him to her village and hid him there while Franco hunted his enemies down. Hans survived the purges, remained in Spain and became a Spaniard. But that is another story and you want to know about Abraham.

'If Abraham Schwartz was there I'd surely have known about it because he would've been in the International Brigades, fighting against Franco like I was. Anyway, Schwartz was not the type to fight for other people's freedom or ideals. He was all for himself. He was supposed to have made a great success of his life, but anyone who knew him would've expected that.

'After the war, some time in the mid-forties, there was a rumour that Abraham had paid a visit here... to Palestine.'

'I'm very interested in this visit. Knowing more about it would help me a lot.'

'I told you it was a rumour. I don't know how true it is. Could be it was true but he never came up here to the village. I would've heard of it.'

'Heard of it? You would surely have seen him with your own eyes?'

'No. Not seen him. I was out of the country. From 1932 to 1937. And then again from 1940 until 1947. I would have heard about it, though.'

'Where did you go?'

'Didn't you listen to what I said? I went to France first. My father wanted me to learn about wine. He had the idea this place was suitable for wine growing, so I was sent to France to learn about it.'

'Did you?'

'No. I learned about politics. I tried everything. Everything except what I went there to learn. I was a waiter and a cab driver and I painted houses. Then I went to Spain with the Germans and after Franco's victory I spent some time in Morocco and then I came back here. I left again in 1940… joined the British Army for the war. I didn't come home until 1947.'

'Yes. I understand. You couldn't have seen him.'

'No, but I would have heard about him. This was a small country then, everybody knew everybody. If he was back in the country he didn't come up here.'

'Why?'

'Why? He wouldn't have dared. He would not have been welcomed here… I told you, he did something bad, but I don't remember what it was. Anyway, he was too high and mighty… too restless a man to waste any time on this place. No, he wouldn't have come back here… Once he left he left for good.'

'You were restless yourself…'

'Yes, but I had reasons. Ideals. In my time young people thought they could change the world. Fight for justice. Die for other people's aspirations. Stupid, huh?'

'No. Not stupid.'

'Schwartz would've thought it was stupid. He wasn't interested in politics. Or other people's problems. Not if he didn't know them personally. He was interested only in excitement and money and women. When I came back from all the wars I settled down. Got married and had a son and a daughter. The boy is the one who became an air force pilot, you know. I can show you where he lies. He shouldn't be there, really. They didn't even call him up, but he volunteered in 1973 and on the second day of the Yom Kippur war he was shot down by a missile. Sam 7, a Russian missile. The plane crashed inside our borders… I don't really know what they brought in the coffin. No, I never left again after 1947. I worked the land and instead of making wine I grew fruit and vegetables. Had a couple of cows, a few sheep, that sort of thing.'

'You still have the land?'

'Of course. But it's rented out now. They pay me bits and pieces. More than enough to keep body and soul together.'

'Your daughter?'

'Not keen on working the land. She married a doctor and they live in Tiberias, down there. My sister lives with them. It's hot there and I don't see them unless she comes up.'

'Must be lonely for you.'

'Never. I had a great life. I travelled… I was in uniform… I worked hard. I talk to people… What do you want with Schwartz?'

'Oh, nothing. I have a client who is interested in him.'

'A woman, I'll bet.'

'No. A man who says he's his son.'

'Schwartz had a son?'

'It seems so. Why not?'

'Somehow I can't picture him staying in one place long enough for that. He would never have kept to one woman or one house. His father told me that after he left, but maybe he was just bitter. Yes, there was something else that made him leave here. Something sinister.'

'Did he have any brothers or sisters?'

'No. Oh yes, yes he did. He had one brother. Killed in 1948. He's lying up here too. Would you like to see? It's not a great stone... neglected. You'd have thought Abraham would've sent some money to look after the place. Have some flowers planted. After all, he was supposed to have made a lot of money.'

'Maybe he didn't know...'

'Maybe.'

'Anyway, wherever he is now, he knows.'

'There's nothing after this. I don't believe in the next world.'

'You don't?'

'No, I don't. Not every old man believes in God. I've seen too much injustice down here. If there was a God he would not have allowed some of what I've seen to happen.'

* * *

Somehow we got talking about religion and right and wrong and destiny and suchlike. I did not find out any more about Abraham Moreno's visit. The shadows of the tombstones and the cypresses grew longer. The afternoon sun wheeled itself towards the west and I needed to get back. I don't like driving at night. Not out of town and certainly not along the treacherous curves of the road to Tiberias. There were rumours of PLO infiltrators and I had a pile of papers to look at. Also, it was visiting day, and I had promised my elder daughter I would take her to a film show. I saw little enough of my children as it was, and I had to change that before they forgot they had a father. Regrettably, I could not blame anyone but myself for living away from them.

I didn't see anybody's grave that day because the old farmer forgot what it was he was going to show me. For a few minutes we stood there in silence and then I started for the gate. Perhaps it was the melancholy of the approaching dusk, but as he walked me to my car it seemed to me he was sad to see me go. We exchanged telephone numbers and I promised I'd call next time I was up. It was only a polite gesture, but I'd underestimated the old boy.

Chapter Three

'I don't like lawyers,' the voice said, and I recognized Danny Katz instantly. 'I am the man from the cemetery.'

'I know who you are. I remember our conversation. I enjoyed it.'

'I still don't like lawyers.'

'Not a lot of people do. We're like doctors. You hate us, but when you need us…'

'I never needed either doctors or lawyers.'

'You're a lucky man, Daniel. What can I do for you?'

'Call me Danny. Only my mother called me Daniel, and only when she was mad at me.'

'Well, fine, Danny, what can I do for you?'

'It's about Abraham Schwartz.'

'You have some news?'

'Yes. I think I do.'

'Want me to drive up? Let me see, now…'

'No. I'm coming down to Tel Aviv next week. I thought we could meet.'

'That would be very nice.'

'My granddaughter is graduating next week. I'm staying in town for the night.'

'I'll look forward to it.'

'You're so polite. A rare thing in this country these days. You sound like an Englishman.'

'I was educated in England. My father was English.'

'That's why your manners are good. I like that. When shall I see you?'

'We can meet in the evening.'

'Isn't a man supposed to be at home with his wife in the evening?'

'I don't have a wife now.'

'I am sorry.'

'I am sorry too,' I said, and my throat clammed shut.

'I'll call you,' Danny said softly, and he hung up.

* * *

From across my desk, Abraham Schwartz's son Alex made a face at me. He was irritated.

'Can't we have some privacy?' he asked. 'You could tell your secretary to stop all calls, at least while I'm here.'

'My secretary has no control over this phone. It's my private line.'

'I wish you'd concentrate on me. You don't give a damn.'

'You know that's not true. Besides, it was to do with you.'

'With me?'

'Yes. Why didn't you tell me your father's name was Schwartz?'

'I thought it'd be more fun for you to find out.'

'You could've saved me a trip.'

'You'll charge me for it anyway. Besides, I need to know how efficient you are.'

'I cannot be efficient without information. You could help.'

'You're the lawyer.'

'You're Abraham Schwartz's son. You want to know about the land he bought in this country. If I'm to find out when he came back here, where and what he owned and how he acquired it, I need to know more about him.'

'I don't know everything about him. I hardly knew him anyway.'

'What do you mean you didn't know him? Wasn't he your father?'

'You'll find out.'

'You could save yourself a lot of money.'

'And deprive you of a hefty profit? You find out. I'm in no hurry.'

'Suit yourself.'

'Can you advance me a few more shekels?'

'That's a bit thick. I've advanced you quite a lot already. What is it for this time?'

'Living expenses. I hate the food here but I've got to eat.'

'If you played your cards right the government would give you a grant… look after you.'

'I don't want anything from your government… or your country.'

'Where are you staying?'

'I'm camping, just like you.'

'Where?'

'Here and there. Give me the money on account. You can add it to your bill when you find my father's property.'

'If there is any.'

'Oh, don't worry about that. There is.'

'No one seems to know when your father came back here. You must remember that.'

'I was born in 1935. I was a small child when my father came back here. He was always in and out. Always travelling.'

'Maybe he made his investments without being here in person. Maybe he didn't come back here at all.'

'Oh yes he did. And he bought some land here. And being the man he was he got the best, and for nothing. Oh yes, you can be sure he came in person… he caused enough trouble here to be well remembered. Some of the shit he left here back then is still fermenting. You wouldn't believe what my father did in Palestine when he returned.'

'What did he do?'

'You find out.'

'Why me?'

'Because you must. You are the only one who can do it. Once you get under his skin you'll be able to think like him… be like him. And then you'll have all the answers and understand why it had to be you.'

'I'm an outsider.'

'You won't be an outsider for long.'

'You have to help me'.

'I can't help you. No one can. The sonofabitch was never anywhere long enough. Whenever he came to the house he'd fight with my mother and leave her in tears. He killed her in the end.'

'I thought you said she was ill.'

'Who do you think made her ill? He was a selfish shit. I don't want to talk about him.'

'That's what you do all the time. You throw me a bone and expect me to find a body. I'm trying to find out how he got to Cuba… if he left his village to go to Brazil.'

'Find out, then.'

'I'm a lawyer. Not a detective.'

'That's your problem,' he said, and he got up to go. I dug some money out of my pocket and handed him a few notes. He made no acknowledgement. He dragged his feet towards the door and as he opened it he turned to me.

'Miami,' he said.

'Miami?'

'Yes. A town in Florida.'

'What about Miami?'

'You find out,' he said, and was gone.

Chapter Four

'Miami,' Danny Katz said. 'That was where Abraham Schwartz was definitely seen first.'

'What do you mean, seen first?'

'After he left the country, that's where he surfaced.'

'How do you know?'

'I have it from a most reliable source, Mr Lawyer. I don't make idle statements. Not like some of these so-called artists in this café. They look fashionable enough, but none of what they write or paint or sing about rings true. I was watching them carefully while I waited for you. If the spiritual future of this country depended on these people, we'd be in real trouble.'

We were sitting in a popular terrace café on Diesengoff Street. The traffic was slow and young people in crawling cars eyed each other hopefully through open windows. Some smiled, others whistled. Danny seemed to be enjoying himself, looking at the outrageously dressed, creative types seated around the metal tables, solving the problems of the world at the tops of their voices.

'Hard to think of you as a coffee-house freak,' I said, and he smiled.

'I told you I lived in Paris for years. We sat around a lot, you know, Hans the German painter and me. And where do you think we sat? People write and paint and invent things in coffee houses. We'd sit there for five or six hours on two cups of coffee, talking art and girls and politics, like these youngsters here. But we went beyond idle talk... what we preached we practised. A group of us went straight to the railway station from a coffee house in Montparnasse... to go fight in Spain. Oh, I've sat in coffee houses all right.'

'What was Schwartz doing in Miami?'

'That's the best part of it. He never got to Brazil at all. He got mixed up with a crowd of people in Miami. One way or another he remained in close touch with them for a long time after that. I shouldn't be surprised if he died there because of the company he'd kept... probably a violent death.'

'I don't think he died there... anyway, not then.'

'I didn't say when, I only said where and why. He kept coming to Miami and I think he might have settled there.'

'He had another life. In Cuba... I suspect quite a long life. He fathered a boy. My client. Born in 1935. The boy got to know him well enough to hate him.'

'Maybe the boy is lying.'

'I don't think so.'

'Well, whatever. What I am trying to tell you is that Schwartz got into a bad crowd. I'm not an expert on this sort of thing, but the man he met in Miami was involved in gambling and prostitution. I shouldn't be surprised if there was worse.'

'Do you have any names?'

'Sure I have names. He lived in the house of one of them… someone called Morton Chandler. A big underworld operator. A hoodlum. The funny thing is that Chandler's son came to our village for the same reason you did. He came to find out about Schwartz.'

'When was that?'

'Twenty years ago. He was on his first visit to Israel and he came up to the village to find out if there was anyone left from Abraham Schwartz's family. He said he got to know him well… said Abraham and his father were close.'

'Did he come to look for Abraham's money?'

'Not at all. He did not need any money, as you will see if you let me tell you.'

'I'm sorry.'

'It's OK.'

'So what did he come to the village for?'

'To find out about Abraham's childhood… his origins…'

'Did you talk to him?'

'No. My daughter did. The one who lives in Tiberias. I told you about her. It's her daughter who graduates tomorrow. My daughter was staying in the village at that time. Came up with her husband for a week or so. Whenever they get fed up with the heat down in Tiberias they come to the village. They leave the child with my sister. That's what you keep old aunts in the house for, right? Yes, my daughter was in the village but I wasn't, I don't remember why. Funny, but when she called to invite me to attend the graduation ceremony, I told her about you and how we met and talked in the cemetery and asked her if she knew anything of Schwartz. She didn't remember immediately, but about an hour later she called and told me about Miami and that Mr Chandler. She remembered the visit quite vividly because of the big car young Chandler had arrived in. Driver and all. She said he'd been to most of the houses in the village before he knocked on her door.'

'What did she tell him?'

'She didn't tell him a thing. Just said that all the Schwartz family were dead. She asked him why he wanted to know, and he did all the telling. He used to know Abraham in person, and he said Abraham had worked with his father for many years.Young Chandler seemed to have liked him a lot… talked of him with some admiration. It was a sort of sentimental journey for him. He said his own father was still around and lived in an old people's home because he had gone senile. You know, that is one thing I'm afraid of… I hope I'll have the brains to arrange for someone to shoot me between the eyes before it happens to me. Anyway, young Chandler's trip to Israel was, so to speak, a pilgrimage. He told my daughter he'd come to make contact with his nation's history and look up the origins of his father's old pal Abraham Schwartz. He admitted quite freely they were up to no good.

'I took the liberty of writing to someone I know in Miami. A retired metal worker who was in the Civil War in Spain with me. I asked him to locate this young Chandler for me. According to my daughter, he would be in his early fifties now. His name is Morton too.'

'There must be any number of Chandlers in Miami.'

'Maybe… but not many astrologers.'

'Astrologers? You mean people who gaze at the moon and the stars? Telescopes?'

'No, not astronomers. You worry me. For a lawyer your knowledge is quite limited. Not astronomers… astrologers. People who tell lies about star signs… you know, your future. What you should or shouldn't do. They have them all over the place now, but the young Chandler was quite successful. Even twenty years ago, when he came here. He stayed in the best hotel in Haifa and was dressed to kill and had hired this limousine. My daughter said he made his money writing star predictions for a few newspapers. An American lady who lives near my house swears by it. She won't get out of bed without reading what the stars say. Imagine! Anyway, she says astrology is big business in America and he seemed to be very successful at it. Shouldn't be too difficult to find him. I get the feeling we're dealing with a prima donna.'

'Why did you say Schwartz might have died violently?'

'People die the way they live. Young Chandler said something to that effect. Maybe he knew more about it… more than he was willing to tell my daughter. He said his father was involved in… I don't remember. I'll have to ask my daughter.'

'You said prostitution and gambling and maybe worse.'

'Yes. Yes, I did say that. You see what age does to one's mind? I'd better ask her about it again, just to make sure.'

'Why don't you call her now?'

'On her daughter's graduation day? A psychologist you're not.'

'No, I suppose not. I suppose I'm in a hurry. I want to get to the bottom of this case.'

'It's a shame you young people never take time. You miss out on the tension, on the waiting… on the excitement of expectation. On the colour of life. You miss observing the fascination there is in human nature… the way it twists and turns to deal with new situations.'

'You're right.'

'You don't have to agree with me. Anyway, I'll let you know what comes in the post.'

He was clearly having a great time. His eyes shone and his skin looked youthful. His strong farmer's frame seemed awkward in his town suit, but his demeanour was energetic and positive. He was looking forward to finding things out about Schwartz and Chandler the astrologist, and did not even know what I needed the information for or how I'd use it when I had it. When the waiter came by again, I ordered another cup of coffee. An idea flashed through my head.

'Do you have any spare time?' I asked.

'Time is all I do have. Not a lot, but I do. What do you have in mind?'

'Would you like to go to Miami?'

'Are you serious?'

'I'm a lawyer. I'm always serious.'

'Sure I'd like to go. There's nothing I'd like better. You know, you're giving me a new lease of life. Tell me, though, is all this to do with Abraham Schwartz?'

'It is.'

'Money, huh?'

'Yes. Money. An inheritance.'

'Smells like trouble.'

'It often does.'

'Are you going to tell me about it?'

'I need to know what happened to Schwartz after he left Palestine. How he made his money, where he lived, who his wife was, his friends. I need to know about his life in Miami and where he went afterwards. I know some of it, but I must be sure. I also need to know exactly when he came back here for that visit . How long he stayed, what he did...'

'What do you want to know all that for?'

'I'll tell you, but not now. Right now the reason is classified. It's between me and his son.'

'You could ask him. That would save a lot of trouble.'

'No, I can't. First of all, his son doesn't know everything, and more importantly I need to have this information independently of him. Cross-checked. Unconnected.'

'You mean you want a neutral, independent source.'

'Exactly. My office will arrange for a passport and tickets and money for you.'

'Not so fast. Shouldn't we wait to hear about Chandler the astrologer first?'

'No. I can find his address before you go. I have a contact in the American embassy. Once we know where he lives, you write and tell him you're coming. The pretext is your being from the same village, a schoolfriend of Abraham Schwartz, the father of the woman he saw when he was in Israel last.'

'You don't need to explain. Believe me, I understand.'

'It must be seen as a private visit.'

'I told you, I understand. You prefer to send me there because they suspect lawyers everywhere, huh?'

'I guess so.'

'Well, what do you know, a new man is born every minute. Sherlock Holmes the retired farmer... Danny the detective. What will they think of next?'

* * *

Danny's American friend from the Spanish Civil War did not answer his letter. His son wrote to say he had died a few years earlier.

I had managed to get Chandler's address through an acquaintance in the American embassy and gave it to him before he left. It turned out that Chandler the astrologer was exactly what my friend Danny had thought he would be. In spite of his father's past he was a celebrity. A star. A favourite of the glitterati. A highly successful astrologer who wrote articles and books and had his own television show. He was always able to find good news for everyone and that made him popular. He lived in Palm Beach and drove a Rolls-Royce and his third wife sent her poodles to the hairdresser once a week.

Danny had a rare ability to listen and Chandler was a compulsive talker who needed a constant audience. Talking about his father's youth and Abraham Schwartz seemed to be a release for him. They hit it off from the start.

* * *

The adventures of Abraham Schwartz could have formed the basis of five action-packed movies. When I first got the news I wondered whether his strange son Alex knew any of it. If he did, it was not surprising he kept quiet. No son of a man like Abraham would have been proud of him. Whatever the case, the story turned out to be one that would cast a shadow over the lives of everyone who was close to Abraham. A shadow that would continue to menace them during his lifetime and long after.

Chapter Five

Dear Mr Lawyer,

You asked me to write and tell you what I've been able to do for you in the last two weeks. When I said that this was going to be a new lease of life I was not kidding you. There is one good thing about growing old. People are not intimidated by you any more. You're safe to be seen with and talked to and condescended to. You're not going to steal their wives from them. You're not competing for their business and are not about to attack them bodily. To start with, they might think you want something from them like that time in the cemetery, the day we first met, when you thought I was after a donation. As soon as people realize you're not after favours or money they relax. In fact, they start feeling guilty about having dared suspect you in the first place. And just in case God is watching from above they start being extra civil to you in the hope that this will be remembered. It's funny how most young people assume every old man has a direct line to the Almighty.

Before I came here I was led to believe this was a sleepy town. I thought I was going to see a slow-moving retirement haven for rich old Jews from New York. A sort of waiting room midway up to heaven or down to hell, if you believe in that. Maybe this is how it was, but it is no more.

The Miami I've seen is very different. It's as if the city has become the capital of South America. It's a huge melting-pot, a magnet for anyone from Mexico to Bolivia. If you don't speak Spanish you'd never get a job here. You still see the odd old-timer here and there, waiting in some queue for a pension cheque or posting a letter. But with the Latins here, especially the Cubans, it is very much alive. If you woke up in the south-west part of the city, or Little Havana as they call it, you'd never believe you were in the United States of America. There are Cuban shops and restaurants and nightclubs and street vendors and there's Latin music blowing out of everywhere. It is said that the Cubans have given America in taxes every penny the country spent on settling them here.

I found all this out from a man I got talking to as soon as I collected my luggage. He was a Cuban gentleman who owns a clothing shop at the airport. He wasn't that much younger than me, yet still he offered to help me carry my suitcase. Maybe he thought I was Cuban. My Spanish is still quite good. He let me use the telephone in his shop and I called Chandler.

Someone else answered the phone. Maybe it was the valet or one of the male secretaries he employs. As soon as Chandler himself came on the line, he told me to stay right in that shop and wait. He seemed excited at the prospect of meeting me, said I was lucky to catch him at home. He remembered my daughter from his visit to our village twenty years before. He said Palm Beach was a long way from the airport but he begged me to wait and I promised I would. I sat down and waited with the Cuban. We talked for a few hours and had a good many black coffees and a brandy and then Chandler's driver arrived and took me to the car. It was as long as three normal cars and looked like a white train. Inside there was a bar and a television and a telephone.

Chandler Junior is every bit the superstar. Everybody knows him and acknowledges him and asks for an autograph. He pretends it all means nothing but he loves it. You'd never believe how these people live. Right from the beginning he had me stay in his house in Palm Beach. Did I say house? It's King Solomon's palace, no less. One thousand and one nights. Kismet. Swimming pool and tennis courts and a private cinema. Pink marble floors and statues and paintings. Closed-circuit cameras that record anything that moves, even lizards. There is an electric gate and a uniformed guard, just like the military police at the gate of any army base back in Israel. Every time we drive in and out the man at the gate makes a note of it. I'm told this is for security. No one walks unless it's from the car into the restaurant or something.

Palm Beach is where many rich people live and I've hit the jackpot. They're spoiling me rotten. I've been turned into a real tourist here and they keep showing me all the sights. I'm enclosing postcards of Parrot Jungle and the Seaquarium so you can see what it's like. Next week they're taking me to Disneyworld. But you didn't send me here to write a tour guide to Florida for you, right?

I went along with being a guest and accepted the tours and all that in order to get closer to Chandler. He is a very considerate and generous man. If he's trying to atone for his father's sins he is doing well.

So far I've not been able to spend much of the money you gave me. I think he feels sorry for me. Perhaps because he sees me as an old man with one foot under the ground. Or else he feels guilty about not living in Israel. You know, the way Jewish people feel sometimes when things are too good for them. He loved his visit and says he will come again soon. He asked about my daughter and was surprised to hear that my granddaughter has graduated. Somehow he seems to think that time never moves on in the Holy Land. In any case, he's a very kind man. I think I knew this immediately because of the way he talks about his father. People who are kind to their parents have goodness in them. He keeps saying he only wishes his father could have been well enough to see how far he's come. Maybe it is a kind of competition. From what I gather so far, old Chandler was no pauper.

As you requested, I started asking him about Abraham Schwartz from day one. When he began talking I told him that his story was far too captivating and important to be restricted to my ears alone. I asked his permission to record it so that I could share it with my daughter and others in the village, those people still alive who knew Abraham before he left. Maybe even share it with a larger circle.

Young Chandler showed great consideration. He got me a small recording machine and taught me how to use it. We have had a few sessions and I'll send you a tape of each as I record it. I'll make copies for security and will bring the originals back with me when I return. I think this will be a great way of communicating. I shall not write again. From now on I'll send you cassettes. You'll hear me. You'll hear Chandler's story for yourself in his own voice. You'll see how much he loves talking about it. You can amuse yourself with these narratives when you get a minute. I hope they'll be of some use to you.

* * *

Having just listened to some for myself I can tell you this, Mister Lawyer: Abraham Schwartz, when he left Palestine, would never have dreamed of the kind of life that awaited him. Or maybe he did. You judge for yourself.

One thing I am very sure of. The way Chandler imagined Abraham Schwartz to have been before they met, his perception of his character and motivation, was more than just wrong. It was miles out. I am sure of that because I know the truth.

Yours, Danny the Detective

Chapter Six

This is a recording made by Morton Chandler Junior for Daniel Katz of Israel.

It is a painful thing for a man to admit that his father was a gangster. Even to himself. To me he was a kind and considerate, loving and helpful father. But I have to face the fact. My old man was not like you, Danny. He didn't make what you would call an honest living.

I know you've heard this kind of story before. How a guy grew up in a poor tenement in New York, where only the tough survive. How the suffering and poverty lasted for ever and how the Jews fought the Irish and the Italians and how no one had enough to eat. But this is no excuse. Plenty of good and straight people came out of such lives too. The bad were in the minority but people remember them because they make headlines.

My father was an exceptionally strong man. Not physically, but in his character. He had a will-power and energy that took him far. I now know that in the life he led outside the family home he was a villain. I've heard that he was cruel and merciless and ruthless in the way he did his business, but I witnessed none of that. I was sent to a private school and during my childhood I only saw him during holidays. I was given a university education. He may have hurt people but I make no judgement of him because I've got no right to do that. I only found out about what kind of a man he really was when he was retired and old and out of it.

Sometimes, when I went to see him in his luxury institution, I'd sit opposite this harmless, frail man in his wheelchair and I'd try to imagine him doing all these things. All the suffering he caused. The vile empire he'd built. I wasn't too successful because I never saw any of it.

My father acquired great wealth. He was never caught while he was active, so he got to keep it all. In any case, he only broke the law in other countries. Over here, he built up a whole group of kosher companies that dealt in legitimate stuff. He managed it all, he said, because of his friend Abraham Schwartz.

There were warehouses, bakeries, trucking and transport companies, that kind of thing. And all those paid taxes, and if you pay your taxes here they leave you alone. To tell you the truth, I don't think anyone really knew he used to be a villain until he went senile, and then it was their word against that of the family lawyers. They tried to interrogate him but by that time my father made no sense at all. Of course, with me being quite famous, the newspapers made a big deal of it. A real matzo pudding. If I had been a nobody, they might not have been interested in my father at all.

They published pictures of casinos and dancing girls and impounded boats and dead bodies in morgues. Pictures of him sitting feebly in his wheelchair with the caption 'Crime sure pays' or some such. I read everything they said about him and it opened a whole new world to me. It also caused me a lot of hurt, and I still visit an analyst to help me.

I've been very lucky in my own life and career and I've been giving all the income from my father's estate to charity. I like to think he would've approved. When you've got it, share it, he used to say.

Having visited Abraham Schwartz's village, your village up there in the north of the Holy Land, having seen the rocky earth that became green fields, the view of the Sea of Galilee, I find it impossible to understand how a man with his background ever got involved with my father. I take it he was a farmer's son, an innocent country boy when he arrived here. Maybe he was too naive to know where my father was taking him. But my analyst says everybody is responsible for their own life, and I'm not blaming my father for leading Schwartz across to the wrong side of the rails.

You can't imagine what your letter and visit have done for me. Knowing you has been a real therapy. You and your generation of pioneers are the salt of the earth. If Abraham Schwartz had stayed in the village he might have ended up like you.

You've seen the kind of life I am leading here. The key word for it is insincerity. It's superficial and vain. It's plastic and saccharine, if you know what I mean. People always think that if they are nice to me the stars will make them healthy and rich and famous.

My one and only trip to Israel twenty years ago opened my eyes. I saw people leading the simple life. People who reminded me of this country's own founding fathers. If I were a young man again I'd go live there, close to the earth. It's a shame I didn't get to meet you then. But you don't want to hear about all this. You came here to get the lowdown on the life and times of Abraham Schwartz, the way it was when I knew him, so here goes.

Whenever my father spoke of Schwartz he'd go all soft with admiration. He spoke of him as though he was his ancestor, his biblical hero. His own Hebrew warrior. Abraham Schwartz was his best friend. Maybe he was the brother he never had or maybe… yes, maybe he was the kind of man he himself would have liked to have been. Schwartz was hard of body and had great looks and awesome charm and he was clever. This simple village boy was to become an international adventurer and a great success, but he had the kind of personality you couldn't be jealous of because he was so likable. There were plenty of reasons for my father to have fallen for him, and most of the time they were as close as two men can be.

By the time I came into the picture Schwartz had changed his name to Moreno. This was on account of his life in Cuba. He didn't look like a Jewish boy at all. Out there everybody thought he was a Spaniard or an Italian. Something like that. He was a very big, strong guy and had the looks and movements of a film star. You saw him once and you never forgot him. He could smile all bad thoughts out of you. He had a pair of blue, piercing eyes with a softness in them that made you feel easy and secure. He was immensely tough looking, yet there was nothing intimidating about him. His voice, too, was something, I tell you. A clear baritone that boomed like a trombone, with a gentle touch that sounded like a Glenn Miller tune. And there was more. Abraham was a great listener and always made you feel you were the brightest guy in the world and anything you said was going to be his Bible.

Schwartz arrived in New York from Southampton, England. I think he worked on board all the way from Jaffa. He never talked about his voyage or why he'd left Palestine, and I figure he just wanted to see the world or something. My father said Abraham would have made it wherever he was, so his departure must have been for personal reasons. I guess they know more about it back in his village. He was a great talker and anyone who listened thought he was opening himself up. But my father said that despite all the talk Schwartz revealed nothing of himself. Towards the end, my father became very curious about what had made Abraham Schwartz leave Palestine. It almost became an obsession with him. That was why, many years later, I came to the village myself to try and find out.

In those days it was easier to get into the States. Being the sort of guy who always fell on his feet, Schwartz landed a job on the first day. Worked carrying luggage and portering in a hotel in downtown Manhattan. It didn't matter what clothes he had on you couldn't help noticing him as soon as you laid eyes on him.

My father saw him as he got out of the cab to book himself in. He had just come in from Florida. He never forgot the sight of this giant, dressed in a porter's uniform but looking like some dashing military officer. He hurried down the steps to open the cab door. He had a smile on his face that made my old man forget the long train journey he'd had. I don't know how they got talking, but Abraham carried my father's luggage up to his room and I guess my father was curious about his accent. He must have asked him where he was from and when he heard Abraham was a Jew from Palestine, he invited him in for a drink and things took off from there. In those days you didn't see a lot of Jews from the Holy Land in the States. People came from Poland and Russia and even England, but they were pale, frightened refugees in search for a better life. The kind of people you see in old Ellis Island newsreels. Very few came from Palestine, and Schwartz did not look like a refugee at all. On his face there was none of that expression of bewilderment or anxiety. None of the new-arrival bit. If anything, he looked like a conqueror.

Abraham and my father hit it off from the start. One was a guest in the hotel and the other worked there, but it didn't matter. They were, both of them, young and confident and ambitious. They talked a lot, and Abraham told my father about how things were back in his village and how he decided to try his luck this side of the ocean. He said he was going to make himself enough money to get on a boat to Rio. He was going to find a whole heap of gold in Brazil and get himself established back in Palestine. But my old man persuaded him out of it. There was, he said, plenty of dough to be made right here in the States, depression or no depression. When Abraham complained about the weather, my father told him to come to Miami. There, he said, the sun was always shining. That was where people went on their holiday and where they played. When people play, my father said, they spend money, and where people spend money you can make a living. Florida was a new place, too, and the opportunities there were great for anyone who was willing to work or take a few risks.

Abraham took his time about coming. He took two or three months. Maybe it was because he wanted to demonstrate his independence, but my father thought it was because of a woman. He had a way with women. There was always a woman behind everything Abraham Schwartz did. They got him jobs, places to live in, appointments, you name it. They cooked for him and drove him around and wanted to do things for him even if, as in Cuba, they couldn't communicate with him. My father said women liked Abraham because underneath his macho frame he was really a child. Maybe.

So he came over to Miami and my father collected him off

the train. For a month or so he stayed with my father while they worked out what Abraham was going to do. He insisted on paying his way from day one, my father said. He contributed a little rent, and although he didn't have a bean he invited my father out for meals and stuff. He'd mow the lawn and help the maid wash the dishes. He wasn't shy of work. They went to meetings and everywhere they went the secretaries swooned over him and the bosses offered him jobs. As usual, Abraham soon found himself a girl. She owned a couple of drugstores on Flagler Street. He went in there one day to buy a box of cigars for my father and that was how they met. She was a couple of years older than him and a divorcee and had a house on the water and a five-year-old son. My father said Abraham took the little feller fishing and gave him Hebrew lessons and worked behind his mother's counter in the evenings. During the day he was with my father, doing the odd job while they looked for a suitable opening for him. He drove trucks, mostly, and he delivered stuff to the bakeries and cash to the banks. It was all official cash, on which the right amount of tax was paid to Uncle Sam. Later on he was entrusted with cash collections that were less legitimate, or, as my father would've put it, a little more complicated.

My father was courting my mother in those days. It was during an excursion to Key West that they all – my father, my mother, Abraham, his girl and her boy – went to Cuba. In those days people went there by boat from Key West without any hassle. It was an entertaining place to visit and was very much in fashion, even before the casinos.

Within minutes of the ship docking in the port of Havana, Abraham got friendly with a local policeman. They got talking while they were asking for directions, and before you knew it the policeman joined up with them to show them the sights. Even then, before he spoke a word of Spanish, Abraham could charm the pants off anyone. Especially in a place like Cuba where the people are easy-going and happy. It was a weekend, and the policeman took time off and stayed with them until they left. They exchanged addresses and promised each other they'd keep in touch. Abraham never lost a chance to make a friend. And the friends he made were always useful. They would remain under his spell for ever.

The sounds of Havana, the music and the food and most of all the girls, took Abraham by storm. The history of the island, the way it used to be the richest colony in the world, fired his imagination. In his mind's eye he saw sugar plantations and rum and coffee and tobacco. He saw old Spanish sailing ships, uniformed horsemen collecting taxes, and pretty ladies on balconies. Everything, the dancelike walk of the people, the bustle of disorder, the serenade of street vendors and the happy faces appealed to him. There's adventure for you, he told my father. Maybe he was getting tired of his woman. Maybe she was pushing him too hard for a wedding. Maybe it was just his need to move on. Whatever it was, he said to my father he'd like to settle down in Cuba.

On the boat coming back to Key West he talked of nothing else. He wasn't worried about making a living there. It was a cheap place to live and he had a few bucks saved up. All the way back he talked abut moving to Havana. About how he'd start some sort of a business there. How the casual way people lived and behaved had reminded him of Palestine. The woman must have sensed there was no part for her in this plan. She went all silent and sulked, and for once Abraham didn't try and make her feel good. He did nothing about her. All of a sudden she didn't exist. My father felt sorry for her, and especially for her son. The kid had got quite close to Schwartz and looked at him the way kids look at their dads, but once he'd decided to up and go that was it. I told you, some people should never get attached to anyone. Look how Abraham screwed up his son's life. And yet my own father, the gangster, was able to pass through this world without hurting his family. I feel warm every time I think of him. I miss him a lot.

Can we stop now, Danny? I'm getting a little sentimental.

Chapter Seven

Danny, my Sherlock Holmes, was sending me riveting reports about Schwartz, but I was having serious problems with his son Alex. I had kept all the information from Miami to myself in order to verify it, and my client was accusing me of doing nothing. It was useless explaining to him that these things take time. I was dealing with a man, born in Palestine, who had emigrated long before this became a Jewish state. A man who had more than one nationality and had never registered residence or paid taxes anywhere. Alex said his father had made substantial land investments here some time in the thirties or forties, but there was no documentation at all.

They have a department that specializes in property belonging to absentees. It is called the Custodian of Absentees' Property, and it keeps all the relevant papers, but I could not gain access without a court order and could not get such an order without evidence. Usually these absentee owners are Arabs who fled Palestine in 1948. In many cases their houses and shops were taken over by Jewish immigrants, but to give the government its due, a good part of that property is registered and held in trust by the department. I guessed Abraham's land, whatever and wherever it was, was held by them. I was not going to approach them without the full picture. I needed proof of ownership. I needed proof of purchase and payment. I needed copies of registration documents and, above all, I needed to prove that Abraham Moreno, né Schwartz, did exist, did come to this country and had investments here, and that my client Alex was his legitimate and only son and therefore his heir. I wasn't getting much out of him. Almost nothing, in fact. I kept hoping he would open up to me once I could show him what I had.

The picture I was getting of his father, his devil-may-care attitude and his vivacious charm, sharpened the contrast between them. Abraham Moreno's son Alex was introverted. As time dragged on, he got into the habit of coming and going as he pleased, never warning us in advance. The more he came to see me, the less he seemed to care about what I was trying to do for him. I tried to tell him of my progress but he showed no interest. The frustrating changes in his moods occurred steadily, almost on a weekly basis. He became progressively more morose, and when he spoke he spoke with anger. He was often disturbed and at such times he'd lose his temper, and while his voice would remain quiet you could sense the fury that lurked behind his dark eyes. He would complain about my uselessness and about the country, he'd knock his fist on the table and then, suddenly, he'd sink back into a dark and total silence. He'd sit there for a while longer keeping me guessing and then he'd leave.

He never took much care of his clothes, and as time went by he became really sloppy. He was going downhill fast, and although he kept outwardly clean he seemed dirty. The staff were commenting on it. They said his appearance wasn't doing much for our reputation. I had asked him to please have a shave before coming to the office, so the bastard grew a beard. He wore different rags each time, and constantly changed his posture, his hand movements and even his walk. If you passed him in the street you wouldn't have recognized him, even if you had met him a few times. I did not know then what a trained master of disguise he was. Naively I thought his actions were those of a man sinking into melancholia. I never suspected that every step he took was planned.

* * *

I had not heard from him in two or three weeks and was beginning to worry. The intifada was in full swing and Arab youths were stoning cars and attacking Jewish passers-by. Alex Moreno knew little about the danger areas and did not speak the language. He knew nothing of our traditions, yet with his pale face and beard he resembled a religious zealot down on his luck. He'd walk the streets like a moonstruck ghost, paying no attention to people or cars. His lethargic lack of interest in the world around him would have made him an ideal target. My concern was more than a question of simply looking after my investment. Maybe the protectiveness I developed towards him later started then. I caught myself smiling with relief every time he showed up, but this feeling lasted only for a few minutes. As soon as he started his baffling criticism of my office and my actions, my displeasure came back with a vengeance.

* * *

One day he flew into my office unannounced. I did not notice him at first because I was deep in a phone conversation with my wife's lawyer. She had intensified her campaign, and the children's behaviour towards me was becoming hostile. As usual it was about money. She had threatened to send the income tax people to my office to look through the files. There are plenty of things in a lawyer's office which are confidential. There are a lot of grey, sensitive areas between a lawyer and his client. Sometimes they deposit money with you, and sometimes secret documents. Mostly they do so to hide something from the company they work for, or from their family. To have the snooping eye of the finance people prying into my affairs would create havoc and she knew it.

The man at the other end of the phone was a friend of mine. We had started in the same law firm together before I became independent, and had been in the same unit in the military. When things had been good his firm had looked after both my wife and myself. He was quite candid with me. He said this time Joan meant business and rightly so. Said I would end up in a whole lot of hot water unless we found a way to placate her. All this was quite properly off the record. He said he loved us both and asked me if there was any chance of a reconciliation. This was a question I had been hoping for, but before I had an opportunity to answer I saw Alex Moreno's face lowering over me. My secretary was hovering apologetically in the background.

I hardly recognized him. He had lost a lot of weight and his filthy clothes hung very loosely on his gaunt frame. His eyes were burning, his beard unkempt.

'Hold on a minute,' I said to my wife's lawyer, 'I'm

having a little crisis here.'

'You'll have a big one if we don't find a solution. Joan has a point, you know.'

From the look on Moreno's face I realized this was going to take time.

'Can I call you back, please?' I pleaded.

'Make sure it's today. I don't think I can hold her off much longer,' my wife's lawyer said, and I hung up. I sat back and collected my thoughts. I took a sip of water and motioned my secretary to leave.

'What do you mean by bursting in like this?' I yelled.

His face muscles relaxed. 'You've never shouted at me before,' he said with a smile. 'That's very good.'

'Very good? What the hell do you mean?'

'Now that you are angry you will tell the truth.'

'The truth?'

'Yes. You're having me followed, aren't you?'

'You're crazy.'

'Don't try to deny it. It doesn't really bother me. There's nothing they can do to me here.'

'Who?'

'The CIA or their dogs the Mossad or anyone else. I don't really care, but I'd like to know why you're doing this.'

'You're deranged. I don't care if you take your business somewhere else. Get out.'

'You're hiding my father's money from me. I have lots of experience with people in trouble. You're having problems with your wife. When someone is in trouble they become desperate and irresponsible, they do all sorts of things. I've told you you can charge me whatever you like as long as you stick to our business. My private life must remain my own. Are you having me followed?'

I had forgotten about it. I had retained the services of a private detective to track Moreno down simply because I was worried about his safety. The trouble was my man was not very good. In his reports he always said the Cuban was a master at dodging and disappearing. I had assumed he had failed, and with the rest of my problems pressing on me I plain forgot all about him.

'Yes,' I said, 'I'm having you followed.'

'How dare you.'

'I've put a lot of time and money into solving this case. I'm only looking after my investment. I never know where to find you when I need you. And, believe it or not, I'm worried about you. But you can relax. My man claims he can never find you.'

This seemed to please him. The shadow of a smile appeared at the corner of his mouth. He said:

'Your man is an amateur. You're wasting your money on the likes of him. I can be lost anywhere. I'm a revolutionary, remember.'

He had never uttered this word before and the vehemence in his voice startled me.

'Revolutionary? Where?... How?... What kind of revolutionary?'

He did not answer. He just smiled, and then he sat down.

'Are you making any progress?' he asked.

'Slowly.'

'I've very little time.'

'Are you leaving the country?'

He ignored my question in his nonchalant way and asked for some water.

'You look as though you've been sleeping in the street,' I said as I handed the glass over.

He drank the water in one short gulp, wiped his beard and sat down.

'I want to tell you something,' he said, almost in a whisper.

'What about?'

'About the time my father married my mother.'

'Why?'

'I want to.'

This short statement said it all. I was in his hands. If what I was hoping for was going to happen, I had to dance to his music. I asked him to wait and I dialled my wife's lawyer.

'Get me some time,' I said. 'I'll find those extra funds within a week.'

The man said he'd try and hung up. Moreno said:

'If that's my father's money things must be moving along.'

'We're very far from your father's money.'

'Are you short of cash, Mr Lawyer?'

'Why do you ask?'

'I want to know.'

'My finances are none of your business.'

'They are,' he said curtly, and I feared I'd lose my patience with him, but I smiled and said:

'Tell me about the time your father married your mother.'

Chapter Eight

Her name was Martha Frankel. She was a delicate young woman and the last year of her life in Germany had shattered the scant confidence she had managed to muster after she successfully completed her studies. Week by week, the familiar sights and sounds of Berlin, the city of her birth, had altered. The friendly, carefree atmosphere gave way to fear. She watched her parents, her elderly teachers and others she had admired being humiliated on the streets. Bit by bit, the theatre and the museums were barred to Jews. Jobs were impossible to get and people were leaving for faraway places: Uruguay, Argentina, even China. They went anywhere that would have them. They were charged astronomical fees for the privilege and many sold their homes and businesses for a pittance. Others stayed, hoping for the current oppressive climate to dissipate.

After she was beaten up while walking in the park, she was sent to Havana. Her father had managed to obtain a three-month Cuban visa for her. They had given the family car to one of the officials in exchange for the document. It was decided to get her out because she was least able to cope with the situation. The voyage would do her good, she was told. She might have to be be alone for a while, her mother said, but at least she'd be out of it. As they parted by the central railway station there were tears. Martha did not want to leave, but her father assured her this was only a temporary parting. Hitler could not possibly stay in power for long. Not in a modern, cultured country like Germany. Nor could the Jews be treated as scapegoats for ever. After all, hadn't they lived there for hundreds of years? Hadn't he himself served in the Imperial German Army in the First World War? This current persecution was but a passing cloud, he whispered as he carried her suitcase into the compartment. If things became worse, they would all follow her to Cuba or somewhere else as soon as they were able to settle their affairs. He had not, her father said, worked all these years just to give everything away because crazy people had taken the country over. She should aim to get to the United States, he said. Or try to get a permanent permit to stay in Cuba. Above all, she must retain a positive frame of mind which would enable her to establish herself wherever she might go.

The voyage was long and the weather kept changing as her spirits sank. There were many like her on board and many sad stories. A married couple and one man jumped overboard during the fifth day at sea. It was said they were a love triangle. A Jewish lawyer, his wife and her Bavarian lover. They were always beautifully turned out, the men in tropical suits and the woman in fashionable attire, appropriate for the time of day. They were polite and well spoken. They had kept themselves to themselves and were always seen together, even on the day they disappeared. The triple suicide gave people something to talk about, but as the journey wore on they were forgotten. Her own moods were now at a constant low ebb. She missed her home and her city and the comfort of familiar faces. By the time they docked in the port of Havana she was despondent. Together with the others, she found a cheap pension in which to stay, where they were made to pay in advance, which left her with very little money. The first thing she did was to write home.

There was a sizable group of them, all refugees, arriving in dribs and drabs to wait for a visa for the States. They hung around the crowded reception areas of the sleazy hotels and sat for hours in bars. They made a strange sight, conspicuous in the latest European winter fashions under the ever-present tropical sun. They walked about the old colonial streets, usually in a group, holding on to their suitcases. They did so in order to be ready when an opportunity to sell something arose. Everything they possessed was for sale, just to be able to buy a few more days in Cuba. Jewellery, cameras, paintings and fountain pens. They divided the rest of their time between waiting outside the American consulate, walking up and down the promenade and sitting in the boulevard coffee houses. They played chess and cards and they all spoke German. They tried all sorts of things to make a living. One dental surgeon and his wife played a violin duet outside the city hall until the police moved them on without ceremony.

At the end of the first month, Martha Frankel sold her pearls and her watch. This paid off her bills, and she bought a small paraffin stove and cooked her meals in her room. She continued to visit the American consulate almost daily, but as with most of the others her efforts to secure a visa did not meet with success. She had no relatives in America, nor was her degree, in German literature, considered to be useful enough to grant her a work permit. Time and again, the vice-consul suggested she go back home, or try to find some occupation right there in Cuba. As a first step, he said, she should use the time to learn the language. He knew of a lady who would be willing to exchange Spanish lessons for German ones.

The meeting took place at the beginning of her seventh week in Havana, and the two women liked each other from the start. The lady, Conchita Madeiros, a woman in her late forties, was married to an official in the Cuban foreign service. Since she had no children of her own, she took pity on the girl, and after the third session offered her a room in the family house. Her husband was delighted with the arrangement because, he confessed to Martha, he was currently acting as a roving ambassador for his country and travelled a lot. His wife was lonely.

You needed to look at Martha twice before you realized the depth of human understanding and kindness that lay behind her bleak expression. She was well read and intelligent and once she overcame her initial shyness with people she could hold her own in conversation. She had a kind and helpful disposition and liked sharing her knowledge, and this made her a good teacher. Conchita Madeiros saw under the younger woman's skin. She saw the fears, the loneliness and insecurity, and recognized a lot of herself in Martha.

They developed a close friendship, and by the end of the second month they had become inseparable. Smiles began to appear on Martha's drawn face. A letter from the family in Berlin spoke of hope. Things were not easy but they could be worse, her father wrote. The economy was booming, and people always come to their senses when there is enough food about. Construction of motorways and factories was mushrooming and the currency was stable. There was, all around them, an air of coming prosperity. At the opera houses they were producing the best music this century. There was money in people's pockets. The Jews had to change their way of life, but there was nothing new in that and things were bound to improve. The family was able to sell a few things and undertake a little business to survive. In principle they were still looking for a place to emigrate to, but if things went on improving that might not be necessary. Outside Germany people spoke of war, but he did not believe there was any truth in it. Outsiders, he wrote, had little or no understanding of the new reality. It was but a reaction to the humiliation inflicted on the country by its enemies at the end of the Great War. The reality might be harsh, but with the long standing of her traditions, her honour and her culture, Germany would come through. He ended by writing that the good Lord would surely repay Conchita Madeiros for her kindness.

In later years she would often speak to her son of that first letter. She kept it all her life. It was the optimistic tone of her father's correspondence which gave her the strength to comprehend and accept the tragedy that was to destroy him and the rest of her family.

In Havana, however, during the winter of 1934, such thoughts were very far from her mind. With her newly strengthening friendship and her quick mastery of the language, Martha began to crawl out of her shell. Conchita Madeiros introduced her to many people, and she was much liked by them. She remained a quiet girl who revealed a quick, dry sense of humour. She knew she could never acquire the bubbly nature of Conchita's friends, but she learned to listen and give advice and support when asked. She never tried to prod and always knew when to be silent. Her words never embarrassed anyone.

It was at a Christmas party that year that she met Abraham Moreno. Her reserved nature was no match for his ardour. The swashbuckling young man with his permanent smile and irresistible charm talked her off her feet. Conchita warned her young friend not to rush into any commitment, but Martha's mind was ruled by her emotions. Abraham Moreno was the first man who ever paid her any attention and his flattery was too tempting to resist. Much to Conchita's concern, Martha ran off with him for an excursion to the beach resort of Baradero, where they spent a few days together. This showed he had no respect for her. In those days a woman who turned up somewhere with a man who was not her husband was considered a putana. A good-time girl. But she was totally smitten by him and did not care. He then took her to Miami and married her there.

After a month-long honeymoon, Abraham and Martha Moreno returned to Havana. He made out that he took her back because she did not like Miami, but the truth was that he wanted to settle in Cuba. He had never stayed in any one place for long before, but Cuba changed all that.

At the time Abraham Moreno was working with an American he had met in Miami. His name was Chandler and he was a criminal. He was one of those people who are born crooked. The kind whose restless nature looks for constant adventure and finds solace only in danger and risk. While Abraham used travel and people and women to satisfy his quest for excitement, Chandler was building an empire. He owned casinos and whorehouses and smuggled liquor and cigarettes in and out of Cuba.

They were good for each other, Chandler and Moreno. Both ruthless, both interested in power, and both corrupt to the hilt. Moreno was not short of money, but he was never one to take orders from others. He obviously thought he had got as much out of Chandler as he was going to get. He wanted to start something on his own.

* * *

What I had learned so far of Abraham's early days in Cuba had come from Chandler's recorded conversations with Danny. The astrologer had his own perception of his father's relationship with Abraham. He made no secret of what the two men were up to, yet he had an obvious admiration for them. There was, in his mind, a certain dignity in their friendship.

* * *

For Alex Moreno, there was no friendship there at all. Just a corrupt partnership between two evil people who used each other. The partners' life, both at home and at work, was propelled by greed.

The more he went into his father's story, the more I realized I must not get involved. I am not a judge. In this, a legal investigation, there was no room for morals. Who was good and who was bad did not matter. I was instructed to look for an inheritance, for documents and hard evidence. I was not supposed to conduct a psychological analysis of the people concerned, or let that influence my actions. I decided to listen to all sides of the story but concentrate on just those facts that would come in useful. I believed that was what my client expected of me.

I was wrong.

I sat there and I listened to everything Alex said. I watched his darkening expression and could almost touch the pain that lay beyond his hate. I offered no comment. It would have been of no value to young Moreno. My personal opinion, I thought, was of no importance. Not to him, not to anyone.

I was wrong there too.

* * *

'In the Cuba of the thirties,' Alex told me, 'you could do anything you wished if you were a foreigner or a member of the rich oligarchy. You'd get permits for anything. Manufacture, import or export. With money, you could buy and sell anyone. Bribes were all that was required, but you needed to know the right people to bribe. Abraham got his most important connections for nothing because Martha's friends the Madeiros were clean and beyond reproach and they knew everybody. Once they were married, Moreno was introduced to their society friends and he charmed them all. He used them without shame.'

Whenever Abraham's son spoke of Cuba, he seemed to be referring to two different countries. The old one, the reactionary dictatorship, a corrupt place fit for vagabonds and gangsters and whores motivated only by money, a cesspool land that neglected its people; the other, Castro's Cuba, a paradise on earth. His eyes would light up and every trace of his usual depressive demeanour would disappear. It was a country created by God. A happy, caring, socialist Garden of Eden that looked after its citizens like a mother. In the old days, once the cutting season was over, the workers were left to starve. How they managed until the new harvest came no one knew or cared. But all that was over after the revolution. Cuba was an admired place. A country every Latin American state wanted to emulate. There was free education for everybody. Free medical care. There was no shortage of jobs, and workers earned enough to live on. He spoke of his own experiences and how he had reached heights any man would be proud of, where he and many others had realized their potential and their dreams. He became excited, but he never told me exactly what it was he had achieved.

In view of the collapse of the communist system everywhere else, and his own years of suffering there, I did not understand his attitude at all. His country was hated and feared. Her experiments in exporting the revolution had failed. Her armies had kept Angola's wars going for years. Without the help of the new Russia, Cuba will soon be starving. It was only a matter of time before Castro fell. And yet, to Alex Moreno, the man was a saint. He would have been ready to go straight back to Cuba if he was allowed to and follow Castro all the way to hell. How could he still believe in all that shit?

It was only towards the end of our association that I found out, but by that time there was little I or anyone could do for him. The man was older than me, yet I shall always think of him as young Moreno. He was a driven man, and motivated by fanatical emotions that often flew out of control. He'd break into a lecture on the merits of socialism with the same gusto he used when cursing our society, his father and, on the odd occasion, myself.

* * *

That time he did not talk politics. He was speaking of how his parents had met and married. A wedding is a happy event, but there was an ocean of melancholy in his eyes and his voice and my heart went out to him. I wanted to cheer him up.

'Cuba must have been a romantic place,' I said. 'Palm trees, sugar-cane fields, beaches and music...'

'Yes, it's a beautiful island,' he responded.

And then his expression changed yet again. His mouth hardened and his eyes assumed the dark glitter of an inquisitor's. He got up and paced the room. His words came in pure staccato bursts.

'I want to know why my father left here in the first place. With his sort of character he would've done well anywhere. I mean, maybe there was no scope where he was born, but he could have left the village and gone to one of your cities and made himself a career. He was a cheat and a liar who was never caught. He could have made a fortune here.'

'Those were difficult times,' I said. 'There was hunger. There was trouble with the Arabs. The British were looking the other way while Jewish settlements were attacked.'

'Spare me all that. Your history had nothing to do with my father. None of that would've touched him. Don't you worry about him. He would've found a way. He was the greatest evader of all time... a coward. He would've wormed and cheated his way out of everything, would've stolen and killed to get to the top. He would've gone far in this country the way it has become. Would've ended up running this little Jewish hell of yours. Oh yes, he would have stayed right here. Someone or something must have forced him to go.'

'I don't have to sit here and listen to you offending my homeland... and yours, too.'

'This is not my homeland.'

'Really? Not yours? What country is yours, then? Cuba? Didn't Cuba torture you and your kind?'

'Who told you that?'

'I'm guessing...I mean, you're here, aren't you? If I'm wrong, why did you leave?'

'I don't want to discuss that.'

'What do you want? You want me to sit here quietly and agree with every bit of...'

'Find out why my father left.'

'That's not what you hired me for. You wanted to find out what happened to his investments and what they were, right?'

'What I'm asking you for has a bearing on that.'

'How come?'

'None of your business. Just do it. Find out why he left.'

'Why were you telling me about the time your parents got married?'

'Because I wanted to.'

* * *

On the surface, Abraham Moreno's son said, it seemed that his father married his mother because he wanted to help her to get into the United States. The truth was he did not intend to live there at all. His time in Miami was running out, and by the time they met Martha had been issued with a permanent visa for Cuba. She had endeared herself to many people, and her adopted family, the Madeiros, were useful contacts for what he had in mind. He wanted to stay in Cuba and she was his ticket. He had seen the country and knew exactly how he was going to make his fortune. There was nothing romantic about my father, Moreno said. He did not know what love was. He had no loyalty or conscience. He was a cold and calculating man, and as soon as her usefulness was spent, he left her to her own devices.

Chapter Nine

The way Abraham Schwartz picked his wife and married her was typical of his generosity, Morton Chandler told Danny's tape recorder.

My father never forgot that because he had arranged the whole affair. They got married in Miami and he fixed the catering and the music and hired the hall and brought their Cuban business friends over for the big event. He was his best man while Mr Madeiros and his wife gave Martha away. Now that Abraham was going to formalize his relationship with Martha, they had dropped their original objections. It started as a Jewish ceremony and culminated in a sumptuous Latin party. The groom was dressed in a tuxedo and a top hat, like some Valentino about to be filmed dancing the tango. He stood like a god under the traditional canopy with his plain-looking bride. Poor Martha was so impressed by all the glitter she didn't know what was happening. Of course, there were people who tried to put him down for marrying her, but my father knew the truth.

Abraham Moreno could have had anyone, and let's face it, compared to all the exotic women in the Caribbean she was a little simple and far from a beauty. He was on his way to making a fortune and had dated quite a few rich broads. She was a poor refugee. He had an American passport and the only way for Martha ever to get into the country was to marry a US citizen. He married her because he was kind.

He must have known he could never be happy with her. Their characters, their backgrounds and their expectations were too different. What's more, their external appearances were like night and day, but they say opposites attract. It did not work in their case because the ocean between them was too vast. She was an insecure intellectual and he an adventurous explorer. She craved a steady home life and he was a gypsy who needed no roots. Maybe his stable, happy childhood in the village had created that supreme confidence he enjoyed most of his life.Yes, maybe his roots were robust enough for him to carry them along, wherever he went. She read books and liked music and poetry and he was a peasant. It's not enough for two people to share the same religion. It takes a hell of a lot more, but if two people desire each other, if there is passion between them, nothing else matters.

The trouble was that Abraham did not desire her at all. My father said he'd told him that himself. And that honest admission impressed him, because Abraham was going to sacrifice his own happiness to give Martha security. That was why he kept on screwing on the side until he fell for one particular woman, and that was fatal. He was never the type to settle down. He had plenty of women, and never got emotionally involved. Not until he met Carmelita Rodriguez, who stole his heart and much more besides. She almost ruined his life, but that's another story.

No, he married Martha to help her out. He was not sure what would happen in Cuba, given its turbulent history, and he thought that only proper American papers would protect her. She could stay in Cuba as the wife of an American and no one could force her to go back to Europe.

Before the ceremony, my father told Abraham he did not have to go all the way. Not if this was not an honest-to-goodness love match. He said Martha was safe enough as things stood. But the prospective husband laughed him out of court. He said my father was naive. He said things could change tomorrow. He said the Cuban government was not stable. Her friends the Madeiros could fall from grace. The man in the palace could be kicked out at any time, and then her permit would be up the creek. Look what happened to all the Jews who were finally shipped back to Germany. My father ended up in total agreement. The ceremony went ahead as planned and they became man and wife.

Abraham married Martha, my father said, to save her life. It was a noble thing to have done.

* * *

Anyway, you remember the policeman they met on that first visit to Havana? Abraham had kept in touch with him. He had moved on to a position of responsibility and Abraham, who knew how to nourish friendships, offered him a partnership in his first industrial venture. In that part of the world there was no law against being both a police officer and a company director. No one looked down on it. In fact, anyone who was anyone in government had some outside source of income. Some kickback deal. This alliance came in very useful. The Cuban policeman was made to feel important and, having been born a peasant, this was worth more than money to him. With his connections in the police force and among the underworld, the partnership turned out to be a great success.

Let's face it, Abraham made my father rich with his schemes, but he never became my father's partner. Not in the gambling casinos or in anything else. He was in charge of bringing the dough back to the States. It had to be done without letting the Inland Revenue Service know, and Abraham Moreno had invented a foolproof system for doing it. That was how my father got to keep his profits, and by investing them in legal businesses back in the States he turned them into a clean fortune. It was so simple you'd think someone else would have thought of it, but no one did.

Abraham had my father's casino profits banked in Havana in the name of a bogus Cuban corporation. The corporation was officially owned by that policeman friend of his, and was free to transfer any of its cash to banks in Miami. There the money was used to buy control of various local businesses. The official buyer was that same fake Cuban company for whom my father was the local agent. As such, he ran the US affairs of the company and wrote yearly reports that were sent to Havana and lodged at the bank there. In those days there was no real control over business in Cuba, and as long as the right people were given their cut, all was well. Abraham's friend the policeman knew exactly who was open to bribes and things ran like clockwork. In the meantime, my father busied himself developing a whole bunch of legitimate companies in Miami. They were then, as they are now, property companies, transport houses, bakeries, one or two hotels, and a real estate agency. They all paid taxes and some of the profits went back to Havana and everybody was happy. My father was, by the time he was thirty-five, an upstanding citizen and a member of all the fashionable clubs in this town.

Remember, my father started as an agent for the bogus Cuban company Abraham had set up. The articles of that company enabled him to buy shares in it, paying for them out of his part of the profit. Within a few years, all these businesses ended up being officially and legitimately owned by my old man. My father and his associates always trusted Abraham to the hilt and, of course, they paid him accordingly. He always wanted Abraham in as a partner, but the guy constantly refused.

He wanted to go into business for himself, and had chosen to make something rather than trade. Abraham had green fingers, my father always said. He could have started an investment company or a bank. He could have started a gambling house or a nightclub. He knew all about that business too, but he insisted on going into something totally different. My father reckoned he would have been successful at anything he turned his hand to. He would have made it anywhere. That was why no one understood why he had left his country of birth. I myself think it was nothing tangible. Just a flaw in his character that stuck with him and made him move from place to place and business to business and woman to woman.

You could never tell Abraham what to do. He always knew better. Don't get me wrong, he was a great listener, but when it came to following advice he was not so hot.

But that was not why they finally fell out.

Chapter Ten

My wife's lawyer had been calling me but I could not face him and had to get my secretary to say I was not in. I did not know where to get the extra money from and was playing for time. His being a friend of mine made things more difficult, but I was hopeful. Sooner or later Abraham Moreno's inheritance was going to materialize, and with that my worries would be over. Once we had at least some of the papers, I could talk the bank into advancing me some money, but until then I had to be a juggler. I had not paid the rent on my flat for months and my landlord was after me too. I found all sorts of excuses for escaping from my desk and never answered the telephone at home before listening to the answering machine first to find out who it was. Whenever I could I'd get in the car and drive around. It gave me an opportunity to listen to Danny's recordings without being interrupted. I always looked forward to his cheerful voice.

One of his cassettes was rather short, and only Danny's voice appeared on it.

Dear Mr Lawyer,

I have sent you my three sessions and since we are coming to the end of the story I figure I shall soon be back. Young Chandler keeps asking me why Moreno left Palestine and, frankly, I don't know. There is something at the back of my mind but, as I have told you before, when you get old you lose the ability to tell your memory when to dance for you. If it comes back I'll let you know before I tell Chandler. Maybe it is important for you too. Yes, I am sure there was something and I used to know what it was, but so many years have passed. I mean, there was my life in Paris and the Spanish Civil War and then Morocco and the British Army. Whatever it was that made him leave could not have been that important or else I would have remembered it.

Or maybe my mind refuses to remember because it wants to stick to good news only.

I have written to my sister and daughter in Tiberias and have asked them to contact you. Maybe you can listen to what they tell you and make something of it. I did not mention this in my letter but I believe Abraham's departure had something to do with a woman. Some scandal. They might come up with the answer without knowing it. I have asked them to give you the names of people who knew him and are still alive. Maybe one of them will go up to the village with you. If you manage to find something before I do please let me know. Chandler's son's curiosity about Abraham's reasons for leaving his village deserves satisfaction. He's done a lot for us.

Yours, Danny

I played the cassette again as the car sped along the coastal road to Haifa. True to his word, Danny's daughter rang a day after the cassette reached me. We had a pleasant chat and I suggested I come to Tiberias and drive her up to the village. We could talk on the way, I said. She wouldn't hear of it. She said I had been so kind to her father in giving him a new interest in life and the least she could do was to help me. Her mother was coming up with her, and there was no need for me to drive to Tiberias at all. Go directly up to the village, she said, and we will meet in the family house. They would go up there the day before and prepare it. She had asked her mother who Abraham's friends were and which of them we should talk to. No, it was no bother at all. This was the time of year they usually went there to escape the heat. I would like it, she said. There was plenty of room and I could stay the night. Or several nights. As long as it took us to talk to the old men she had in mind for me. Those who might remember Abraham from their youth.

I had thought about taking young Moreno with me, but he had gone into hiding. There was nothing new about his disappearance, but this time he was gone for longer than usual. I had not seen or heard from him in over a month. The detective agency I had put on his tail came up with nothing.

I was making some progress with the Custodian of Absentees' Property. I had started dating a girl who worked there and had taken her to some fashionable eating places and to the movies. I was too besotted with my wife to think of anything intimate. Every time we met I brought her flowers, but I never took her home. The day before I went up to Abraham's village she finally came up with some encouraging news. The properties Abraham Moreno had bought were purchased in 1946, and so far two had been found. She could not tell me where they were because all she had seen was the ledger. There was a handwritten registration there without any documents to back it up. It meant, she said, that they did exist.

She didn't need to tell me more. From what I now knew of Abraham Moreno he was bound to choose the best possible location. Whatever else was wrong with him, he did have foresight. With the great wave of immigration that hit this country, prices of good building land had rocketed. The properties were sure to be worth a fortune if the legality of the situation could be established.

It was time for me to inform Abraham's heir of his obligation to me. I expected at least ten per cent of the value, over and above my fee and expenses.

I know it is in fashion to knock money, but I have learned all about its importance. When you have money you can buy independence. You don't have to hide from anyone or worry about how long they'll wait before they send the bailiffs in. You can buy people's respect and, contrary to whatever else you've heard, you can buy better health. Money buys you time to exercise. You can afford to eat the right foods and get the best medical help when you're in trouble. At that time my credit and resources were non-existent, and with the information the girl had dug out for me the sweet smell of cash was coming closer.

More than anything, I craved a reconciliation with Joan. I had managed to postpone a further confrontation with her by borrowing one last sum of money from the bank. I had given the manager the lease of my office as collateral and promised to pay it back within four to six weeks.

We had to let the office cleaners go and I thought about sacking the receptionist. I was late in paying the electricity and telephone bills. I gave up my parking spot. I was so short of funds I began to chase clients for outstanding payments. I also demanded cash deposits from people who came in with new cases for me to handle. Tel Aviv is a small town, and my behaviour was soon going to become common knowledge. This sort of thing does not do a lawyer's reputation much good.

Something else had given me the shakes.

That morning, before I set off, I had a visit from two gentlemen who barged through reception, telling the girl they were personal friends of mine. Once inside my office, they sat down without being asked and introduced themselves as members of the security services. I must have shown signs of anger or shock because they took pains to calm me down. Nothing personal, they said. Nothing damaging to you personally.

They wanted to know about my client Alex Moreno. Where he lived and what he did and how he paid his bills. I said I had advanced him some money. I said I had no idea where he was and, in any case, I was not going to discuss it with anyone.

They did not seem very impressed by what I had to say. They were a cocky pair. They made no verbal threats but said I'd better comply with their requests as any good citizen would. They said Alex Moreno had been in some trouble with the American authorities and our side had been asked to look into this. When I asked what crimes young Moreno had committed in America, they gave me a blank look. I was supposed to understand that America is our ally and when they need our help in security matters we don't ask questions. We just perform. One of them handed me a nondescript visiting card and asked me to contact him as soon as I heard from my client.

I have never been fond of the security services and their methods, and as I drove up north to meet Danny's daughter I tried to dispel the eerie atmosphere their visit had created. Attempting to work out why Abraham Moreno had left his village was as good a diversion as any. There I was, chasing solutions to Abraham Moreno's long-gone passions and mysteries, instead of finding concrete proof of his identity. Danny was a born detective, but he could not guess what kind of information I required from him. I badly needed to find out where Abraham had stayed when he came here, when the properties were purchased and from whom, and how he had paid for them. I needed evidence that he was now dead and that my client was his only son and sole heir and therefore entitled to his father's estate. The problem was I wanted all these enquiries to be undertaken discreetly. If the press had got hold of the story they would have solved it for me long ago, but then I would have forfeited Alex Moreno's trust. He wanted everything done in a cloak-and-dagger way. Perhaps I was wasting my time trying to find out why Abraham had left. Maybe going up to Danny's village was a mistake, but I could not help myself.

Chapter Eleven

The man Danny's daughter had found for me was at least eighty years old. He was Abraham's only living classmate from his schooldays. He had known him well and he talked of him with great affection. I was almost pleased old Moreno never lived to hear his own son Alex's distorted view of him. It must have been distorted, for I had the evidence of young Chandler and Danny and finally a man who grew up with Abraham through his formative years. He was an adventurer, he loved women, he was a nomad, but all three said he was a kind, generous and fearless man. Perhaps, I thought as I listened, his crime had been his charm.

We sat out on the man's verandah and in the distance we watched the landscape Abraham Moreno knew and walked. The Golan Heights dropped towards the placid Sea of Galilee and farther down, across the water, green farming plains led to a hazy Tiberias. The man's wife served us tea and dry dates and roasted peanuts.

'We used to go down that hill there and play with the Arab children, Abraham and me,' the old man said. 'They taught us a lot of things you didn't learn at school. They knew how to set traps and how to kill snakes and which shrubs and fruits you could eat. They knew how to make medicines out of the grass and the flowers. How to make flutes out of bamboo and how to play them. How to train sheep and where to find watering holes. They were mostly quite happy to let us in on what they knew.We shared the same grazing fields and the view and the need for rain. We shared, too, a suspicion of the real rulers of the country, the British. We would invite the Arab boys to our house and we went to their tents and there was peace up here. Of course, there were disputes but they did not see us as a threat. The shattering animosity between us only came with politics. In the early years they did not mind us being there at all. I can safely say we were friends, the way cousins are.

'Abraham was their favourite. There was nothing they wouldn't do for him. Every time we'd meet they'd hug him and kiss him and generally treat him like he was one of their own. He would have made a great prime minister, I can tell you. We would have found peace with the Arabs long ago if he'd stayed because they believed in him. Yes, even after the trouble started he'd go on hikes and fishing trips with them. It took two days and a night to get down to the other side of the Sea of Galilee, where the fish were abundant.

'By the time he was fourteen he had grown so big he had become a giant almost. Ibrahim il Taweel, Abraham the tall one, the Arab boys called him, and the name stuck. He'd come back and have us all listen to his exploits. How they'd lived on stolen bananas and fish and wild birds. How they were going to build a small sailing boat and go over the water to the other side of the lake to hunt for wild cattle. How he shot and killed a hyena that came upon them in the night and nearly mauled one of the Arab boys.

'He had learned how to read and write, and then it seemed the usefulness of school came to an end for him. He used to say you can learn everything else out of books. That was where the teachers themselves had got their information from. Books and experience. Experience, he said, was not to be found in a classroom. Only out there with the animals and the bushes and the trees and with people. He only turned up at school when the lessons were interesting for him. Farming methods and chemistry, that sort of thing.

'Before he was sixteen Abraham had become an expert on helping animals in distress. He could cure cows and horses, hens and ducks. He could set backbones on limping sheep. It was an art he was taught by an old Arab he had befriended after he had put out a fire that had broken out in the man's village.

'It wasn't just putting the fire out. He had saved the old man's granddaughter. It seems the fire began inside a bread oven in the centre of the village and started spreading. It was summer and at that time of the year everything is so dry it goes up in minutes. The fire sprawled into the house next door and then someone said there was a girl inside. The heat was unbearable and people stood around and wailed. The men were all out in the fields and all around the burning house there were old ladies, young children and men too old to work. Abraham covered himself with a wet sack and went in and pulled the little girl out of there. He had the presence of mind to wrap her up in a carpet. She screamed her head off but was otherwise unscathed.

'The story of his act soon spilled over to all the other villages and made him a hero among the Arabs, men and boys alike. He was given a hand-made decorated knife and a rifle from the girl's family and was welcome among the tribe for all eternity. This was an act of valour and any young man would have bragged about it, but not Abraham. He never told us about what had happened. It was the old Arab himself who did, when he came up to our village to defend Abraham after people here accused him of having stolen the knife and the rifle. I was only fourteen or so, but I can still remember the occasion. Just like it happened yesterday.

'All our elders were there, among the golden bales of hay, sitting in a large semicircle to listen to the old witness. The rifle and the knife were laid on a jute sack, between Abraham, who sat sulking on the right, and the old Arab on the left. He stood proud and erect, his arms taking to the air in all directions like a windmill. It was, the old man said, a sad surprise for him to see how a valiant man like Abraham was not trusted in his own house. It was, he said, a great honour to be given not just a knife but a firearm too. More than just an honour. It showed his people had given Abraham the rarest kind of trust; as if he'd been one of their own, even though by blood and faith he was not. It was only then, when the old man told the people of our village why he had given Abraham the rifle, that we ourselves found out about the fire and the girl's rescue. Before the old Arab had come, even Abraham's own father had suspected him of theft. No one in our village had such a weapon. It was a brand-new Enfield rifle which one of the villagers must have bought or stolen from a British soldier.

'I know all about that gun because Abraham gave it to me twice. The first time when he took off for three years and the second time on the night before he left here for good. After that I kept the gun for almost twenty years. Most of the time I hid it from the British. I would have kept it for ever. I finally gave it to the Israeli Army after the 1948 war, when private weapons were no longer allowed.

'Oh yes,' the old man said, 'Abraham would have gone far in politics, had he stayed in this country. He would have brought peace with the Arabs because they loved him, and more importantly, they trusted him.'

'Why ever did he leave?' I asked.

A cloud crossed the old man's face.

'I would rather not talk about that,' he said, and through the thick silence that followed I could sense his agitation. 'Don't ask me about that.'

'You must have missed him a lot after he left, I mean.'

'Oh yes. We all did. I don't know anyone who did not like and admire him. He was good looking. More than that. He was handsome. So handsome even people who had known him all his life commented on it every time he walked into the room. You couldn't get used to his looks or take them for granted the way people do when they see someone every day of their lives. And yet, believe it or not, no one was jealous of him. You see, he was too nice, too generous and brave, but he never took to showing off to make you feel inferior... And having him around was always fun because he was so wild you never knew what he'd do next. Of course, he might have upset a few men later on, but while he was a young boy in this village you could not be angry with him. Not even my father, who was our schoolteacher. Not even him. I think my father, God bless his soul, was an admirer of Abraham even if he could never admit it to anyone because Abraham missed so many classes.

'The only person who disliked him was his own father. Envy, I think it was. Maybe Abraham's father knew he could never reach the heights attained by his son.

'Then came the year when he left for the first time. I think he was about seventeen then, but he looked like an adult. A car stopped in the village one day. You may be surprised I remember that, but a car was a thing you hardly saw in those years. Everybody came out to admire it. This would have been 1924 or 1925, a few years after the First World War. It was black, the way all cars were then. It was an open car and a man and a woman were in it, asking for directions to Tiberias. The road in those days was not paved all the way down the mountain, and Abraham Schwartz volunteered to take them to the lake. From there the road was good almost as far as Tiberias itself, with the exception of the bit by the Scottish church. I was there that day, and I saw the man look at him. I saw the woman look at him too. I believe the man was an eye doctor and the woman, much younger, was his wife. Abraham spoke a few words of English and he told them he was going home to collect a few things. I remember wondering about that. After all, if he was going to be back the very next day, he didn't need to take anything with him. Still, when he came back with his bundle he told me to go to his house and take his rifle. Told me to keep it for him until he came back. I still hadn't caught on. Anyway, the fact was Abraham Schwartz was gone for two years that time.

'The village was not the same after that, as though there was no fun in the air once he was gone. We were out of school and were expected to take full responsibility for farming the land. Those were hard years, I can tell you. With work and guard duty and building houses and roads, no one slept more than four hours a night. So time ran very fast, and although I often thought of Abraham I had no time to go and look for him as I had promised myself I would. The Arab boys from the village always asked about him, but no one could give them a straight answer.

'And then one day he was back. The first I knew about it was the familiar knock on my window. It was maybe three o'clock in the morning, and I knew it had to be him because no one else would do that at such an hour. I opened the shutter and saw him. All he did was ask, have you kept my gun for me, and I said I had and we hugged and he came in.

'Oh, how excited Abraham was when he came back the first time. Just like a child. You would have thought he had seen the whole world in the two years he had been away. His English, he said, was now almost perfect. He had been working as an interpreter for the man who had come to the village in the car. The man who had taken him away. He was a Scottish eye doctor who worked in Haifa and Jaffa and Jerusalem and all over the place. He was so pleased with the young boy he wanted to adopt him and send him to Edinburgh to study medicine. He suggested sending his wife along to look after Abraham and help him there in Scotland, but Abraham wouldn't agree to that. He was too decent. To work for the man and learn English and see places was all right, but to take deliberate advantage of him went against the grain. There is more to this. I didn't really intend to go into it but it is a part of the story so I'll tell you. You see, he had been with the doctor's wife for some time. She was the first woman he had known. Maybe he refused to accept such a commitment from the doctor because he was sleeping with his wife and felt guilty about it.

'After Abraham came back that first time he talked about his absence for one whole week. The stories we heard about his travels and how people lived were something, I tell you. He had seen all the big cities of Palestine and beyond. He had been to Damascus and Cairo and Beirut. He saw great buildings and cars and trains and ships that carried as many people as we had living in our village. He saw markets with goods from all over the world. Not just old junk and meat or vegetables. Real markets with real stuff. Clocks and radios and motorcycles and shiny metal instruments and decorated jars. He had been to restaurants where you got dressed in a jacket and were served by waiters. He had been to the cinema houses and had seen many films. And he remembered everything and told us all about it. We'd listen to him in the evening, having worked hard all day, and sometimes he was still talking when dawn came. When you are young you can go on for ever. It was like some fantastic dream.

'Within a week of his return it was as if Abraham had never left us at all, so no one asked him what made him return.

'It could be he came back to the village because the affair with the doctor's wife was becoming too much for him. The doctor was a dedicated man and Abraham was not the kind to hurt anyone. His conscience might have bothered him. Or maybe he'd just had enough. I did not ask and he did not tell. The doctor's wife did not forget him. I saw her back in the village on a few occasions after he had come back. They went for long walks together, and once she took him away in the car, but he was back the next morning, working in the field with his father and brother. And then one day Abraham left without saying goodbye to anyone. He put the rifle in a hiding place we both shared, where we'd keep cigarettes and spare coins and other things we didn't want our parents to know about. He put the rifle there with a note saying he was giving it to me for ever. That was how I knew we would not see him in the village again.

'Time passed. The doctor's wife came back to the village a few times more and she looked for him all over the place. That was after Abraham had gone for good, and I thought it strange she didn't know about it. She had grown older, but she was still a tall and elegant lady. She asked everybody about him until I took pity on her. I told her he had left the country never to return. I think she came back one more time during the war and your father, Danny Katz, saw her. He had joined the British Army and was here on leave at the time. He too had told her Abraham was not coming back. No one saw her again. Maybe Danny did, but he never said. Didn't Danny tell you?'

Danny's daughter and I exchanged glances and shook our

heads.

'My father must have forgotten about that,' she said.

* * *

The old man's wife came out of the house and surveyed her husband's face. He had fallen asleep just then, as if he had waited to recall his friend's return before allowing himself to doze off. Then he opened his eyes and smiled.

'Do you think Abraham had enemies?' I asked.

'You must be crazy,' the old man said quietly, as if stating an indisputable fact. He said he would never believe there was someone on this earth who hated Abraham Schwartz.

I could have told him about someone who did. Would listening to his father's childhood friend have changed Alex's mind?

Maybe.

But then again, Alex Moreno's loves and hates were too deeply rooted for him to change.

Chapter Twelve

Danny's sister had prepared a sumptuous dinner, but after all the bits and pieces her daughter and I had been offered at the old man's house I could hardly eat. And then my secretary rang. She apologized for calling that late but she had only just arrived at her flat. She said the police had brought Alex Moreno into the office. He had been taken into custody earlier in the day and had given my name as a reference. She had no idea what the charges were. As I was not there, they said they would keep him until I was back. There was a number I could ring if I wanted to, she said. I decided to wait until morning.

* * *

I called my wife's number and my daughter answered the

phone.

'It's you,' she said, as if the sound of my voice was the last thing on earth she'd expected to hear.

'Yes, darling. How are you?'

'I'm busy right now.'

'What are you doing?'

'I'm watching television.'

I did not want to upset myself. I said:

'I'll call some other time, then. Maybe tomorrow.'

'If you like,' she said without much enthusiasm, and hung up.

My daughter must have been listening to her mother on the telephone. My wife often talked to people about my affair. She'd reveal all the sordid details at the top of her voice. I often asked her to stop doing it. I said it was wrong to make the little girl lose respect for me, or even to hate me. How long was she going to punish me for my mistake?

And yet, in quiet, lucid moments, I understood her well. I understood her frustration, and her anger. Had it been me I would have done worse.

* * *

History repeats itself. They say people from broken homes create broken homes for themselves. My father left my mother before I was two years old. I never found out why, because he never talked about my mother at all. I used to think there was an accusation of sorts in his demonstrative silence. He was so very British. He had been born in London and came to Palestine in the early thirties, but in many ways he never arrived. His way of life did not change with the new country. He'd don suits and ties in the height of summer and wore a panama hat and read the London papers. He never assumed the brash, open mentality of the home-grown Israelis. He was very reserved and cordial and laid-back, did not make any effort to learn Hebrew but tried to make a living as an English teacher. In his spare time he did a bit of writing and had some of it published in the Palestine Post and other English-language publications. He met my mother and they got married just before he enlisted in the British Army.

It was only much later, when he talked about my affair, that I saw him lose his temper. In spite of his leaving my mother without ever telling me why, his behaviour when my own marriage hit the rocks was strangely biased. He took Joan's side lock, stock and barrel. Maybe he backed her because she, like him, was born in England. I will never forget the occasion.

He was sitting with me on the terrace of his beautifully restored flat in Jaffa, shortly before he died. There was magic in the air. Birds of all shapes and colours and sizes hovered about, as though welcoming the returning fishermen. Behind the minaret, a giant orange sun slipped slowly down, leaving a golden glow that touched the pink horizon. In the distance you could hear the bells of the Italian church. I wondered at how, in this small area, the world's three main religions had survived for centuries side by side. And yet, with all that tranquillity around us, I was facing my first and last confrontation with my father. I do not know where he found the strength to berate me the way he did. From time to time he had to stop and catch his breath. His grey eyes burned with anger. Why did I have to look for other women when I had a perfectly wonderful wife at home? She was beautiful, she was clever, she had great taste. She could have been the best art dealer in London with her qualifications and sensitivity. Had she not followed me back to this country? Had she not given up a promising career for me? He called me an animal. Go get her back, he shouted. Crawl, apologize, eat humble pie and tell her you made a terrible mistake. Tell her you will atone. Do anything you can, just get her back. If you fail to do it you're going to regret this for the rest of your life. You're going to lose the love of your children.

He was livid, but remained a gentleman even then. He never mentioned what he had done for me throughout my life. How he invited me to live in his house in London. How he supported me while I studied at university. How he took me on all those holidays to Spain and elsewhere, and how he helped with the wedding and buying our first flat. There was none of the old guilt-producing 'I told you so'. But he did warn me. He said I was going to end up on my own. He whispered 'like others did', but stopped himself right there. That time was the closest he ever came to pointing an accusing finger at my mother, but he had managed to put his point across without doing so. My mother has a lot to answer for, I thought. Otherwise he would still be there with her.

* * *

It had been an extraordinary day. The old man's stories had brought back a part of my country's history I had forgotten existed. Israel is a modern country nowadays. We have a fast career- and money-chasing society like they have everywhere else. There are divorces and suicides and people who make it and people who fail. Money rules here as everywhere. I'm as much a part of it, as much to blame for it, as anyone. The Dannys of this world, and Abraham's old schoolfriend who told us of the old days, are a fast-dying minority.

Once upon a time there were ideals here, ideals that moved people to change their way of life, to leave their countries and their cities and work the land. Simple days of hope. Those who were different or too frail to take the hardship left to seek their destiny elsewhere. Abraham Moreno had left too, but for reasons I was yet to discover.

* * *

I sat out on the verandah and looked towards the valley. I wondered where and why it had all gone. Would Alex Moreno have fitted in then? Probably. He had no place in this new country because he had mixed his private emotions with other people's dreams, and that blinded him.

Danny's daughter came out and sat by my side.

'I've told my mother about this afternoon and what we

heard,' she said with a smile. 'Of course, there was little about Abraham she did not know already. She was a few years younger than him, but she remembers it all. He must have been quite a character. No wonder Father and you are fascinated by him. So was that young American who came here, Chandler. He is very good to Father and treats him like family, but I suppose you've heard about that already.'

'Yes. Will your mother talk to us about Abraham? I may not be able to stay here tomorrow.'

'She might. I hope so. Let her finish washing the dishes first.'

'What do you think made him leave?'

'I wish I knew.'

'You do know he came back to this country again. Once. Some time in the forties, just after the Second World War. He was a big and successful man then. It's that time I'm interested in. Someone must have seen him.'

'My father?'

'No. Your father was away in Europe. He was still in the British Army.'

'Didn't Abraham come up here to the village at all?'

'Not that I know of. I was hoping the man we saw today would tell us.'

'Why didn't you ask him?'

'I didn't think he wanted to be interrupted.'

She nodded. We chatted long into the night before tiredness caught up with us. I did not get a chance to see the old man again that time. In the morning my secretary rang and said that Alex Moreno was still in custody. She said I had better come back immediately.

Chapter Thirteen

It was one of those nondescript grey-green and black police stations that have smells and sounds all of their own. A mixture of ink, lubricating oil, fresh writing pads and the stale mixed scent of coffee and cigarette smoke. People came in and out, some frightened and others looking guilty. Everyone was told to sit in front of the duty sergeant's desk and await their turn. The clatter of iron doors opening and shutting mingled with the click-clacking of old-fashioned typewriters and the roar of revving motorbikes in the yard. I waited for almost an hour before they called me.

The officer in charge took me into his room. He offered me a seat and poured me a cup of coffee. He had soft, intelligent eyes and spoke with compassion. He apologized for the inconvenience and said there was no need for bail. This could be cleared up in minutes. I was tired and heard myself talking to him in an aggressive tone of voice.

'What are we, a police state? That was the sort of place my client escaped from. How can you hold anyone without charge?'

'I was going to let him go, Mr Lawyer,' the officer said quietly.

'So why is he here?'

'He had nowhere else to stay.'

'What was he arrested for?'

'Disturbing the peace. Got himself involved in a fist fight outside a bar in Jaffa. Apparently he was cursing the country, telling people off for treating the Arabs like second-class citizens.'

'He's got a point there, hasn't he?'

'Maybe he has, but not in front of a bar in Jaffa, with a load of drunken right-wingers just out of a party conference.'

'You mean a kick-the-Arabs-out sort of conference?'

'Yes. That sort of conference. He was lucky we were there. They would have torn him to pieces.'

'I see.'

'Your man Moreno is a card, you know.'

'In what way?'

'I interrogated him myself last night when they brought him in. He isn't new to this sort of thing.'

'He's never been arrested here before.'

'I don't mean that. He behaves and talks like a policeman. Was he a policeman?'

'I don't think so. What makes you say that?'

'Something in the way he looks at you… in the way he talks, anticipating what your next question is going to be, working out how to answer before you even ask. Waiting for you to blunder. He has a quiet air of authority about him. I'd say he has been an interrogator… at some point in his life at least.'

'Difficult to tell… he lived in a dictatorship. How did you converse?'

'Spanish is my mother tongue. I was born in Peru.'

'How lucky.'

'Surprisingly, it did not make him more forthcoming, my speaking Spanish.'

'Were you able to get anything out of him?'

'No. Just that he's been living rough, that he'd tried to find a place… When I took him to his cell he didn't make a fuss at all. He lay down on the bunk and fell asleep as though he'd been in jail before.'

'He has. He was in jail for years.'

'Poor guy. You know, I have a feeling the big back-room boys have an interest in him.'

'Really? I wouldn't think so at all. Why?'

'When I started to take his details down he said something along those lines. He said the CIA were after him, and Mossad, that sort of junk. D'you think he's been hallucinating?'

'Must have.'

'What's a man like that doing in Israel? I thought all Cuban refugees settled in Miami.'

'Maybe they didn't want him. Maybe he didn't want them. He's a Jew. He can live here. Law of return, you know.'

'I don't think he likes it here very much. Why doesn't he leave?'

'He will leave. As soon as he's got what he came for.'

'What's that?'

'Money.'

'Money? Here in Israel?'

'Yes. His father was born here. He came back years after he'd emigrated and bought some property here. That's what he's after.'

'No shit.'

'No shit. When can I have him?'

'Any time you like.'

* * *

We sat in the car quietly. Alex looked like a beaten animal. For once he did not argue with me. I took him to my flat and while he bathed I put his shirt and socks and underwear in the washing machine. You become quite proficient at looking after yourself when you're alone. While the clothes were drying I made coffee and we sat there waiting, staring at each other.

'Thank you,' he said. I had never heard him say that before. Not even when I gave him money. I looked at him and tried to see the ex-policeman. I searched for the interrogator, for that super-intelligence, but all I saw was a dejected, defeated man. I felt deeply sorry for him.

'You can stay here with me for a couple of days,' I ventured.

'We'll see. Did you have a good time up in my father's village?'

'How did you know?'

'I know. Did you?'

'Yes. As a matter of fact I did. That Abraham Schwartz of yours was quite a guy.'

'Yes.'

'They love him up there still. Always did. He used to be honoured by the Arabs, too. Saved a girl's life there. No one ever forgot him.'

'It's good you're getting to know him. Very important. You don't know how important.'

'Maybe you should get to know him too.'

'I knew him.'

I heard the dryer stop and I got up and brought the clothes back. I started to iron his shirt but he shook his head.

'It won't hurt you to look orderly for a change.'

'Leave me be. I was watching you just now. You're learning all about my father. Like I told you, the only way to get to know someone is to try and get under their skin… become like them. This is quite possible; even if the person is dead you can enter their soul. Once you get under his skin you'll learn to think like him and know his secrets and the way his mind worked. You'll find everything we are looking for. Even documents. And I must tell you you're doing well. So well you're beginning to… You almost remind me of him.'

'You're sick, Moreno.'

'You do… you really do make me think of him.'

'It's only because I'm in a position of some authority here. I give you money, wash your clothes… I'm being a parent. Besides, all we do is talk about him. That's why I make you think of him. You even hate me sometimes, for being in a position to help you.'

'Could be. Not today, though. I don't hate you today. How is Danny doing in Miami?'

'Haven't been to the office yet. I came straight for you. He's sent me some material, but I'm expecting more.'

'I've been listening to his cassettes. Chandler is a dreamer.'

'Why?'

'Listen to him talk about his father and mine… a pair of angels. Did you hear him describe my mother? Plain girl, the sonofabitch said she was. She was a beauty. She was highly educated and well read and loyal and…'

'Don't get yourself upset. Everybody has their own point of view. Chandler was only quoting his father. Maybe he got a little carried away. You're not taking the circumstances into account. He's telling his story to Danny. He's trying to impress him. Remember what Chandler is. He lives in a glitzy world… for him a woman is only beautiful if she's a show girl from Las Vegas. Beads and feathers and black nylons. Saccharine. Maybe he's inventing things his father said. Maybe it's all wishful thinking.'

'Of course it's wishful thinking. Chandler senior was a gangster, a murderer. His name in Cuba was mud, even then. He had bodyguards. Didn't move without them. I remember him well. He used to come to our house outside Havana. He'd corner my father. Monopolize the conversation… talk about business and getting rid of people. But most of all he talked about women and his adventures with them, and all that with my mother there in the room, and me too. Shameless, I tell you. He'd talk about the way he and my father screwed all that money out of the stupid Cubans. A family man, young Chandler said his father was… ha! Some family man. He was a hypocrite. He had women all over the place. Even in Havana. He had a mulatto mistress, old Chandler did. She was a famous dancer and a singer. At first he'd leave her in the car outside for hours. Later he'd bring her into the house and my father forced my mother to entertain her like she was Chandler's wife or something. Can you imagine how difficult that was for my mother? She came from a decent, middle-class family in Berlin. She could recite Goethe and Schiller. There were books and music in her house when she grew up… she wasn't used to that sort of thing. Having to sit and entertain a man's mistress while she knew his wife. I bet you young Chandler knows nothing of that.'

'Every man has many sides. I wish you'd see your father the way he was in his youth. He wasn't all bad. He couldn't have been loved as well as he was by people who'd known him all his life unless there was a good side to him too.'

'It's beginning to work on you, his charm. From the grave it works on you. They said it was irresistible. But not to me. I had the last laugh, though. I saw him when he crumbled. When he was humiliated, when all his power and influence and money had gone. He wasn't charming then, I can tell you.'

'When? Where? What happened to him?'

'I don't want to talk about it now. I must tell you something else, something that will teach you about my mother. The mulatto dancer Morton Chandler brought with him, the mistress he kept in Havana? Her name was Carmelita Rodriguez. And do you know what happened? She became my father's mistress too. More than his mistress. She was... they were together for years. For ever. Until the end. She was the love of his life, if there ever was such a thing. Shameless, that. After all the things old Morton Chandler had told my father about her. What her body was like, what her scent was like. How she was the best screw in the world. How her skin drove him mad. I'm not inventing this. I heard it with my own ears and so did my mother. After hearing and seeing all that he took her on himself. I don't mean they shared her. My father fell in love with her and she became his exclusive woman. Old Chandler accepted that without a fight. What sort of a man does that make him? He simply passed her on to my father as though she was a second-hand car. They moved in the same circles and saw each other all the time. She came to our house whenever Chandler came. My father pretended she was still Chandler's mistress, but you didn't have to be a genius to see what was going on between them. The way she looked at my father. The way his eyes followed her all over the room. The way their lips sent silent messages. I saw and I understood, and I was only a child. Can you imagine what my mother thought? She was a sensitive woman. She knew. Probably long before I did. Later on he didn't even bother to pretend. Used to kiss and hug and fondle the Rodriguez woman in our house… with me and my mother there. My father was an insensitive, cold bastard. But I got my own back, I promise you.'

'How? What did you do to him?'

'I don't want to talk about that now,' he said, and then his expression changed. He got up and touched my shoulder. He was shorter than I but he looked down at me and his voice was clear and soft and sure. He sounded like a councillor or a schoolteacher. He spoke with authority. He said:

'Let's go to the office. Don't you have to work for a living? Isn't your wife at war with you? Don't you owe money all over?'

He said all this in the recriminatory tone of a parent or an older brother. He seemed to know everything, and I did not even bother to ask him where he had got it from. Slowly, without my noticing it at all, he was moving in on me. Right into me. He knew what I was going through. Someone at the office must have been feeding him information. Or else he had another source somewhere.

And yet none of that worried me because one thing was certain. He was not going to use whatever he had found out about me to do me any harm. In his warped way, Alex Moreno was trying to protect me. And maybe not just because he needed me. Maybe he even liked me a little.

'Do you want something to eat?' I asked.

'No.'

'Let's go to the office, then. There's a new tape from Danny. I'd like to hear it.'

Chapter Fourteen

Abraham Moreno settled down in Cuba, Morton Chandler's voice said.

My old man would go and see him over in Havana and he came to Miami and so the connection was always there. They talked to each other on the telephone daily. Abraham got himself into the canning business. Imported the equipment from the States and started to can fruits and vegetables. He bottled sauces and juices and syrups. He did well because he understood farming and farming products and he understood farmers. They loved him and they let him have top choice of their produce. Most of all, he did well because he had planned it all long before the first machine was even ordered. On top of that he was making money brokering. You know, agenting... getting import and export licences for Americans who wanted to sell stuff or buy stuff. He negotiated contracts for the laying of small railway lines for the sugar mills. Supply agreements for the ship chandlers. Purchased uniforms and small arms for the police. You name it. On top of that, he was still sending laundered black money out to Miami for my father to invest and my father paid him two per cent on everything. He was doing real good.

Then they fell out. It was, my father said, because Abraham got romantically involved with a friend of our family, a Cuban dancer called Carmelita Rodriguez. You can understand that, can't you? I mean, my father and my mother were there when Abraham first met Martha. They were at their wedding... they organized it, for Christ's sake. My father could not accept Abraham's behaviour with Carmelita because it was he who had introduced her to Abraham in the first place. She was married to a Cuban friend of my father's, and when she came with her husband to Miami to perform in one of the hotels she became quite close to my mother. After she went back to Cuba her husband had to go on long trips negotiating sugar deals in Europe or somewhere, and my father used to look her up when he was over there. Bring her little gifts from my mother, that sort of thing. There was nothing intimate between them. My father may have been a gangster but he was faithful to my mother to the last. This I know for a fact because we were a close family and I saw everything that went on in the house.

Anyway, Carmelita Rodriguez worked nights and during the day my father would take her to the countryside or the beach. Often he took her with him to Abraham Moreno's place in the country. I think that was where Moreno and Carmelita first met. He made a beeline for her and she fell. Soon she divorced her husband and became Abraham's lover full time.

Of course, he lived to regret that, but for a good many years Abraham Moreno was a one-woman man. My mother was upset about this, her knowing Carmelita in person and having been at Martha's wedding and all that. My father, too, was not happy, because it brought bad blood between him and the guy Carmelita Rodriguez had been married to.

Abraham Moreno and Carmelita Rodriguez? It was a real movie. One of those fatal attractions you saw coming, like a sudden little gust that becomes a tornado. It blows and blows and all around you big trees begin to shoot out of the ground. My father said my mother insisted he stopped talking to Abraham until it was over. I think the feud lasted about two years or something, but they got together again. My father said there was no stopping Abraham's infatuation with Carmelita nor hers with him. You can't break a true friendship over a lost cause. My father and he became inseparable again, and no trouble came between them until the real big bust-up, but that's another story.

My old man accepted the situation, and from then on the woman Rodriguez was always there. She really got under Abraham's skin. He used to travel around with her like they were man and wife. He bought a small record company just to produce stuff with her singing and even that made a bit of dough because she hit the big time. He would have gone to Hollywood with her. Nowadays, with all the Cubans living over here, she would have made a real fortune. Anyway, the only time they were separated was when he went off to Palestine. She did not want him to go because she was jealous, but he swore blind he would never look at another woman. She did not believe him and neither did my father. Abraham could not be without a woman and they couldn't keep their hands off him. But we are talking about 1940, and his trip to Palestine came later. After the war. Somewhere around

1946, I reckon. By that time his boy, Alex, was old enough to keep Martha company. He was a frightened little kid with mysterious eyes and hidden thoughts who hovered all over the house, clinging to his mother's skirts. My father was a little scared of him.

'Stop,' Alex Moreno bellowed. 'Stop now. I don't want to hear any more of that shit. Did you hear what Chandler said? How his father was never unfaithful? Do you think Danny believes that?'

'It's up to me, not him. He's working for me. In any case, whether old Chandler was or wasn't faithful is unimportant.'

'Did you listen to what he said? His father had nothing intimate going with Carmelita Rodriguez. He was her boyfriend. I told you he was. I saw old Chandler screw her once in the back of his car, outside our house. They were having a quick one before he came in. That was in the beginning, before he started bringing her into the house. Until then Carmelita was left in Chandler's car, waiting like a dog while he came into the house and sat around for hours. I don't want to hear any more. The Chandlers never liked me. You heard it yourself. Scared? How could a gangster like Chandler be scared of a boy of five or six, you tell me that.'

'Don't get so excited.'

'I'm a Latin. We get excited.'

'You're a Jew.'

'Jews get excited too.'

'So your father came here after the war…'

'Maybe… he must have. Unless Chandler got it wrong.'

'If he was here after the war, how come Danny didn't know about it?'

'Don't ask me. Danny's your friend. I've never met him. From what I've heard of him, he would know. He's an honest man. An anti-Fascist. He fought against Franco in the Civil War.'

'How do you know?'

'I know. Anyway, maybe Danny isn't telling you the whole truth.'

'Why?'

'People have reasons for hiding things. Maybe he'll tell you when he's ready.'

'Tell me, Alex, were you ever a policeman?'

He looked at me and suddenly he smiled. He smiled so rarely that I was taken aback and I watched him. He was handsome in a strange way, and as the smile worked its way across his face he seemed gentle, but only for a second.

'I don't want to talk about that now,' he said. I could have sworn he was going to admit he had been a policeman, but maybe he did not want to volunteer any information, like any good interrogator. Of course, I knew why he did not want to hear any more. The rest of Chandler's tape was going to be about him, his mother and his childhood, and he hated that time. It made him suffer. It made me suffer too. Inside, I cried for him.

'You need some money, Alex?'

'No, lawyer. You haven't got any to give.'

'My credit is good still.'

'Not for long. I'll go back to your place, if you don't mind. I'll wait for you there.'

'Let me give you the address.'

'Just give me the keys. I know the address.'

'Want to have dinner with me tonight?'

'You have no money for that sort of thing.'

'How do you know?'

'I know.'

'Well, there's nothing you can do about it.'

'There is.'

'You, Alex?'

'Yes. Me, Alex.'

'How?'

'Will you get me a telephone number in Miami?'

'Sure. You want to call someone?'

'Yes.'

'Why don't we call Danny? He'll do it for you.'

The firmness was back in his voice. He was in the driver's seat.

'I want to call Miami now and I want Danny out of this one. Don't tell him a thing about it. This is private. It's my treat.'

My secretary came in. Moreno gave her the name of someone called Juan Miret. He lived on Aventura Boulevard. The time in Israel was seven in the evening. In Miami it would have been midday. It was Sunday.

'Will he be at home?'

'Yes.'

'What does this Miret do for a living?'

'Oh, he's got a shirt factory. A shoe business, a couple of supermarkets. A financial company of some sort. He employs a lot of Cuban refugees.'

'Has he done well?'

'None of your business.'

'Friend of your father?'

'No. Not my father's. He used to be my friend. He once needed me.'

The call came through before I managed to ask him what he meant. It was a very short conversation. Moreno spoke in yet a new tone of voice. That of an absolute ruler. The assurance, the power in its staccato tone, astounded me. He spoke curtly and to the point, like a man accustomed to leading and being obeyed. He gave Juan Miret my address and my bank details. He dictated the information to the other man as if to a child, pronouncing every letter carefully and repeating it twice. He made Miret repeat it too. How he knew my personal account number I could not imagine. He then instructed Juan Miret to send some money. He said he would leave the amount up to him. He did not promise to pay any of it back and did not thank the man, nor did he say adios before he hung up.

'It will be here tomorrow,' he said when he was through.

'What was that for?'

'A down-payment, Mr Lawyer. You're not exactly rolling in it right now, are you?'

'This is highly irregular.'

'Irregular? You've been chasing all your clients for cash, haven't you? You've laid out quite a bit on me already. Any minute now the bank will kick you out of this office. Isn't the lease now mortgaged to them? I can't have you losing your reputation, can I?'

Nothing was going to surprise me about him again, or so I thought.

I had the shakes. I sat there and looked at my hands. He got up. I handed the keys to my flat to him. He took them and walked out without a word.

I needed a diversion badly. Danny's tape and Chandler's voice would provide plenty. I asked my secretary not to put any more calls through and turned the tape recorder on.

Chapter Fifteen

The little Moreno kid was one hell of a gloomy customer. A permanent case of the blues. He was nothing like his father. He didn't have the energy or the charm or the charisma. He had one of those anonymous faces. The kind you'd need to think hard about before you knew whose it was. He stayed indoors and never saw the sun and was always pale. Abraham loved him in his way but little Alex was not a guy you could hug or fool around with. He was far too serious, too deep, even as a child. He was small for his age and wasn't a great looker but boy, was he smart. He was going to cause incredible trouble for everybody because he knew about things. He knew who bribed whom and who invested where. He knew every corrupt official there was to know. I mean to say, they all came to Abraham's house and they spoke about things quite openly, negotiating hush money over a cigar and a drink, the way it was done in Cuba in those days. He looked at everyone and listened and you could see the little wheels rolling inside his head. He was memorizing voices, body language, faces. He was collecting information like he was making up files about people in his head. My father said he didn't miss a thing and was going to make good use of it all and he was proven right, but that happened much, much later. Abraham wanted to send him to school in the States. A boarding school for boys. I think it was a kind of military academy. He thought the training and the discipline would toughen him up. Who did they think they were kidding? Alex Moreno was as tough as nails. He needed no military academy. Georgia, yes. It was in Georgia, but where the academy was doesn't really matter because the boy never went. His mother wouldn't have it. He was real quiet and would walk around like a cat without a sound. Sometimes you'd be sitting in the house there, my father said, and he'd creep up on you and suddenly he was there behind you or by your side. He was polite, though, but he never smiled. My father figured that with the way Abraham carried on he had little to smile about.

You would never believe it, but Abraham's mistress Carmelita Rodriguez liked the kid. Maybe she felt sorry for him. We all did. She'd bring him presents and he would accept them and take them out of the room. He'd burn them later, up in the garden, with his mother watching. Like they were having a kind of voodoo ceremony. Martha and her son shared many secrets, but she never used them against Abraham because she loved him and never forgot what he had done for her.

It was a strange set-up. My father never understood how come Abraham even came back to the house, but it was on account of the child. He and Martha had little to say to each other by then. He was besotted with the Rodriguez woman. My father said every word, every glance, every touch that passed between them was pure sex. Even years later, when they weren't so young any more.

She lived with him in his place in Vedado, one of the finest neighbourhoods in Havana. On weekends they would stay in bed for hours. They entertained lavishly and many important people came to their place. Ministers, ambassadors, businessmen. You name it. They were not married but with her fame and his money, nobody gave a damn. They were never apart. He always took her to his country house where Martha and the kid lived. They had their own bedroom there and Martha said nothing and accepted it all, but the boy... well, the boy must have been keeping a silent score. No, they were never out of each other's sight. When she sang, wherever it was, he had his own regular table, and he was jealous. Boy, was he jealous. My father said Abraham once got a young officer into trouble just for sending her flowers after a show. The poor guy was kicked out of the army. You could do things like that in Cuba then. But she was jealous too. My father swore she had no reason to be. Not until later, when he went off on his own, but that too is another story.

They travelled to the States and Mexico and all over South America for business. He was setting up deals and selling cigars and putting up canneries under licence. He had a herd of cattle. Two. One in Cuba and one in Argentina. He knew a lot about animals. He was a fine horseman. My father often saw him playing cowboys down on his haciendas. Like a real expert, Abraham used to comment on their skins and energy. They were all healthy beasts and he won a whole bunch of prizes for them. He once told my father he would have become a rancher had he stayed in Palestine. So they travelled around and he made more and more money. Sometimes he would get her a singing engagement if he needed to stay in one place for any length of time. She was quite famous by then and so beautiful you wouldn't believe.

He was a naturalized US citizen and needed to reside over here for a few months from time to time to keep that going. Abraham was very proud of his American papers and was always worried about losing them. He had managed to get himself naturalized without living in the States for the full required period. How he managed that was a mystery. I figure my father had something to do with it but he never said. And mind you, it was no phoney. It was the real thing. A full-blooded green passport. Later on he lost it. The way he lost it was tragic, my father said. A tragic mistake. No one would ever have guessed something like that could happen to Abraham. The US authorities would never have revoked his passport. Not with the connections he had with the embassy and the work he was doing for them on the QT. Still, that's not what we're talking about today, right? I've got to say it, though. Truth is stranger than fiction, take my word for it.

As the world steamrollered itself towards the Second World War we in America were out of it. Not until Pearl Harbor did anyone think we'd go overseas and fight again over there in Europe. No one knew what was going on with the Jews. There were rumours and Martha used to tell horror stories but no one believed her. No one except for her friend Conchita Madeiros. She even tried through her husband's Foreign Office connections to find Martha's family, but they had disappeared without a trace.

Conchita Madeiros once took Martha on a little trip to Miami. That was when my folks got to know her real well. Martha was deeply ashamed of the way her marriage was going but while she and Conchita Madeiros were visiting here she made out everything was swell. Of course, the whole town knew the truth, but Conchita never let on. She was a real lady. She was Martha's best friend and they stayed at our house without ever letting slip why they were over. They'd take off for a few hours every day without saying where they were going. I think they consulted some doctor or a shrink but my father was never sure. Their kid Alex went along with them, only he was not that much of a kid any more. That was when I saw a lot of him myself, seeing that I was home for the summer break. My folks wanted me to take him out and show him a good time but he was not interested. He did not drink and could not dance so we went to the movies a couple of times. In any case, he preferred to hang around with Conchita and his mother.

Conchita Madeiros was the only woman who had formed an affectionate relationship with Alex. She was demonstrative. He even allowed her to kiss and cuddle him when he was little. She loved him and she spoiled him like he was her own. He used to like staying with her, even without his mother. He was very close to Mr Madeiros, too.

He was too much of an intellectual to be a father figure, but they talked a lot. No one knows what that sophisticated diplomat talked to Alex about. They liked each other and went out to the theatre and libraries and Madeiros once bought the kid a gold watch. They were very thick together and spoke on the telephone each day. Conchita and her husband were like a replacement family for Martha, and things would have been great if it had lasted. But in January 1949, after a big New Year party in the house of some diplomat, Conchita Madeiros and her husband were killed when their car crashed into a wall by the port. The car caught fire and blew up. They were well-known people and the story was all over the papers. Martha was never the same again after that.

After the accident there were all kinds of rumours about the Madeiros. You know how it is in a small community. People like scandal and gossip even if it hurts. There are jealousies and jealousies produce plenty of dirt. They said he had kept a mistress. They said he was a gambler and had lost all his money. Then they said Conchita had taken a lover because Madeiros had had a long sordid affair with his male secretary. They even said they had a suicide pact.

They were all so wrong it wasn't funny.

Abraham told my father what the score really was. I only heard about it many years later, but I never forgot it. Every story has an end. You know how things tie up when the circle finally closes. On the private side, Mr and Mrs Madeiros were first cousins and could not have children because they were scared of in-breeding. On the public side, Mr Madeiros' back-stairs activities were about to be exposed by Cuban Intelligence. This upstanding, upper-class diplomat was, on the quiet, an important member of the Communist Party. After the war, during the late forties, the Cold War was raging and anything red was a curse. Abraham said Madeiros was going to be put on trial for his activities as a spy. He had used his position to pass on heaps of information to the Russians through their embassies in South America. He would have been shot, or at least tortured and imprisoned for life.

My father believed Abraham was the one who had

warned them.

Abraham said they did themselves in to avoid the disgrace of a scandal.

* * *

It's funny how things turn around. Their lives and their convictions and what happened to them simply occurred too early. Batista's Cuba was not ready for them. It would have condemned them as criminals. In Castro's Cuba they would have been heroes. Today's Cuba and what it has become would have disillusioned them. I bet they'd be living right here in Miami. Crazy, huh?

Anyway, my father said Abraham had always known about Madeiros' political beliefs and yet after their death he used his connections to keep that bit quiet. Because of Carmelita's fame he was intimate with every journalist in Havana and no one printed a word. My father said he did not want Martha to know that her friends were not what they seemed. Abraham never allowed anyone to say a thing about Conchita and her husband when Martha was around.

He was protective of her still. No wonder she was crazy about him until the end.

Chapter Sixteen

I had not seen my mother for a while and decided to pay her a visit on my way home. She lived in a spacious three-bedroom flat overlooking the sea. It was built in the thirties and she bought it when the war was over, a couple of years after her divorce. I never found out where she got the money from. At that time she was not working for herself and I didn't think my father had any money to give her when he left. Whenever I asked her about it she said she had borrowed the money from a friend. It is still a very fashionable place and it took for ever to find a parking place. The lift was small and constantly occupied and I got tired of waiting for it. I walked up three flights of stairs and stopped by her entrance to regain my breath.

'You look like you've been in the wars,' she said as she opened the door. I had a key but for some reason I always rang the bell first.

'I have.'

'Is Joan making trouble?'

'No. It's work.'

'Anything interesting?'

'Yes. This profession takes you around the world. Better than the navy.'

'Tell me about it. You know I like hearing what goes on. Where did you dock today?'

'Havana. Cuba. I spent the afternoon in Cuba.'

Something funny happened then. She did not wait to hear the rest of it the way she usually did. She cut me off and asked me if I wanted a cup of coffee or a drink or something to eat. She said it quickly and her voice faltered. Maybe she was worried about me. I was hoping she would, for once, ask me if I needed anything, and that would have given me the chance to ask her for help. But nothing like that happened. She looked at me like I was a ghost and then she cleared her throat and asked the same question again. Did I want some coffee or something to eat? As if she wanted to make sure I had heard.

I did not catch on then. I should have noticed that something had startled her but I suppose I was tired. It had been a long day and I had other things on my mind. I had driven back from the Galilee and had wrestled my client out of the clutches of the police. I had listened to Danny's most recent recording and had witnessed a hundred changes of mood on Alex's face. More than anything, I had heard the way he had spoken to that Juan Miret fellow in Miami. The way he more or less ordered him to transfer money into my account. The fact that nothing about Alex was what it seemed had finally caught up with me. I needed time to understand what was going on.

My mother asked me if I was staying.

'No. I'm taking a client out to dinner. Just popped in to see how you were.'

'That's sweet of you, my dear,' she said. Her voice returned to normal. She spoke slowly, measuring every word. I had always thought of her as a cold woman. In many ways she was as reserved as my father was. Or maybe she assumed his manner the way people sometimes do. She did not have many friends but she was not lonely because she liked her own company. She read a lot and listened to music and she went to the theatre. She had never remarried but I knew she had men friends. No great love stories, just men friends. She was a slim, attractive woman and I used to hear her with them across the corridor in her bedroom when I was a boy. All her lovers were married men, and, years later, when I asked her about this she admitted it was because she did not want to be attached to anyone again. I could never imagine her emotionally involved. She was too efficient. Too career-minded. I think she simply used them, the way women claim men always do. I often wanted to ask her why Father had left her but did not dare for fear of hurting her. She had run a travel agency for many years, but three years ago she had passed it on to her young assistant in exchange for a share in the profits. I had drawn up a good contract for her and, as it was a successful, centrally located business, she was not short of money. We had a cool, correct relationship and I knew I could rely on her help. But I did not ask and she did not notice I was in any need.

'Not even a glass of water?'

'No. Thanks all the same.'

She shrugged her shoulders and came and stood over me.

'You must not overdo things. Have you seen the children? You must make sure you do as often as you can. Otherwise they only get one side of the story. That can be bad when you get to court.'

'I'm not running a competition and there's no question of any court. Joan is a highly intelligent woman. She knows that whatever she says about me to them will boomerang back on her one day. I'm sure she isn't saying a single bad word, and if she did I'd understand. You can't blame her for being bitter. I would be. I wish it had never happened.'

She sat down and we looked at each other. I thought about what I had heard that day and wanted to go home, where Alex was waiting for me, but something kept me there with her. I don't know what it was. Her usual self-assurance seemed to have received a jolt. Could it have been my rather aggressive defence of my wife? I tried to work out what had been said but I couldn't think straight.

'Do you think things would have been different had you stayed in England? You were happy there. Maybe Joan would have preferred to. I mean, she is English...'

'It's a bit late to think of that now, Mother. I've been back for ten years.'

Had it been that long? My liaison with my father's country of birth had started when I was a very young boy. After the divorce, my mother used to send me to England for the school holidays. As with any affair, England and I started as strangers would, an adventure pretending to be a relationship. When we got to know each other, the country and I became close. And when we started to trust each other, we fell into intimacy. There was a time when I was not sure where I belonged. The two civilizations must have enriched me, but I was too busy having fun to be aware of it . I began to master the language and got myself involved with the laid-back rhythm, the history and the culture of the British people. There were, too, summers of fun when we went to the zoo and pantomime and on weekend hikes in Scotland. Mostly, though, we went to Mallorca, where my father had bought himself a small flat. I made lots of friends on our holidays, but our own relationship was never simple.

There was something distant about him. He was considerate and polite and wanted me to have a good time, yet he always seemed to be holding something back. Maybe I embarrassed him in some way. He was a slim, elegant man. I did not get on well with city suits, while he always looked like he was born in one. He was of a fair complexion and well mannered and the epitome of an Englishman. My own accent and manners grew indistinguishable from those of the people around me, but not my looks. I was a lanky Mediterranean with unruly black hair and and the remains of a loud laugh. He was a journalist of some note and a television personality. I was proud when people recognized him, although because of the strained distance between us no one took us for father and son. Maybe he felt that too. Maybe that was why he always took such pains to tell everyone that we were. And then again, perhaps doing so was his way of exorcizing his guilt for leaving my mother and me. Later, after doing my military service in Israel, I went back to London and studied law. That was where I met my wife Joan. When we married and came back to Israel, my father took early retirement and came to live in the ancient port of Jaffa, south of Tel Aviv.

I am sure he only came because of Joan, with whom he had become very close. He continued to write a syndicated column for a group of American newspapers even after he retired. He was writing his autobiography when the cancer struck him, but he put up a long and bitter fight. He died a year ago, just after I was found out and kicked out of the house. The manuscript was not among his papers. I suppose he destroyed it.

I have always missed those things between us that were left unsaid.

* * *

'I tried to call you last night. You weren't in,' my mother said.

'I spent the night in Rosh Pina.'

'What's in Rosh Pina?'

'It's where a gentleman I'm investigating lived before he left the country. It's a long story. I'll tell you about it some time.'

'You do that, dear,' she said, and I knew she had closed

the subject. Again I thought something was afoot. I could not put my finger on it. Maybe something was upsetting her. Maybe she was not feeling well. She always made a special effort to appear interested in what I was doing, but that evening she seemed glad not to hear me talking about work. Maybe she was tired. I wish I had stuck to my hunches. I should have investigated the matter further right there and then. I would have saved myself a lot of pain later.

'You'd better go home, dear,' she said in her business voice. 'Aren't you taking a client out to dinner?'

'Yes,' I said, and got up. We hugged and I kissed her lightly on her cold cheek. As I shut the door behind me I heard her record player blaring her favourite Beethoven concerto.

* * *

He was waiting for me in my flat when I came in. As soon as I saw him I knew there was something different about him. Something totally new. He was, for the first time since we had met, almost happy. His face shone with the expectation of something good about to happen. His voice was soft, his movements slow and relaxed. He had an apron around his waist and had made a chef's hat out of a white pillow case. I burst out laughing. He had prepared a rice and chicken dish with olives, red peppers and saffron. Arroz con pollo was the name of the dish, he said. It was typically Cuban. How he got the ingredients without speaking Hebrew I did not know. He had a couple of beers in the fridge. We had a feast that night, and we talked easily of this and that. We steered clear of Abraham Moreno and his past and properties. Alex turned out to be a vivid storyteller and we laughed a lot.

And then I remembered something from Danny's recording that had stuck with me. It was the story of Martha's friends the Madeiros and how it ended, and I asked Alex to tell me more.

This had, strictly speaking, nothing to do with our business but for once he did not refuse. In fact he talked with great enthusiasm and pathos. It became evident that the Madeiros commanded an exceptionally intimate place in his heart. Intimate enough for him to drop his customary guard for the first time and reveal something of himself.

Chapter Seventeen

'It was Gustavo Madeiros who taught me about the real Cuba,' Alex Moreno said. 'He was a patriot. A man who had a love affair with his country all his life. What you've heard about Conchita and the German lessons my mother gave her and the way they took my mother into their hearts and their home was true. Gustavo Madeiros was an educated man. He knew about history and economics and poetry and he tried to pass his knowledge on to me.

'I was not an easy youngster to teach because I did not trust people. Our home was often intimidating, and always a lonely place. I heard my father's lies and saw the decadence and greed among his friends and I lost my faith in grown-ups. My mother constantly forgave him for being indifferent to her and her needs. She accepted his philandering and in her quest for peace she became his doormat, but there was no peace. There was, instead, a relentless atmosphere of aggression in the house. I never knew who was coming for dinner or the weekend and worried about whether they would be civil to my mother or ignore her. These people were not my father's friends. He had used them and they had used him. Until I understood what Madeiros was about, I did not believe there was such a thing as unconditional friendship. With my suppressed anger and frustration I would have ended up in an institution, hating all of humanity. If it hadn't been for Gustavo Madeiros, I would have had no role model at all, no confidence and no beliefs. He showed me a life and gave me a reason to live it because he helped me rise above my petty bitterness and self-pity. He showed me there were real victims out there, casualties of genuine injustice.

'He was born into a privileged family who owned sugar mills, but instead of going into the family business he chose an academic career. He was interested in politics only because he dreamed of improving the life of the workers. Whenever Cuba went through a financial crisis, it was the workers who suffered first. If sugar prices went down, they were out of a job.

'He came from the ruling classes and he knew everything there was to know about them. The way they thought, their aspirations and the way they intended to maintain things as they were. That was why he had to keep his political thoughts to himself. Had they known he was a communist he would never have been able to have had the career he had. He would never have been able to help others, including my mother and me. He did not intend to be a leader because he was not interested in power. Only in justice. He was more of a philosopher, and would've been the country's conscience had he lived. I wish he had been my father. He was a wonderful teacher because he cared and because he was blessed with a rare ability to communicate. He chose to stay and teach after he graduated because he sought the company of young people, and in a way he remained a student all his life. Being always surrounded by them started the rumours about his homosexuality, but that was a lie.

'Students were always suspect in the old Cuba. They were at the head of every resistance movement we had from the beginning of the century. Many of them were executed by successive reactionary governments.

'Cuba's romance with democracy started while the Spanish still ruled the island. There was a Captain General in Havana who represented Spain, and there were many Spanish settlers there. They came to find their fortune, and having become rich some went back and lived like kings. Many of them stayed. They kept coming, even after Cuba's independence. Of course, their loyalty, to begin with, was to Spain, their mother country. Within a generation, most of their descendants became real Cubans. Gustavo Madeiros was of pure Spanish stock, and no member of his family, including the first Madeiros to arrive, had ever returned to Spain. Unlike other soldiers of fortune, they had, from the start, developed a sense of permanence about their life on the island. There is, to this day, a Madeiros mausoleum at the San Cristobal cemetery in Havana. That is where Gustavo and Conchita are buried. Death is a great equalizer. The two revolutionaries rest there with their foreign-born, wealthy ancestors.

'The prejudiced social set-up of Cuba in the 1920s was to cause everything that happened later. Gustavo Madeiros saw all that, and if I said he was born long before his time I would be speaking the truth. In the new Cuba, a Cuba he had dreamed of, he would have reached the very top.

'He came into politics because of his concern for others, while I got there because in Abraham's heart there was no concern for anybody. Gustavo Madeiros must have seen the way my father treated my mother and me, and once or twice he tried to talk to him. It was, of course, useless because my father was not a man you could give advice to. He was arrogant and he knew it all. He surrounded himself with corrupt people who were in positions of power. He was the paymaster and they always agreed with him because they wanted more. He used them all and believed that the carnival of injustice would last for ever. The rich would grow richer and the poor would become slaves again.

'No one declared their true profit. Taxes were fixed by corrupt officials and later on, after the revolution, the government valued those companies according to their official tax returns and offered to buy them for the people on that basis. Funny, huh? But I promise you not one of these capitalist pigs laughed.

'My father made money and avoided paying taxes and exploited people. He loved big, ostentatious cars and gold watches and cuff links. He loved to be noticed and he continued to flaunt his whore Carmelita Rodriguez for all to see. She didn't bother me much. In fact she was probably a kind woman, if misled, and always tried to get on with me. I rejected her because her being with my father made my mother suffer.

'I once spent a whole afternoon with her in our garden. My mother was in town and my father had been on the telephone for hours and we talked. She was wearing a thin summer dress that stressed her curves. Her long, shapely legs danced in front of me, close to me, and I fought hard against the urge to touch her. I admit she was a beautiful woman, and when I was a teenager I had fantasies about her myself. Don't give me that look. There is nothing unusual about a young boy feeling sexual desire for an older woman. Maybe I had those fantasies because by conquering her I would have beaten my father, but she saw me as a child. On the whole, I was trying to hurt him, but he didn't give a damn. He was too insensitive even to notice my pain and my hate for him. As far as Carmelita was concerned, I had forgiven her everything. You see, she was his victim too and a real Cuban, and she would've gone over to our side had she known how he betrayed her and what he was really like. Love is blind, they say, but in the end it was Carmelita herself who delivered my father into the trap.

'But we are talking about Gustavo Madeiros.

'Sometimes, Gustavo took me up into the mountains with him. I had hardly ever been away, and these excursions were a new experience for me. We had a place in the country too, but going there did not feel like going anywhere, because my mother and I were living there most of the time. It was only one hour away from Havana and was a proper house with furniture and a radio, and there was a telephone and servants and neighbours.

'Going up-country with Gustavo lasted hours and sometimes days and it opened a totally different world for me. After six hours in the car, we'd arrive at a deserted sugar plantation his family owned, where there was a disused rum distillery. I liked the place because it was cool, and there were so many trees I'd always imagine we were in Europe. It was not a conventional place in which one could stay. We'd more or less camp in what must once have been a great house, but now only some of the rooms had a roof. We'd get our water out of a well and cook our meals on open fires outside. Up there I was free of the shame my family life had thrown at me. I could play hide and seek and I enjoyed going there because it was such a great secret. Lonely children love secrets, and I think I liked it best of all because Gustavo had made me swear never to tell my father about it. We would stay only for one or two nights, but they seemed to last for weeks on end. He'd take me up there on the pretext of an outing, but once we got there it became something else.

'It was far from everywhere and safe because it was private. I noticed he kept looking over his shoulder as soon as we were on the outskirts of Havana. He watched his back all the way, even though he was above suspicion. He only relaxed once we were deep in the countryside, in the vicinity of his family's old domain. Near the entrance to the property were the remains of a village. Gustavo told me that once, before he was born, the people who worked the estate had lived there. It was burned down by the Spanish when they quashed the first Cuban revolution. He said most of the people were killed and the rest exiled. The fences were long gone, but the old iron gate was still there. Standing on its own in the middle of a meadow, as if to remind you of what once separated the masters from the slaves.

'At the estate we were welcomed by a group of young people who slept in tents and had guards placed all over to watch for strangers. At first I thought they were boy scouts, and when I asked Gustavo about them he smiled and said they were not unlike boy scouts. They too, he said, were dedicated to helping others. They were happy people who sat and sang around the fires at night. In the daytime they kept themselves busy with lectures and they organized committees of action and practised with firearms, and he trusted me not to tell anyone what I had seen. I never betrayed him. They were laying the foundations of what came later, but I was young then and did not understand it all.

'We couldn't have gone up there more than five or six times in all, yet the holiday camp atmosphere at the place enthralled me. The enthusiasm and energy and happiness the young people exuded took me over. I felt I belonged there with them, although I didn't quite understand what they were doing. I was away from the dismal house and my father's behaviour and my mother's sadness and I sometimes felt guilty, but I was happy. I often thought of the place and it remained vivid in my mind even after he died.

'Many years later, when we were fighting the revolution, a strange thing happened. We used to move about in small squads attacking remote government installations. These were hit-and-run affairs because in the early days we didn't have the men or the resources to sustain any open battles with Batista's army. One time, after we blew up a small military transmitter, we were ambushed, and in the skirmish between our group and the soldiers I was wounded. We split into three units and took off into the darkness. It was a long retreat and my comrades carried me all through the night. When we reached the regrouping place it was dawn. I had bled heavily before they bandaged me and must have lost consciousness during the trek. When they put me down I woke up, and as first light came up I saw the old gate, like in a dream, and recognized the place.

'It was that same deserted village where the students had trained, on Gustavo Madeiros' family property. There was a new concrete water tower near where the distillery had been, and on it was the old family crest. The trees were all burned since the area had been bombed by the government's air force. I was so happy to be back there. It was as though I was a boy again. I got up and looked around and then I went out like a light.

'When I came to I found myself being cut open by a young surgeon who talked to me all through the operation. There weren't enough painkillers and they kept pouring rum into me and asking me many questions that made me concentrate and helped me tolerate the pain. The surgeon said my face was familiar, and just as they started to sew me up he looked down at me and smiled. He asked whether I had been in these parts before. I said I had. I said I used to come up there long before Fidel's rebellion. He wanted to know who had brought me to the place, and when I mentioned Gustavo Madeiros he gasped. If there were any saints in a revolutionary movement, he said, Madeiros was one.

'I told him about our excursions and how I had been up there as a child, meeting the students with Gustavo. Watching them run and roll and crawl and shoot and listening to them talk. He stroked my forehead and said he could well have been one of the students I had met then. He said he would've dropped out and become a political agitator, but Madeiros had encouraged him to finish his studies. He said doctors would come in useful when the big battle came, and in that he was right. You and me, Moreno, the doctor said, are on Madeiros' old property and we're here because of him. If that's not a sign that we were on the side of justice, he asked me, what is? It was a shame Gustavo never lived to see how close to defeating Batista we were.

'Madeiros never treated me like a retarded child, the way my own father did. He would listen to me and explain things to me, even though some of my questions must have been naive. He took me shopping. He took me fishing with him. He was out of the country a lot, but whenever he was in Havana he made a special effort to see me and talk to me. I only wish I had had more time with Gustavo Madeiros. But that was not to be. He and his wife Conchita were killed by government agents. They messed with his car and made it look like an accident, but they were murdered. Had he lasted a few years more I wouldn't have become the mess... yes, the mess I used to be... and still am.

'You, Mr Lawyer... you have helped me more than you know.'

* * *

That was the only time I actually saw him lose control and cry. I had to restrain myself because I wanted to take him in my arms and hug him like a child. It was the closest I ever got to him. That time and one more time later. On that first occasion he did not wait for me to hold him. He got up and went into the kitchen and soon I could hear him washing the dishes. I drank all the beer and half a bottle of Scotch and fell into bed with my clothes on.

In the morning, he was gone before I awoke.

Chapter Eighteen

My secretary welcomed me with an anxious face. The good news was that there was another cassette from Danny. The bad news was that the bank manager had phoned first thing and wanted to speak to me urgently. He had called twice since. He had made her promise she'd let him know as soon as I walked in because the matter was most important. Should she tell him I was out if he called again? I said I was going to grab the bull by the horns and call the bank right away.

The manager came on the line and sounded relieved and extremely affable, the way bank managers are when they sense that you are out of trouble. I could not understand why he was being so friendly, and then he told me. The sum of fifty thousand dollars had just arrived for me from a Mr Juan Miret in Miami, Florida. All commissions had been paid by the sender. This amount would cover my overdraft many times over. He could now release me from all the obligations

I had signed. Did I wish to put the rest of it in a deposit account? I said he had my permission to do what he thought best. In view of the strengthening value of the dollar against our currency, he suggested I wait for a better rate before I paid the loan back. In the meantime, the dollars would serve as collateral instead of my office lease. They would pay enough interest to cover the cost of my loan and much more besides. I was clearly out of the sack.

I thanked him and he said any time. Then my mother called.

'Good morning, son,' she said.

'It was nice seeing you yesterday. You looked well.'

'I can't say the same about you. You worry me.'

'I was just tired, that's all.'

'See that you get some rest.'

I knew from the tone of her voice that something else was on her mind. She would usually start with a nonchalant 'by the way'. I was waiting for it.

'Is there anything I can do for you?'

'Why do you ask?'

'You don't ring me this early usually. What is it?'

'Nothing.'

The charged silence was back again, and then it came.

'By the way, you said something about Cuba yesterday. What business could you have with that place? I didn't know we had any connections with them. They don't even recognize us, do they?'

'I have a client from there. An immigrant.'

'An immigrant from Cuba? Lucky man. It must be terrible there… No one is allowed to go. I read they keep finding new ways of escaping from Castro. They sail small boats. Some Cuban exile from Key West landed a small plane outside Havana a few weeks ago. He took off again with all his family. They flew a few inches over the water to avoid radar. The paper said the man had trained for years. A Cuban immigrant in Israel? Don't they all go to Miami when they manage to leave?'

She was a travel agent and well versed. She read all the papers back to back.

'No. He's a Jew. His father was born here.'

'Are you serious?'

'I am serious.'

'What does he want with you?'

'His father is supposed to have bought property here. We're looking for it.'

'Oh.'

'Interesting case. Very confusing, though. His father was a man of great charm but a little mysterious, too. He's supposed to have come back here many years ago but didn't stay long. Didn't even go up to his village. From one side I hear it was in the thirties and another source insists it was in the forties, after the war. It's difficult to work out. Could be he didn't come at all. Maybe he bought the properties from over there. He was a rich man. He…'

Maybe she was pleased I was going to make some money at last. I could hear her breathing hard, then nothing. She must have covered the receiver with her hand.

'Are you all right, Mother?'

'There's someone at the door,' she said. I could have sworn I hadn't heard anything but I waited anyway. After a few moments she was back on the line.

'I've got to go now,' she said in her matter-of-fact voice. 'I'll call you later.'

The presence of money in my bank account had brought relief and with that came courage and finally calm. With my new composure I remembered I had wanted to talk to her about something. Ask her why my father had left her. Talk about it over the phone to save embarrassment. It was a question I had kept inside for years.

'Hang on,' I said, 'while I make sure the door is shut.'

But she had hung up before I'd managed to say any more.

I called my secretary in and told her to make a cheque out for the rent and to stop writing to people about money.

'Can we eat this week?' she asked with a hesitant half-smile.

'We can.'

I had plain forgotten about Danny's cassette.

'Let me speak to my wife's lawyer,' I said.

Then I heard the door creak open and Alex Moreno stuck his face into my office.

'Come in,' I said.

First he grinned, and then he became serious again and sat down. I told my secretary to forget about my wife's lawyer and she fled. Moreno seemed relaxed and I was hoping he'd be in the mood for some small-talk. Maybe say something about the money that had come from Juan Miret or even comment about my getting drunk the previous night, but he just sat there silently and looked at me. His hair was well groomed and he looked clean and rested. His eyes exuded the benevolence of an indulgent uncle. He seemed younger and very much on the ball. I thought of asking him to stay with me for a few days.

'Forgive my outburst last night,' he said. 'I don't know what came over me.'

'It's understandable. You were talking about sad times.'

'I lost control. I'm sorry.'

'Don't give it a thought. It happens to everybody. It's human.'

'You don't have to be so condescending.'

'I'm sorry. I didn't mean to be. I was only…'

'I don't want to talk about it.'

'Fine. Tell me, do you know when it was your father came here?'

'You find out.'

'I've hit a blank there.'

'I don't want to talk about it.'

'That fellow Juan Miret must love you.'

'I once did him a favour.'

'You?'

'Yes. I was in a position of power then.'

'What sort of a favour?'

'I don't want to talk about it.'

'Some favour. He sent fifty thousand dollars, for God's sake. How much do you want?'

'I don't need any money.'

'Come on, Alex. Of course you do. That's what you're here for, to find your father's money.'

'You've got it all wrong.'

'You mean you don't want me to look any more?'

'Of course I do. You find it.'

'It's a hell of a lot more than fifty thousand. What will you do with it when I've found it?'

'You'll see.'

'You keep me in suspense. When will you tell me?'

'Not now. I've changed my mind.'

'What do you mean?'

'Give me a few coins. Make it three hundred shekels. On account.'

'That's not even two hundred dollars.'

'That's all I need.'

'You're full of surprises, Alex.'

I gave him the money and then he got up and turned away. He did not give me another look; without a word he walked to the door and was gone.

I called the girl at the Custodian of Absentees' Property. I tried to put on a friendly voice but she sounded gruff. She was more than a little mad at me for not having called in almost a week, and before she curtly hung up on me she mumbled that there was nothing new.

I needed some entertainment. I stopped all calls and put Danny's cassette into the tape recorder and switched it on.

Chapter Nineteen

The war years created a boom for anyone in business, Morton Chandler's obliging voice said. Cuba's politics and economy were closely tied to the United States.

Abraham Moreno came to see my father once, unannounced. They stayed together in the house all day while my mother reluctantly took Carmelita shopping on Miracle Mile. No business was discussed. The sole reason for the visit was his son Alex. It was common knowledge that he was having problems with him, but no one knew how bad the situation was. Alex was sixteen or seventeen then, and he did his best to make his father's life a misery. He ran up debts all over town. He drove cars without a licence. He insulted waiters in every restaurant Abraham frequented and got into fist fights with a few. Broke some furniture, too. Of course, with Abraham's direct line to the chief of police, none of this ever reached the courthouse. But Abraham's image became that of a guy who could not restrain his son. Simple policemen mocked him behind his back. What was more difficult to deal with was the fact that Alex ran around with people who were in trouble with the government. Anarchists and communists and suchlike.

These were boom years, but it wasn't all a picnic. If you were on the side of the Batista clique you had to be above suspicion. There is no smoke without fire, and Abraham was paying through his teeth to keep Alex out of jail.

'All he wants is some attention,' my father said when he heard this.

Abraham shook his head. 'He'll have nothing to do with me. When I come into the house he looks through me as if I were made of glass. Life is too easy for him.'

'Did you discuss him with Martha?'

'Useless. She'll only take his side.'

'I can't blame her,' my father said.

'Neither can I.'

Abraham did not live on the moon. He knew exactly what the problem was and had probably accepted that his son was lost to him.

'How come you don't have any problems with your boy?' he kept asking.

My father said it was because he was bringing me up in a normal household. A home, a mother and a father. Mealtimes were spent together as well as weekends and holidays. Besides, I was away in a boarding school and that, my father said, was where Alex should be sent.

'Martha wouldn't hear of it,' Abraham said. 'It would only be a repetition of what happened when I wanted to send him to a military academy when he was small. It's different now, and believe me, I understand her. The way I treat her she needs her son with her. Alex is bound to grow up and leave her one day, and while he's young he keeps her company. I would never force him to go now. She'll have to face many lonely years when he does.'

'Can't you and Martha patch things up a little, for Alex's sake?'

'How?'

'Leave Carmelita.'

'I can't. I can't live without her.'

'You must. You can't be that weak, Abraham.'

'I can't help myself.'

The visit achieved nothing. From the reports my father was receiving, the situation was getting worse. Alex had become a law student at the university and was seen in more and more clandestine meetings. Whenever there was a raid he was snatched and returned safely to his home. He once ran off to Mexico, where he was seen with anti-government exiles, but Abraham had him brought back and the file destroyed. Alex resented his father's interference but this last incident took the biscuit. Soon after the Mexican trip he left the house and took an apartment in Havana. It was above a small shop in Obispo, very near the Floridita, the bar made famous by Hemingway. Only his mother knew where he lived; she used to bring him food and money. His father did not see him for almost a year. He did not want the police to look for him because by then his own position on the island had become sensitive.

I am jumping the gun. I was going to tell you about the time Abraham and my father finally fell out, but I got stuck with his son. Alex and his student days were all in the future. A lot had happened in the meantime, while the boy was still a boy and lived with his mother.

* * *

The war in Europe was drawing to a close. The horrible truth about the fate of the Jews started coming out. These were difficult times for Martha, who had never lost hope of seeing her family again. One of my father's cousins was serving with the Marines on the European front. He was wounded and shipped home and spent a week with us just before he went back to Germany. Later they transferred him to intelligence and my father wrote and asked him to try and locate Martha's family. As soon as the war was over he found out what had happened. He discovered that they had escaped to Prague but were deported from there in 1943 and sent to a concentration camp. The Germans kept meticulous records of these deportations. There were files on everything. Who was caught and where they were sent and when they were finished off. There were heaps and heaps of material, and six months into 1947 my father's cousin came back to Miami. He told my father that not one member of Martha's family had survived. Somehow, I don't know where she took her strength from, she managed to hide her feelings, but I believe her blues started then. A year later, after she had lost her friends the Madeiros, she must have snapped. She had no one, and with her son constantly battling with her husband she sank into a depression from which she would not recover. Abraham put her in a hospital where he sometimes visited her, but his own troubles were waiting just round the corner.

One day he was called by the chief of police to an informal meeting. After all the niceties were dispensed with, the official told him that it was time for him to choose. They were aware of his long residence in Cuba and his generosity, but there was growing public pressure on the government to reduce the industrial power held by foreigners. The end of the war had brought new opportunities for Cuba to renew its trade with Europe. American influence was far too strong. There was too much corruption; too much money made out of gambling and prostitution was being siphoned away and turning the island into a colony. The government expected an anti-American backlash. The students were bitter. Something had to be done.

It might be advisable, the chief of police said, for Abraham to consider renouncing his American citizenship. The political and economic future of Cuba was uncertain. The world had changed and sugar beet production would soon resume. Cuba would have to look for new alliances and he should play a part in the process. It would show his commitment to the country that had made him rich. The man reminded Abraham how, years ago, the Spanish immigrants had done just that. As a citizen, he would become a true son of Cuba. He could ask and would certainly receive a diplomatic passport and his tax concessions could be extended.

Abraham said he would have to think about it. He told my father that the chief of police ended the meeting by suggesting that Abraham contact his deputy as soon as he had made his decision. He was never allowed to see the chief again. It was then, my father said, that Abraham decided that he was going to go to Palestine to make some investments. He said he was keeping his options open. A war between the Arabs and the Jews was going to break out in the Holy Land and the uncertainty presented a good opportunity for finding bargains. The Jews were a nation of immigrants and some were bound to leave. My father said Abraham was in no doubt who would finally win.

That was what my old man was told, but he did not believe a word of it.

There was, he told me, another reason for Abraham's sudden decision to visit the old country. He never found out what it was but it became an obsession with him.

This trip, which he took in 1946, was to be the turning point in Abraham's life. On top of that, it signalled the beginning of a change in their friendship. It was as though his short return to his native land spelt the end of a lifelong lucky run. But not before one last explosion in his emotional life. Right there, in Palestine, the country of his birth, Abraham Moreno fell in love. A last, explosive fling of passion before he settled down with Carmelita Rodriguez for the rest of his time.

It was a short affair with a married woman whose husband, Abraham said, was badly wounded during the last days of the war and was convalescing in some hospital in Europe. Millions of soldiers were being transported all over the place at that time, and travel restrictions meant that she could not visit him. She had been faithful to him all through the war years, but I suppose, my father said, she could not resist Abraham Moreno.

He was, at that time, into his forties. He was still a giant of a man. A few strips of grey were spreading above his temples, which added maturity to his Latin lover's looks. Above all, he was an exotic figure. No one had ever heard of Cuba in Palestine.

He did not visit his village. I still wonder about that, even after all these years. I mean, his brother was still there. The one who got himself killed in the war of independence a couple of years later. He must have had friends there, too, and what about a man's natural curiosity or pride in having become a success? Surely that would have been the place for him to do a bit of showing off, right? Still, for one reason or another, he did not go up there. I reckon we'll never know why. He made his conquest and took off again. The biggest problem to hit him then was that his new mistress became pregnant. She had tried to find someone to abort the child but had failed. Of course, he did not know a thing about this until he was back in Havana, where her letter awaited him.

There followed weeks of distraught transatlantic calls. He begged her to divorce her husband and come to him. When she refused, he offered to fly her over and arrange for an abortion. This business was bad news and was going to complicate his life further. He was married. He still lived with Carmelita Rodriguez, and he had a son. The woman said she would not leave her husband. He would need her after spending so many months in hospital. She would have a new beginning, she said. It was all a big mistake. For a few weeks Abraham wandered around aimlessly like a madman. He drank heavily and kept away from his office, his wife and Carmelita Rodriguez. There were more calls to Palestine and more letters and then the woman stopped writing to him. True to his nature, Abraham soon forgot what had happened. It seemed the magic was over. He went back to Carmelita and the non-stop party that was his life continued.

That was, my father said, what finally upset him and caused a real rift between himself and Abraham. You see, my father was a family man. He could not imagine a man shunning his responsibilities when a baby was involved. The whole idea of an abortion was repulsive to him. But Abraham said the woman back in Palestine was not interested in babies. She had stopped writing, he told my father, because she had probably managed to find someone else to help her get rid of it.

My father said he did not buy that at all. He was sure there was much more to it, and as things turned out he was right. It was the first time in many years of co-operation and friendship that Abraham Moreno had kept a secret from him and had lied to him, and that was too much for my father.

Chapter Twenty

'Yes,' Alex said, 'I knew he came here after the war. So what?'

'It makes all the difference. We now have a definite date. At least we know where to look. You could have told me.'

'Why? You're clever. You've managed to find it all out, all by yourself.'

'Am I going to find out you were here too? Are you going to tell me you were there when he bought the properties?'

'You're not. I wasn't here. He didn't even bring Carmelita with him. He talked about this trip to my mother and I remember how happy she was. How she hoped that coming face to face with the place of his birth would bring him to his senses and his origins and maybe back to her. She even hoped he would settle in Palestine and bring both of us out here too.'

'When he came back, did you hear him talk about the...the baby?'

'You must be mad. He was insensitive but not a fool.'

'You mean you didn't even know about the woman?'

'I don't want to talk about it.'

'Why not?'

'Look, my father had women all his life. What does another matter? He couldn't help himself. He was too weak a man to stand by any commitment. Even towards the end, when he was getting old and sinking, he managed to seduce someone to help him. He was never faithful to anyone. Not even to Carmelita Rodriguez. You heard that yourself.'

'Did you ever talk to him about it?'

'Are you out of your mind?'

'Didn't you want to... defend your mother. I mean...'

'Look, there was nothing new about my father and his whores.'

'Was the woman a whore?'

'I don't want to talk about it. Do you want to talk about your father, Mr Lawyer?'

'I don't mind.'

'Tell me about your father, then.'

'Why?'

'I want to get to know you better.'

'What for?'

'I need to.'

'Why?'

'I have my reasons.'

'I bet you have. All right, Alex, I know what you're going to say. You're going to tell me I have a rejection complex because my father left my mother. I don't think I have because I was too young to notice.'

'I wasn't going to say anything like that.'

'My father was very good to me. He preferred England, that's all. He never really got used to life out here.'

'You didn't know him too well, did you?'

'Not when I was a child, no. My mother had a travel agency and had someone look after me until I got to kindergarten. Then school and the army. I really got to know him when I was in my teens. Used to spend the summers in England with him and his parents. Did I say I got to know him? I wanted to get to know him but there was a sort of wall there.'

'What was he like?'

'I can't really say. He was a reserved, quiet sort of man. We didn't have any deep conversations about emotions or passions, that sort of thing. It was all factual, you know. This is how you swim and this is a beautiful mountain and what do you fancy for dinner. My mother isn't all that different...Do you know what I mean?'

'I think so.'

'And yet, there was much more to him. He was a journalist. He wrote beautifully. During the desert campaign he was a war correspondent and I read some of his reports. He had intense feelings, but these only came out on paper. He could describe a field hospital and when you read it you saw the sunsets, you heard the groans, you could smell the ether. When he wrote about a front-line kitchen you became hungry… he was a very atmospheric writer.'

'What did he look like?'

'What does it matter?'

'You get a better picture of a man when you look at him. People grow to become like their image, Mr Lawyer. What did your father look like?'

'He was not too tall… fit, elegant. He played a good game of tennis when he was young… later it was golf. He had a classic forties face you know, a straight nose, his hair combed back with a parting in the middle. He looked like an Englishman. I don't know what else to tell you. I got to see him more afterwards. See him, you understand, not know him. That was when I came to study law in London. I lived with him then… before I moved in with Joan…'

'Joan?'

'My estranged wife. Oh, my father liked Joan, and he showed it. He could talk to her and let his hair down and come out with what he felt inside. With her he somehow found a way of showing he cared about things… I don't know how to explain it. I suppose he had more in common with her than with me. Maybe it was my fault, but I did try. She didn't have to try at all. It came naturally to her. Everything about him changed as soon as he saw her. His eyes would light up, his voice would soften… he knew what she was thinking before she said a word. Joan was… was like the daughter he never had.'

'Why are you not together?'
'She left me.'
'Why?'
'I had an affair. She found out.'
'You're a womanizer.'
'No I'm not.'
'Of course you are. Your wife wouldn't have kicked you out otherwise. You have no idea what pain betrayal causes to a woman in love.'
'How do you know?'
'I know. I saw it. I lived with it. You are a womanizer.'
'It was only that one time, for Christ's sake.'
'You like women, don't you?'
'Everybody likes women.'
'Did your father chase women?'
'Oh no. Not at all.'
'Why you, then?'
'Abraham Moreno was the greatest Casanova of all. You didn't take after him, did you? We don't always take after our parents. Very often, Alex, we rebel and go the other way… we want to become exactly what they were not. Like you, for instance.'
'If you say so,' he mumbled, and then he got up. He stared at me for an eternity, and I thought he was going to say something, but then he turned away and without another word he was out of the door. Then my secretary called and said my wife was on the line.

Chapter Twenty-One

'Are you going?'
'Going? Going where?'
'Don't you remember? It's the anniversary of your father's death. I'm thinking of taking the girls if you're not

coming.'

'Oh.'

'I loved him very much, you know. I miss him dreadfully. He was the only one who cared for me, who understood me, took me seriously. He was the only one who made me feel at home. Made me feel I was part of some family. If he hadn't come to this country when we left England I wouldn't have lasted here.'

'Thanks for telling me.'

'You're most welcome.'

'When were you thinking of going?'

'Three o'clock. Four maybe.'

'You go, then. I'll drop by this evening. I'm very busy.'

'From what I hear you're making a lot of money.'

'Money?'

'Yes. You've paid up, in case you forgot. Things must be good.'

'Borrowed. All borrowed.'

'You're a liar,' she said before the phone went dead. I called her back.

'What do you want?' she asked.

'It's time we talked about the future.'

'You dare talk of a future, for you and me?'

'I think we ought to get together again.'

'You must be out of your mind. After all the pain you've caused me, after all the misery…'

'I would like to try again, Joan. Show you…'

'Show me what?'

'Show you that I love you.'

'Is that why you bed half the girls in town?'

'Who told you that?'

'You're a pig.'

'Are the girls there?'

'Of course they are. Who do you think is looking after them?'

'I wish you wouldn't talk to me like that when they're there. They love me. I'm their father. It won't do anybody any good. No girl wants to think of herself as the daughter of a pig.'

'You have an answer for everything.'

'I want to come home, Joan. I love you. I can't live without you.'

I could almost hear the anger gathering on the other end.

'You're a shit,' she said.

'Please, Joan… I could leave the office now. We could go together.'

'Go to hell,' she said, and put the phone down. I didn't call back. Every time we spoke it ended just like that. As if the mere sound of my voice was enough to set her off.

* * *

I thought of the old carefree days back in London when I was a student. Of how we first met in the small coffee bar across the road from the lecture hall. You could get a cup of coffee and a sandwich for fifty pence. It was a popular place and always crowded. The boys used to go there to meet girls.

I could not help noticing her. Hers was not the kind of beauty you picked up on immediately. It was more the animal thing she exuded. Her walk maybe, the supple way she carried herself, or that apparent coolness which evaporated when she spoke. I saw her first as she walked in my direction. She was tall and slim and red-haired; her eyes were mustard green and they flashed at me for a second as she walked past. She later told me she thought I was strikingly different with my wild black hair and my keen, burning eyes and whatever else it was I had. She was having a cup of tea with a fellow I knew slightly and I came up to them and introduced myself. I was never a particularly shy man, and with three years' service in an Israeli combat unit I was, as she put it, oozing confidence. I suppose it was just bravado. Or insecurity. Or something to balance my inability to communicate with my parents. They were talking about a film they had both seen and I entered the conversation. She did not say much at first but she appeared to listen and accepted another cup of tea, and then the man looked at his watch and excused himself. He said he had an important lecture to attend and he left. The funny thing was that as soon as he was gone her shyness was gone too. She looked straight at me and then her smile flared up. It was a strong, uninhibited smile that was meant for me alone and rendered me defenceless. I went all silent and watched the change in her demeanour as she opened up and started talking. I watched her lips and imagined stroking her hair and my mind caressed her skin. She must have noticed the way I looked at her but nothing in her manner acknowledged it.

She told me about her course. She was studying history of art and was working part time in a gallery in Cork Street. She was going to make art-dealing her career. There were, she said, only a few dealers who actually knew about art. The rest were only concerned with the money side of it. I could hear her voice, but I'm not sure I listened to what she was saying. She was impossibly attractive, and I looked at her and thought about where I'd like to be with her right then and what I'd like to do with her. I'd always thought it was a waste of time for two people who are struck by mutual attraction to sit and talk for the sake of doing the so-called right thing. Someone ought to invent a little bulb that lights up when both parties agree to move to the next stage. I heard somewhere that it takes a person fifteen seconds to decide whether or not they want someone. It took me about three. The chemistry was there right then, even before I got close enough to her to really see her and smell her.

I had been dating girls, like everyone else. I did not have a steady girlfriend. Maybe I was afraid of a serious relationship. Maybe I seemed too cocky to attract permanence, but as soon as I saw Joan I experienced a surge of new emotions itching to come out. Something inside was screaming at me. Saying this was different. This was the one. In an instant I knew what was happening to me and what was going to happen to us. I could have told her then, during that first meeting, that she was the woman I was going to marry. But she was an English girl who was not accustomed to the uninhibited Israeli way of communication. In most places our blunt language is considered downright rude, and I fought like mad to hold myself back from telling her what I was feeling. I suppose I did not want to put her off.

I don't know how long we stayed there. Maybe an hour or two. After we parted I could not get her out of my mind. She insinuated herself into my head and did not leave. I felt her close to me everywhere and always. She had given me her telephone number and I started bamboozling her with endless conversations at all hours. I called her at the gallery during her lunch breaks until I realized I was overdoing it. But she never told me to stop. She agreed to come out with me once and then a second time. Then I took her to the theatre and she took me to opening nights and we'd walk along the river and we'd talk. Soon we saw each other every evening. One thing led to another and we started to spend Saturdays together browsing through the antique stands along Portobello market. We never bought anything because I had very little money and she had no place to put anything. She was an orphan and shared a furnished room with another student whom I never met because I was not allowed into the place. We learned a lot about each other and I was burning for her but she remained quite remote. I tried to kiss her on the second date and she politely turned her head away and gave me her hand. Her hand-holding-only attitude continued until the time I introduced her to my father.

When I said I was seeing someone seriously he abandoned his usual cool and asked to meet her. He suggested lunch at the Veeraswami Indian restaurant on Regent Street. He was very well known there, of course, and the enormous turbaned Sikh at the door knew his name and welcomed him with a salute. As soon as we sat down he dazzled her with words. I don't know how he did it because he never talked much, not even then. Nonetheless, he managed to impress her with his modesty and his intimate knowledge of Indian cuisine. He had spent time in India as a war correspondent, and she accepted his choice of food without a murmur. There was, from the very beginning, a harmony between them. A ballet of movement and smiles that needed few words. She was to say later that she never understood how a quiet man like him could have fathered someone like myself, and I always agreed. I don't know how he did it.

It was not a one-way street. They warmed to each other instantly. After he had ordered there followed a quiet conversation that lasted all through the meal as though I were not present. I sat there and I looked at them. I looked at his elegant hand movements and listened to his cultured voice and saw his reserved smile. And then I looked at myself in the ornamented mirror on the other side of the room. Through the tropical flowers I looked dark and uncouth and menacing. I envied him, his choice of words and his beautiful English voice. I wished I could have been like him.

Their conversation became more animated as the food and wine arrived. The alcohol seemed to unlock their inhibitions and they talked about art and the theatre and he told her about India. He was blossoming. I felt so inferior to them both it almost hurt. I tried to make myself think of my own achievements, my own good points, but I was having big problems there because I couldn't find any. She talked easily to him about studies and careers and the right places to shop and eat and live. There was none of the restraint she had shown with me. Joan and my father were instant partners. It was a friendship among equals, and after that first time he was always to take her side. Even when there were fights, and especially after she kicked me out. It was a relationship that was to last until he died. I remained the outsider to the end.

He very much encouraged our going out together and took us both on holiday to Italy that summer. It was while he was on some assignment in Florence that we first made love.

It was a revelation. All the walls and the hesitation fell away from her. She wanted no foreplay and no warning and no warming up. Somehow she was in my room and we were on the bed and naked. We did not talk. She took the lead and she pulled me into her and then all hell broke loose. She heaved and gyrated and her hunger was bottomless. She screamed and shouted obscenities and my excitement became intense and I knew I had to hold myself back. The bedsheets were soaked with our sweat and soon I joined this carnal dance and it seemed we were soaring from one high point to the next without an end in sight. She seemed to be making up for all those long, distant moments we had shared. On and on we went, and whenever my excitement was about to overcome me I had to think of all sorts of things just to keep from exploding. I would never have guessed what passions lurked behind her quiet exterior, but that afternoon I found out and I was hooked for ever.

After that all I needed to do when we were alone was to look into her eyes. That wild mare would come out from under her long, cool lashes and I would recognize it instantly. We did not talk. We didn't even kiss. Sometimes there was no bed around. Sometimes it was while we were walking in a lonely part of the park or up some stairway. She would just look at me and put her hand on my shoulder, pull me towards her, and the reverie would be back.

That first afternoon in Florence, when my father came back, he took us out to dinner in a small restaurant overlooking the River Arno. While I sat apart he told her about his assignment. It was a reunion between a group of British officers and their Italian prisoners of war. The men had not seen each other since the African campaign and you would never have guessed they were enemies once.

They were just men, frustrated by middle age, traumatized by responsibility and scared of sickness and of getting old. Here they were playful and they fondly remembered the good old exciting days when they were at each other's throats. They showed each other photographs of their slim youthful selves in uniform. They exchanged family stories. It was the first time I heard my father talk the way he wrote. He became excited. He spoke of emotions and tears and the smell of sweat and battle fatigue. He spoke of the baffling experience of men who came back from the war. The death of camaraderie, the money-making rat race and the hiss of broken promises. He talked like a man possessed.

All through the evening Joan held my hand under the table while her eyes were fixed on him. As he spoke, her excitement would sometimes result in her squeezing me. I felt the tang of jealousy dig deep into my very soul. A week later, when we were both watching his programme on television, he was mesmerizing still, even on the small screen. His enthusiasm was gripping and it fired those well-dressed old soldiers he had interviewed and made them come out of themselves. They were laughing and crying and whispering and shouting and not once did my father lose his control over them.

I could never look like him or talk like him or have the confidence he had behind his unassuming voice. I'm a loud-mouthed nothing, I thought, and wanted to say something, but her eyes were glued to the set.

Once, a few years into our marriage, I told her about the way I had felt and she laughed. She took me in her arms and she said:

'I love his soul and his manners and culture but I lust after your body.'

That summed it up, I suppose. Maybe she never really loved me. Maybe she married me to sleep with me and have my father to confide in. Maybe that was why I kept looking at other women.

I shall never forget how, after our first daughter was born, she said something strange. It was the time of my final exams. My father went to the hospital every day. He was waiting there when the doctor came out with the news. When I got there in the evening to catch a first glimpse of my daughter he had just left. The room was full of flowers and Joan looked at me and then she said it:

'I simply can't understand how your mother ever let a man like that out of her house.'

'He left,' I said, and I sat down on the bed.

'A woman knows how to keep a man if she wants to,' she said.

'She never told me.'

'Did you ask?'

'Not yet.'

'You have a strange relationship, your mother and you.'

'Maybe.'

'She should have kept him in the house.'

* * *

Well, Joan certainly knew how to keep me out, I thought. But I did not have that rejection on my mind. I was thinking about my father. My wife and daughters were going to lay flowers on his grave that afternoon. Perhaps Alex Moreno was not the only man obsessed with his father.

* * *

The telephone cut through my thoughts like a knife. My secretary said my mother was on the line. I knew what I had to ask her but she did not give me a chance to say anything. Whenever there was something on her mind she had to spell it out right away. She could never wait to hit you with it.

'Aren't you going to your father's grave today?'

I was right where she wanted me. On the defensive.

'Joan is going with the girls. I… I'll drop in later. Funny you should remember.'

'Why? He was my only husband.'

'Not for that long,' I said, and regretted it. 'Tell me, Mother, why did he leave you?'

'I don't want to talk about that now.'

'You sound just like Alex Moreno.'

'Alex Moreno? Who is Alex Moreno?'

'The Cuban client I told you about. You sound just like him.'

'You never told me his name was Moreno.'

'What difference does that make?'

'Is he the man who'll make you all that money?'

'If it works out, yes… it is.'

I was going to ask her about my father's departure again but she interrupted me.

'I'd like to meet him,' she said, as if nothing else in the world mattered. She forgot all about the cemetery.

'What for?'

'I'd like to.' It was an order.

'I'll see what I can do. It's not that easy.'

'Why not?'

'He doesn't meet people.'

'Arrange it and let me know,' she said, and hung up.

The phone rang again. It was Danny. He sounded so excited he could hardly put words together. He rambled on with his trivial enthusiasm and I kept telling him to relax, and then he stopped. I could hear him take a deep breath as though he were preparing to reveal some explosive news. The fact was, he said in a whisper, he had managed to find Carmelita Rodriguez. He had not met her yet but was well on his way to fixing it.

'I'm not sure what good such a meeting would do.'

'I can't say, Mr Lawyer, I can't say. Morton Chandler is in New York for a week and I'd like to meet her. She is bound to know something about Abraham's end. Besides, I'm as curious as hell to meet the object of his lifelong passion, aren't you?'

'I haven't given it much thought.'

'I'm disappointed in you, Mr Lawyer.'

'What makes you think she'll talk to you?'

'She's hit on hard times and could use some money. She'll talk.'

'You'd have thought Abraham would've left her well provided for.'

'Well, I can't answer that. It is odd though. Abraham was never mean with his money. Anyway, I hope to see her tomorrow. I'm going to Miami first thing in the morning.'

'Let me have the news.'

'As soon as I've got something,' he said, and then we

talked a little about this and that. He sounded like a young man in a hurry. Maybe he was too excited to stay on the line. We said goodbye.

My father used to tell Joan he thought a lawyer's job was boring. Had he been alive and in the picture he might have changed his mind.

Chapter Twenty-Two

I was just passing through the heavy cemetery gates when the two little girls saw me. They broke away from their mother and ran into my arms. Joan stayed well back but I caught her eyes. They mocked me. They said, so you've decided to come after all.

'We visited Grandpa,' the little one said.

'We put beautiful flowers on his stone,' said the other.

Any stranger watching us from afar would have thought this was a picture of a happy outing. We used to be the perfect family before I screwed up. Whenever we could we did things together.

* * *

We all went to England one summer. It was at the time of my father's sixty-fifth birthday. He was about to retire from his high-profile television job and planned to go and live somewhere on the continent. Probably Mallorca, where he had recently sold his flat and bought himself a small farmhouse. He wanted us all with him for the occasion.

Joan and I had married six or seven years earlier and she had followed me to Israel. Our elder daughter was born in England and the second in Tel Aviv soon after we arrived. We settled down to family life in an apartment we bought in the fashionable northern part of the city. My mother said people judged you by your address and my father helped with the down-payment. I did not want to be further in his debt, and as soon as my law practice started to thrive I made sure he was paid back. Maybe because I hankered after a separation from him, independence from his civilized manner and his attachment to Joan.

As I had been educated in England and was fluent in the language, the immigration agency introduced me to a number of well-to-do Anglo-Saxon immigrants. People who come to this country find it difficult at first, not least because of the famously bad-mannered locals. Israelis are seen as arrogant, charmless two-line merchants. No one has time. Money is hard to come by and you are called up for reserve duty more than once a year. Whoever and whatever you may be, when the military calls you drop everything and go. You get very little compensation for lost time. All you can hope for is that there will be no war.

I am told I am a laid-back Israeli. This was an important factor in my becoming a fairly successful lawyer. The newly arrived, English-speaking clients felt they were dealing with one of their own. People recommended me to their friends and soon I was much in demand. The more prosperous I became the less I saw of my family. The girls were small still and Joan had a lot of work on her hands. I suppose I was too arrogant to notice how tired she was. My excuse to myself was that she was better off without me messing around the house.

Later on she took to criticizing me. She accused me of being too familiar with my clients and especially their wives. She said I was becoming too personal with them.

A lawyer, I said, especially in this part of the world, often needs to get on to a personal level with his clients. She did not accept this. She said I was a flirt. I tried to explain it was my nature. People knew I was open and frank and the sort of man who likes to touch people. I was from the Middle East, I said, and our friendliness does not imply flirtation. How many male clients would stay with me if they were worried about their wives? I asked.

She just cut me off and said she wished I could have been more refined.

Of course, dumb and insensitive as I was, I did not comprehend how difficult it was for her to get used to this country, to cope with the language and the climate and the people. I was too charged, too stimulated by fulfilling my ambitions. Being safely tucked away in the comfort of my own element I did not notice her struggle to survive it. I did not praise her for the way she had managed to deal with an alien way of life. For the way she mastered those important little things like shopping and driving and communicating. How, in this dusty environment, so different from where we had started, she retained her awareness of my needs and steadfastly supported me.

'What happened to the human power of imitation?' she asked. 'If you'd been a human being you would have tried to have been like your father, especially if you were so envious of his talents. You could have learned to imitate his gentleness, his consideration, his quiet self-assurance, his respect for other people's feelings.'

She went on and on and I found myself on the run. I told her that I hardly knew him in my formative years. I did not get a chance to imitate him or play games with him and try to be like him because he wasn't there. How could anyone blame me for that? I said she knew he had left my mother and had gone back to England. I had grown up in Israel and had assumed the open, local character. I said I could not help that. Hadn't she told me it was that very streak in me which had attracted her?

I remember trying to hug her but she went all stiff. I began to feel embarrassed and started talking out of turn.

I said she could only accept physical contact if she was the instigator. I said her inhibitions evaporated only when she had sex in mind. She told me to keep my hands to myself and get the hell out of her house. I exploded. I said she did not need to sleep with me just to prove I was hers. I said there were plenty of fish in the sea.

She called me an animal and I went out. I drove around aimlessly. When I got home she was asleep.

That time it took weeks for things to get back to normal again.

Anyway, after the summer of his sixty-fifth birthday, my father changed his mind about emigrating to Mallorca. He sold his newly acquired farmhouse there and decided to settle in Israel instead. It was his second attempt to make a go of life in this country, and this time he stayed. He said he had always wanted to live in Jaffa, a city that had hardly changed since he'd seen it first, many years before. He could work on his memoirs there. But that was not why he came. Joan was the main reason for this decision, and secretly I was bitter about it.

Clearly, on some levels, she needed him more than she needed me.

The other woman came into my life shortly after I convinced myself of that.

* * *

He may not have been a father to me but he was a full-time grandfather to my daughters. Mother was not particularly interested in children. Of course, she saw them during holidays and never forgot their birthdays, but her meticulously ordered apartment was not a place for children to roam in. At some stage they became too apprehensive to go there in case they broke something.

Visiting my father's place was different. It was a party. He had bought and restored a ruin in Old Jaffa, and the place was an instant hit with them. There were interesting bits and pieces there and he took great pains to tell them what each item was and where it had come from. They could ramble about to their hearts content. He let them help him paint old furniture and polish brass doorknobs. Sometimes, to their delight, they were allowed to stay the night.

While he was around, Joan saw a lot of him, and so did my daughters. He did most of his work at night and always had time for them during the day. With my daughters he had the patience of an elephant. He'd walk with them and read to them and sing songs with them. Maybe that was why Joan took to life in this country as well as she did. Perhaps her unhappiness became acute only when he was no longer there.

I must not hang all my failures on others. It was I, nobody else, who shook her to the ground when she found out I had had a fling with that other woman. That got me into serious trouble with my father too. I would have liked to have made it up with him but he did not give me a chance.

During the last month of his life he refused to see me.

Still, until all that happened we were a normal family. I worked hard and the practice did well. I bought Joan a car and she started going to art school while the girls were in kindergarten. She wanted to become a photographer and my father encouraged her. He had a few of her pictures published in an American magazine. She was very proud of that and never cashed the cheque they'd sent her. It is framed now and still hangs in her kitchen, above the fridge. On weekends we went to the beach and on excursions. I helped clean the flat and did the shopping. We entertained and went to parents' evening at school. I went into the military every year and took part in policing the occupied West Bank and southern Lebanon.

On one occasion I was wounded. We ran into an ambush; it was a dark night and I was hit in the shoulder and fainted. The others must have gone on, and when I came to I found myself lying on my back inside a long prehistoric cave. I had no idea how I got there. I had water and rations and I nursed my wound. Above, I heard the shepherds calling for their sheep and the sound of bells. Then, having regained some strength, I took off into the night. I moved south, in the direction of the border. I had been missing for three days and received a hero's welcome when I arrived at our lines. Everybody was happy to see me. I was flown for treatment by helicopter and was debriefed by Intelligence. Joan came to the hospital every day. Some of my clients came too and showered me with flowers and fruit and magazines. My father came once, but his health had taken a turn for the worse and he had to be led away almost as soon as he'd arrived. True to his upbringing he sent me some chocolates and a note apologizing for his forced departure. He wished me a speedy recovery. I would have preferred him to have put his arm around me, but this was not to be. Anyway, I must admit I enjoyed the attention. The only one who made no fuss at all was my mother.

She said she had known all along I was safe.

* * *

So there we were, at the cemetery, me holding my daughters and Joan fiddling with her handbag a short distance away. I suggested we all went out to dinner somewhere, but she said she had cooked. The girls wanted to go for ice-cream and she relented. She said I could take them provided I brought them back in time for dinner.

'You'd really prefer to take them straight home, wouldn't you?' I said. 'After all, they may not be very hungry after the ice-cream.'

'I didn't know you cared,' she said mockingly.

I kissed the girls goodbye and said we'd go for ice-cream some other time.

That night I needed company. I waited for Alex to call or come over to the flat but I remained alone. I had expected my mother to ring but she did not. It might have been her bridge night. I was hit by a massive wave of self-pity. Here I was, on my own, supposedly irresistible and a flirt and on the verge of making some real money. I had nowhere to go except for this grey little place I had to call home. I could not get to sleep and managed to doze off only after a few very large swigs of whisky.

The phone rang. Before picking it up I opened my heavy eyes and looked outside. I was drowsy as hell. The sky was dark still but there were no stars. It must have been three or four o'clock in the morning. I was so tired I wanted to sleep for ever or die. I hoped the nauseating ringing would stop, but it persisted. It was Danny. I lashed out at him:

'Are you crazy? Can't you sleep at night?'

'I'm sorry, but I was so shocked by the news I had to call you.'

'What news?'

'Did you know your friend Alex Moreno was a big-shot policeman?'

'Policeman?'

'Yes. He worked for Castro's secret police. He was trained by the Russians. He even spent time in Angola. He... You don't sound very interested, Mr Lawyer. Are you asleep?'

I must have said something rude to him because the line went dead and I fell asleep with the receiver in my hand. It was still there in the morning.

Chapter Twenty-Three

The room was inexplicably icy. My mother and Alex Moreno sat across the glass-topped coffee table staring at each other without a word. They looked like two marble figures on a chess board. A white queen and a black bishop. There were tea and biscuits and she had bought a chocolate cake from the bakery across the street. I had had no lunch and was starving, but as no one had touched anything I was forced to hold back.

* * *

He had dropped into the office at lunch-time and kept me there until three o'clock. It was one of his talkative days, and although he hardly gave me a chance to speak it was obvious he was interrogating me. He talked, and he constantly looked for a reaction in my face and my eyes. When I did say something he listened not to what I said but to the way I said it. He is a cool customer, I thought to myself. This was the time he spoke of his career after the war against Batista had ended. After Castro and his men came down from the Sierra Maestra mountains to take Cuba over. It was not a career I would have been proud of, but he took great delight in my embarrassment. He told me about his exploits in Castro's police.

It was as though he knew what Danny had called me about that very morning.

You read about these interrogators. Especially the Nazi ones and the KGB. Both have now passed into history but the movies are still full of them. Their cruelty, their boots, their batons and leather coats and dark glasses. Their delight in people's suffering, all in the name of patriotism. Of course, they still exist, but they have different names now. There must be a good few of them in this country too, but no one knows them except their victims. Interrogators are a special breed, and as I listened to him I asked myself whether they are born that way or grow to become what they are because of their experiences. I tried to equate this quiet, shabby man with that species, and it filled me with trepidation. Was it his childhood? His compassion for his mother and hatred of his father? What was there in Abraham Moreno that could have pushed his son into that vile profession? Hard as I tried, I could not think of an answer.

He described many of his gruesome successes with obvious relish, and as his story unfolded I caught myself wishing I had never set eyes on him. I was hoping he was lying. But why would he do that? Was he simply trying to shock me?

'You hate my sort, don't you?' he remarked once or twice, and I thought to hell with it and said I did.

'You'll understand me when this is over,' he said, and I thought I saw a flicker of the deepest sadness quiver behind his eyes.

'Do I have to understand you?'

'Yes.'

'Why?'

'You must know all about me. The good and the bad. Especially the bad.'

'To hell with you.'

'I say it again. You must learn all you can about me.'

'And I say it again too. Go to hell.'

'What would you do without me?'

'Don't be sarcastic. Without you we wouldn't be sitting here now. I wouldn't be searching for your father and his money and his past and you wouldn't be telling me all these horror stories… you wouldn't be digging my soul out.'

'Well, I am here. The place isn't exactly crawling with clients. Anyway, you accepted the job.'

'Shouldn't I just be looking for your father's money? Wasn't that what you hired me for?'

'No. I'm not interested in money. Not my father's money, not any money. You know this well.'

The man was an oddball. He made no sense at all. Of course, all was to become clear, but not that afternoon. How I wish it had. Everything would have ended very differently. But that afternoon in my office, before we went to see my mother, his story tortured me. I turned to him and asked:

'What are you interested in?'

'I'm interested in you, Mr Lawyer,' he said, almost with affection.

'Why? What's so special about me?'

'You'll see,' he said, and then he smiled. He was succeeding in confusing me totally.

'What are you doing this afternoon?' I asked.

'Why?'

'I've been invited for tea with my mother. Would you like to come?'

I expected him to refuse, but he looked down at himself and then turned to me and said:

'Am I dressed for the occasion?'
'It's only my mother.'
'I always wanted to meet your mother, Mr Lawyer.'
'Why?'
'We have a lot in common.'
'What do you mean, Alex? You don't know her. What would you and my mother have in common?'
'One day I'll tell you.'
'Tell me now.'
'I don't want to talk about it now. Shall we go?'
On the way to her flat the bastard insisted on buying flowers. I paid.

* * *

So here they were, my mother and Alex, grilling each other with their eyes, as if looking for a weak spot on which to pounce. I knew I could not make him out, but I had thought I knew my mother. Yet everything changed that afternoon. Perhaps he made her change. He obviously had this effect on people. She appeared calm while underneath her skin there was a pulse of suppressed aggression. The silence lasted for ever.
'I'm starving,' I said.
'It's all my fault, señora. I'm afraid I've kept the boy from his lunch,' Alex said. The gentle, paternal silkiness in his voice was mocking her while at the same time it was protecting me. This duplicity was so skilful I was too shocked to notice he was speaking English. A language he never admitted he knew. It was heavily accented, but faultless all the same. I could have cursed him for having forced me always to stick to Spanish, but this new manner was too fascinating. His face was polite and patient and the easy charm that accompanied his smile was a revelation.
'I can understand his hunger pangs,' he said softly. 'This is as good an afternoon spread as I've ever seen. And you did it all, I'm sure, at short notice. My compliments, señora. And my eternal thanks for having invited me.'

My mother smiled. It was her usual calculated I've-got-you-covered smile. The silence had been broken but the artificial atmosphere was getting colder by the second. My mother pointed at the other pot on the corner of the table and said he probably preferred coffee to tea. He nodded and she poured a cup for him. He bowed his head and, as she poured mine, he looked at me and winked. In that split second an understanding was established between us. As though he was letting me in on his secret. On what was happening. He was guiding me without words and I was proud of him because he was clearly on to her. So was I. We both knew she wanted something of him and we waited to see what it was.

She pushed the milk towards him and he smiled.

'We take it black in Cuba,' he said. 'Black and thick and very sweet.'

'My son likes it white. He is half-English.'

'He is more polite than most Israelis,' Moreno said. 'You have brought him up well.'

'Thank you,' my mother said, 'but that's because he lived in England.'

'Maybe,' Alex said. 'I imagine he only went there on his holidays. The rest of the time he was here with you and it couldn't have been that easy. This being a hard country and your being all on your own...'

'He's been telling you his life story, has he?'

'No. I asked. I know all about this kind of story. You see, I was more or less brought up the same way. My father was never at home. Sometimes he was away for months. There was only my mother.'

I thought how different his mother was to mine. How my mother built up a real career while his mother stayed at home. How she was a victim while mine was a winner. I tried to conjure up a meeting between them and thought how my mother would have despised the other woman's nature. She would have seen it as weak.

While I was lost in my thoughts my mother and Alex embarked on a real conversation. They talked about the pros and cons of parenthood. Alex was telling her about the care Cuba took of single mothers. He talked with enthusiasm, but she did not react. The more uninterested she appeared to be the more he told her about the communist paradise he had left. She was bored. She would have made some excuse to end the gathering, but I knew she would not do that before she had achieved what she had invited him for. I watched them closely. They were probing each other. They were a matching pair, both playing cat and mouse at different times. Each waiting to make their move while the other was nearing the trap. To my horror I concluded that they were both enjoying themselves.

Alex was describing some tourist attraction in the old city of Santiago de Cuba when my mother interrupted him.

'I nearly went to Cuba once.'

'Really? When was that?'

'Oh, after the war. Nineteen forty-six.'

'What did you want to go to Cuba for?'

'It's a long story. I was invited by an American client of mine… to do a job.'

'What kind of a job?'

'The client wanted me to run a travel agency for him in Cuba.'

'Why did you change your mind?'

My mother pointed at me.

'He changed my mind,' she said. 'I was pregnant with him.'

I thought I'd put a word in then. I asked:

'Where was my father when this little plan was being hatched?'

'He was in India,' she said angrily. Then she collected herself and said we were out of coffee and got up to go to the kitchen. I turned to Alex.

'Where the hell did you learn to speak English?'

'Take it easy… I learned English at school. We do have schools in Cuba.'

'Come on, Alex. Why didn't you tell me?'

'You never asked.'

We sat in silence for a bit. It made no sense to get mad. With his quiet confidence he was gaining the upper hand and I was too tired to pry any further.

'Formidable woman, your mother,' Alex said. 'But no sense of humour.'

I waited for him to say something else. I thought he would come clean. Admit we were, the both of us, waiting for her to reveal her cards. Admit we were on the same wavelength for once. But he did not bat an eyelid as he watched me. I devoured all the biscuits and had three slices of cake. I gulped down two cups of tea and burned my tongue. He shook his head.

'Careful, Mr Lawyer. You'll screw your stomach up.'

'Your constant surprises confuse me.'

'I am sorry. Please take it slowly.'

'Why the sudden concern?'

'You didn't have it easy either, did you? Your mother makes me feel very close to you,' he said. There was real compassion in his eyes. I looked at him and searched for the cruel secret policeman he had unveiled for me earlier, in my office. But that man was gone and so was my frustration. Here by my side sat a caring man. 'Very close,' he repeated, and I thought I understood what he meant and touched his arm. He started to say something and then the sound of my mother's footsteps butted in. We recoiled like a pair of naughty schoolboys caught stealing. She found us sitting quietly, both staring at the sea.

She had put a fresh layer of lipstick on and I knew he had noticed it too. She sat down and poured us some more coffee and the conversation flowed. She told him about her days in the travel business and he told her about the various South American countries he had visited. She was all smiles and charm after that. So was he. She gave him her telephone number and said he could call her any time. He said he would be delighted to.

When we got up to leave she walked us to the door and

shook his hand. She gave me her cold cheek to kiss and as I turned to go I saw her smile at him. I felt her eyes on my back all the way down the stairs. Then I noticed I had left my briefcase in her flat and asked him to wait while I fetched it. When I came down again he had evaporated into thin air.

Chapter Twenty-Four

At the start of his latest tape, Danny told me off. He said he would avoid speaking to me on the telephone again unless I apologized.

Your performance the other day was abrupt. You strike me as a well-mannered young man so something must be upsetting you. This sort of attitude, coming from you, would usually be considered rude. However, at my age I have no time to waste on anger, so I forgive you. And as I am still on your payroll I hasten to send you this recording. Morton Chandler will be back in about a week but frankly I think we have got all we are going to get out of him.

I have left Palm Beach and am now in Miami itself. For the last three days I have been staying in the part of town they call Little Havana. I took a room in a charming little hotel with the impressive name of El Gran Tucan. They only speak Spanish around this part of town. The language has come back to me with a vengeance. It is as though I have spoken nothing but Spanish ever since the end of the Civil War. I have finally met with Carmelita Rodriguez and she is a mine of information. She has come down in the world yet you can still see what a beautiful woman she was in her time.

The place where she works is an eating house on Eighth Street. It is packed with Cuban emigrants. When you see Chinese people crowding a Chinese restaurant you can be sure the food there is going to be good. Carmelita's restaurant was unbelievable so I went back there every day. I sat and inhaled the atmosphere, the sight of Cuban faces and the loud sound of gossip and laughter. The air was full of cigar smoke and people read Spanish magazines. I listened to the orders being shouted at the kitchen and sampled every dish in the house. The arroz con pollo. The rice and peas. The beans. The marinated fish. The fried plantain and the fruit juices and the coconut dishes. And yes, the coffee... oh yes, that impossibly marvellous sweet black coffee. If I were young and in Moreno's shoes, I would have stayed in Cuba just for the food.

I must be boring your orderly legal mind. I can hear you saying why doesn't the old fool just send me a picture of the place and a copy of the menu? You are right, but I need more than facts. I need the colours and the sounds and the smells that breathe behind the facts and give them life. OK, OK, so you don't require any background information. I am sorry, Mr Lawyer. I am here at your cost. I am working for you, so here it is.

I was introduced to Carmelita by the manager of the place with whom I had struck up a friendship. As soon as she and I started talking I brought up the question of money. I tried to be diplomatic about it. I said I knew how famous and successful she used to be. I said I needed to talk to her and expected to pay her for it. Her reaction was one of modesty.

If I was after a story, she said, there wasn't one to tell. Maybe she thought I was an old-timer, one of her fans. She more or less dismissed her erstwhile fame as though it did not matter. What mattered now was the place we were in, where she worked. She stood there calmly as if to take my order and I said I was surprised she needed to work at all. Had she not lived for many years with a man who should have made sure she never wanted for anything? She looked a little puzzled by that and I thought we had the wrong woman.

I then came straight out with it. I asked:

'Were you not the lady who shared the life of Abraham Moreno?'

Well, let me tell you, Mr Lawyer, when she heard his name she crossed herself and then she pocketed her pad and sat down by my side. Her movements were slow and she went all pale and her chest heaved as she struggled to find some air . She tried to whisper something. She looked around as though we were breaking some military secret and her face contracted. Then it lit up again and she asked me where I knew his name from. She asked whether I had known him in person and how. When I said I was born in the same village as he was, in the Holy Land, she nearly fainted. I said we were children together. She crossed herself again and said, Dios mio.She tried to kiss my hand as though I was the Pope himself come to have a chat, but I did not let her. She apologized for sitting with me and for being so familiar. I said I would like to help her if I could, and money, it seemed, might be one way of doing that. She held on to my hand and then she said she could not possibly take any money from me. I said of course she could but she shook her head. Then she became very chatty. She could make ends meet, she said. From time to time they begged her to sing something in the eating house and then a hat was passed around. There were always a few dollars in it. She said the older customers remembered her well. They knew just the kind of song to ask for.

Anyway, we sat in the corner of the restaurant and she wanted to know all about Abraham. What he was like as a child and what his family was like. What his house looked like and were there any trees in his street. I answered all her questions and that made her feel at ease. I told her all I knew. All you have been told about Abraham. His friendship with the Arab boys and his saving of the little girl. I described our village to her and the Sea of Galilee. Whenever I mentioned one of the holy places she crossed herself.

Thirty years, she said. For thirty years she had lived with Abraham and knew nothing of his beginnings. He never talked about his village or the Holy Land, as though he had no life before Cuba. She knew him because she loved him and she saw the way his character evolved. His ambitions and his hard work and his rise to untold riches. She was always with him. Theirs was a true love story. Something that happens only once in a lifetime. Sure, she had been married once and had known men before Abraham and even after, but never during. He was not capable of fidelity, she said. It simply wasn't in him. But she forgave him everything because as soon as he took her in his arms and smiled and looked into her eyes she could not be angry with him. She should have been, and now in her older years she sometimes was. But when she was younger and by his side she did not have the strength to leave him.

She had witnessed the misery he had brought on his wife and his son and she saw what that misery had produced in them. Love, Carmelita said, either weakened you or made you strong, and Abraham's wife Martha loved him, too, and was grateful to him for saving her life by marrying her. But she was too weak to fight him when she needed to. Abraham was charming and when he promised things he believed them himself, but his memory was short. Maybe he could not help it. He was an earth wanderer who needed his freedom. Something always pushed him, yet he stayed with her, with his Carmelita, until the end. She had brought the end to him but she did not know it. It was all planned by his son Alex and by the events that befell Cuba.

Well, Mr Lawyer, I wanted to know about Abraham's son and I kept bringing him up. At first she did not want to talk about Alex. He was an evil man, she said, and crossed herself. Life had made him evil. He had become, in his quest to punish his father, a terrorizing official. He had caused much pain and death to innocent people. If he was alive somewhere, Carmelita said, he could only be an empty shell. God had surely taken his insides away from him before granting him absolution. A man cannot live with the memories Alex had to live with.

At first, whenever she spoke of him, there was fury in her voice.

Later on, in mid-sentence almost, her expression softened. After that she spoke of him with a considerable measure of regret.

You could not blame Alex for what he had done, she said. She had seen how much he suffered when he was a child. He had some good in him. Maybe a lot of good. But his father's selfishness and her own existence as his mistress must have destroyed that. It was his loneliness as a child and his resentment of Abraham that made him a rebel and a heel. She was as much to blame for that as Abraham was. She used to come to their house when Martha was there and flaunt herself and never hid her love for Abraham. In her way she had tried to win Alex over. She was kind to him and every time she came to the house she showered him with presents, but he would not reciprocate.

She had no business trying to do that, she told me. The only excuse she could find for her behaviour was the narrow-mindedness of her youth and her ignorance. She was naive and callous. She should have known he could not compromise his loyalty to his mother. She only learned about sensitivity much later, alone and close to old age, because one could not be sensitive and live with Abraham and still remain sane.

Carmelita stopped talking. She lit a cigarette and beyond the grey smoke I saw her wise, vivacious black eyes gazing at me. She put her hand on my shoulder and said:

'You must forget what I said. What matters in life is not the beginning of things but the way they end.'

'What do you mean?'

'Señor Danny, it was young Alex who saved me in the end. He saved my reputation and my life.'

I was going to ask her about this but just then an old man with a guitar approached. He was playing some tune and as he played he drummed his free fingers on the wood.

'Dance, Carmelita,' someone shouted. 'Dance for us!'

From the look in her eyes I saw that she could not refuse. She rose and her face lit up and then, before my very eyes, she became someone else. The elderly waitress had vanished in an instant. A clue to her past glory was coming through the commotion, and she took her apron off and moved towards the centre of the place. She danced. Boy, Mr Lawyer, how she danced. She was an apparition. Her movements were so swift and rhythmic and sensual that the years flew from her face and her body. The patrons formed a circle around her, and I had to get on top of a table to see. She sang and she gyrated and her shapely legs hit the floor with energy and power I did not realize she still possessed. I began to forget who I was and where I was.

The place was what young Morton Chandler would certainly call a dump. There were no decorations and no soft lights. No ten-man orchestra or chandeliers or tuxedos. Just an eating house full of foreign immigrants trying to become Americans. But while Carmelita Rodriguez danced they were pure Cuban, no more, no less, and proud of it. While Carmelita sang the eating house turned into a theatre in old Havana. Or some other Latin place. The sort of joint old Xavier Cugat would be playing in, you know. Or maybe you don't. Anyway, watching her sing and dance I could well imagine that younger version of her as it tantalized those vast long-gone audiences. I could imagine the lines of people waiting for the next show.

I am getting excited and I know it. My frame may be tatty but my heart is where it was when I was born. Worse, I am becoming sentimental, and those same emotions that pulled me and the Germans out of the coffee house in Paris all the way to the rocky battlefields of Spain are with me and I cannot stop them.

Even for you I cannot stop them. I have long been an admirer of Spain. In my time I went to fight for her. Spain has always meant love and jealousy and music and passion and wherever her sons went they took these emotions with them. In South America, everywhere you go you will see what they left behind. Yes, I know, they did some awful things to the natives, but a lot of good remained. The excitement, the language, the names of people and places and a crazy social order that screams for reform and needs constant revolution. But then there is fun, and fun is more important than anything. The poorest man in the remotest village knows how to enjoy it and how to forget the squalor he lives in if you give him a drink and a guitar. Any short trip in a bus somewhere in Latin America becomes a Spanish carnival. All you need do is listen to Spain's music and see her daughters dance and you will understand what I mean.

I know, Mr Lawyer. I know that I am boring you to tears, but I cannot stop myself describing this for you now any more than I could stop watching her then. I have forgotten the name of the place, but I could find it walking in the dark. I was bedazzled by the music and the noise. My youth was back and Spain was back. And somewhere around my loins a hint of a sweet itch made me remember the past passions of this, my tired old body.

When she was finished she came back to our corner. She apologized for having to work and I said I would wait for her. Perhaps she would like to have dinner with me later. There was a lot to talk about and a lot for me to listen to. Now that she knew all there was to know about Abraham's village and his beginning, it was her turn to tell me about his end.

What came next was too stirring for me to mention and still is. I shall have to stop now, but I will give you the rest of it when I get off this merry-go-round. Thank you so much for putting me there. Goodnight, my young Mr Lawyer. There is a lot to tell still, but Carmelita is waiting for me in the small bar they have downstairs. I am feeling tired yet so happy I could fly. I have had a drink to fortify me but all it did was make me feel dizzy.

Later, perhaps tomorrow or the day after, when I am sober and safely back on earth, I shall make another recording and tell all. I shall tell you about Abraham and about his end and most of all about his son Alex. Yes, your mysterious client.

From what I can make out I am pretty damn sure he has come to Israel to see you and no one else. He had you, and you alone, on his mind for many years. I am sending this in tonight's post. I shall give it to the concierge on my way out.

Chapter Twenty-Five

There was too much tension inside me. Danny's last remark had aggravated me and I could not find peace. The old man had said I had been on Alex's mind for years, and I was weary of second-hand information. I wanted the man himself to tell me what Danny had meant. I was hoping to play this latest tape to Alex and get his reaction but he had gone underground. He often did that, and always when I needed to see him. All I could do was sit and wait for him to call, but that day he made no contact, nor did he the next. Perhaps I was jumping the gun. Perhaps I should listen to the next tape first. I waited two or three days for the promised sequel, but nothing new turned up. I was thinking of calling Danny but I was too confused to work out where to find him. My frustrations reached a new peak. I must have been a nightmare to work for.

I called Morton Chandler's house, but there was no sign of him there. Mr Chandler was in Las Vegas for a short vacation, they said. Playing the tables relaxed him. They knew Mr Danny was staying some place in downtown Miami, but he had not told them where. The man was very polite and helpful. He asked whether I wanted Danny to call me if he made contact. I said yes please and we hung up. I had other clients to attend to but I found all sorts of excuses to do next to nothing for them. I was nervous and I played around with some overdue dictation most of the morning. I didn't make much sense but my secretary was kind about it and took everything down. Then, after a scant lunch of a takeaway hamburger, I remembered the name of the Cuban hotel Danny had mentioned. El Gran Tucan, it was called.

With the able help of a kindly American operator I got through to the number. The hotel telephonist said Señor Danny was out. When I asked to be put through to the porter, the telephonist said he was the porter too. And the concierge, he added, anticipating my next request.

'When will Mr Danny be back?'

'Later this afternoon.'

'Do you know where he is?'

'Yes. He is out with Señorita Carmelita Rodriguez.'

I thanked the man and he wished me a nice day. Then Alex called. I was so relieved I shouted.

'Where the hell have you been?'

'Is there a fire somewhere?'

'No,' I said. 'I worry about you, that's all. I need to see you.'

'What for?'

'I have a tape from Danny I would like you to hear. I want to discuss it with you.'

'Is it about my father?'

'It's about you.'

'Is it the truth?'

'What do you mean, Alex?'

'Is Danny's source reliable?'

'I believe so.'

'Do you believe what they say is true?'

'I think so. Yes, I do.'

'In that case I don't need to hear it. I know the truth. I know all about myself, Mr Lawyer. You listen to it again by yourself if it amuses you.'

'I've heard it already,' I said.

'Then do some other work. Am I the only client you have?'

With these words he hung up on me. I had no idea where he was calling from. I never got the chance to ask him about Danny's remarks. And then the man himself called me.

'I hear you're asking about me all over the place.'

'Yes, I am.'

'You sound angry.'

'I'm that, too.'

'Why are you angry?'

'Because you left me hanging at the end of your last tape. What was it you said about Alex and me?'

There was silence at the other end.

'What do you mean?' he asked.

'You said he had been after me for years. Or something like that.'

'Did I?'

'Yes, Danny, you did. I can play it back for you right now.'

'I may have done. I was drunk and when I'm drunk I always talk rubbish. You knew I was drunk. You must have worked that out from the sound of my voice.'

'You're lying.'

'You say that again, Mr Lawyer, and you lose your detective.'

'I'm sorry.'

'That's better.'

'I thought you... You did say Alex had had me on his mind for years.'

'Did I say that?'

I thought he had but I was no longer certain. I could have played the tape a second time to make sure but I was afraid of upsetting him. To lose him at this point would be a calamity. My whole line of questioning collapsed because I had no idea what I was trying to achieve. Danny went on talking. He spoke fast, as though he were in a tearing hurry.

'I can't understand what you're saying, Danny. Slow down. That night you said…'

'I don't remember a thing about it now. When I recorded that I was on my way out and when I came back I was sick half the night.'

'You said you were just about to go out with Carmelita.'

'I'm sure I did… but I was so drunk the evening with her was a write-off. When I get drunk I make all sorts of assumptions. That may have well been one. I'm sorry I misled you.'

'When are you sending me the other tape?'

'Tomorrow. The day after that… As soon as I speak to Carmelita again.'

'Fine.'

'I'm supposed to see her later today.'

'Fine.'

'I'll come back to my room and make the recording immediately after.'

'Fine.'

'I'm sure we're in for some interesting details.'

'I'll wait to hear from you, then.'

'Goodbye.'

I still believed he was hiding something. He was too precise and too factual. None of his habitual mentions of local smells and colours had come up in the conversation. I had been deliberately short with him, but he did not comment or complain. He was certainly making an effort of some kind, and I decided to forget about it for now. I would not ask any more questions, nor volunteer any clues or information. I would wait for Danny to offer a second revelation that might explain the first.

Then my mother called. As usual she came straight to the point.

'He's an interesting man, your Alex Moreno.'

I was still thinking about Danny and managed only a weak 'Yes, Mother'.

'And he is going to make you all that money?'

'Yes. When we find his father's papers.'

'Is his father dead?'

'Yes. He's here because his father bought some property while he was here after the war. That's how I came to know him. I've told you this before.'

'When did Abraham Moreno die?'

'How do you know his name?'

'You told me… the time you came back from the Galilee, remember?'

I did not remember but I was miles away. I did not even notice how her voice had changed. It became less precise, hesitant almost.

'When… when did his father die?' she asked again.

'I don't know.'

'Ask him.'

'What difference does it make?'

'I suppose… I suppose it doesn't matter really. How did he die?'

'I've no idea… but I'll know once Danny sends me his next instalment. Danny is in Miami. He met with Abraham's mistress. She will tell him and then he'll tell me and then I'll know.'

'Alex's father had a mistress?'

'Yes. It seems they all have those where he comes from.'

'Does that mean she has a claim on some of his money?'

'Maybe. I don't really know. I haven't seen a will.'

I suppose I should have been happy she was interested. We chatted for a bit about the law and how it differed from country to country. About what a mistress can inherit from a man she had lived with and how. The old composure was back in her voice. Again, I only thought of that later. As usual, the significance of her verbal delivery was going to come back to me only on another occasion. When I found out what lay behind it.

I was tired but she expected me to do the talking. She always did when there was something up her sleeve. I obliged.

'Thank you again for the tea party, Mother,' I said.

'If you want you can come for dinner some time. You can bring this Alex with you. Make friends with him. It will come in useful when it's time for him to pay.'

'I don't know where he is. When he contacts me I'll suggest it to him.'

'I only need a day's warning.'

'I know.'

'Where does he live?'

'I don't know. You seem to have taken to him. Why this sudden interest in my clients?'

'Oh, nothing. I think he likes you a lot, that's all. That is good. Especially when it comes to paying your fees. You can tell he likes you. From the way he looks at you.'

'I don't believe he likes me at all. He needs me, that's what it is.'

'He seems a disturbed man. Is he married?'

'I don't think so.'

'Is he a homosexual?'

'You're reading too many tabloids. I don't think he is... I don't know.'

'I've got to go now.'

'Goodbye, Mother.'

The long-awaited recording from Danny arrived as soon as I put the phone down. I asked my secretary to hold all calls.

Chapter Twenty-Six

Mr Lawyer, I'm sending this by special messenger without extra cost to you. I went to the Hialea race course with Carmelita yesterday and made three hundred dollars. She used to be a great gambler and I must say I could easily become one myself. It was grand to see horses again. I mean well-bred, pampered racehorses. They are beautiful beasts, shapely and fast and very different to the big, heavy animals I knew when I was a boy. We used them for the plough and for the occasional ride on Saturday. Only the British police and some of the Arab boys had horses just for riding.

Anyway, it seems Martha died in 1952. Immediately after her death, Carmelita was arrested for her murder. The Cuban papers were full of it. She was a famous woman and the details of her affair with the dead woman's husband were splashed all over the place. Most people loved her, especially the men, but she had enemies too. It seems that the media loved success then as now. But then as now they loved it best when they could bring the famous down to earth.

For days there was nothing else to read about. Not a mention of sugar prices or politics or wars. The papers were full of Carmelita's downfall and her impending conviction. There were pictures of them together, all three of them, she and he and Martha. Pictures of them going to parties or to concerts or just sitting around. Someone managed to print a photograph of Carmelita with Abraham's arms around her while Martha sat on a couch across from them, reading a book. How convenient, the caption said, for the mistress to be the one who first discovered the body. She spent a long time in a cell by herself while evidence was being collected. The press had already judged her and none of the people she knew came forward. Abraham managed to bribe the prison authorities to move her to a comfortable cell, but these were trying days for her. The widower was not even questioned. Man was the undisputed king in that part of the world and could do no wrong. Especially at that time. Men were priests and presidents and even God was a man. Some people would have loved to have seen Abraham in the dock but he had been away on a trip to Miami when Martha died and was therefore above suspicion.

Carmelita was a well-known performer and the authorities feared she would leave the country. And there was a political side, too: they wanted to show the masses how even the high and mighty must face justice. So she stayed under lock and key and no bail was granted. As the trial date came closer she began to feel she had no friends. There were demonstrations outside her window. Mostly by women who stayed out there for days and tormented her with their accusations and chanting and abuse. How she had taken a woman's man away. How she had broken his family. How she had wormed her way into the woman's house while she was sick and alone. No churchgoing family was safe while she was free. Her guilt should have been easy to prove. By her own admission she had spent a lot of time with Martha and that gave her plenty of opportunities to kill the poor, defenceless woman.

That was not the way it was, Carmelita told me, and I believe her. She has an amazing grasp of the psychology behind the facts. From her story I learned about her powers of observation and the depth of her feelings for Martha, the woman she was accused of killing. You judge for yourself, Mister Lawyer.

This is what she told me.

Martha had been ill for a long time. She had suffered from shortness of breath and arteritis and at times she could hardly move. Yet she cooked for Alex and delivered the food to him at his flat in the old part of Havana. She insisted on cleaning the house all by herself in spite of Abraham's pleading with her to use her maid. She worked her fingers to the bone because she was prone to sink into a depression unless she kept herself busy. The problem was she could never find enough to do, and her craving to be needed remained unquenched. It was almost as though she had lost the will to live once her son had gone to live on his own. Her entire family had met a horrible end during the war in Europe and she constantly brooded about them and how it had been when she was a child. Her friends the Madeiros were dead and she hardly knew any people in town.

Pushed under by loneliness, she began to change. The stage within her, where once she could act out her emotional and intellectual life, had vanished. Her ability to draw on her own strength was gone and Martha found herself in a vacuum that wrenched her towards a most unlikely quarter, her husband's mistress. She would call her over the telephone sometimes, when Abraham was away. Carmelita responded, and within weeks this strange relationship found the two women talking to each other every day. Martha's attitude towards her rival assumed a new light. She began to accept her.

With time, her stance evolved into something more than mere acceptance. Having spotted Carmelita's own vulnerability, Martha grew to trust her, and finally to confide in her. She invited her to the house and talked to her about her life, and about Abraham, the man they both loved. His estrangement from his son, she divulged, had hurt him deeply, but having learned how to live with it he had convinced himself a person could overcome any pain. He was a man who judged everybody else by his own standards. He thought other people were as talented as he was. He thought everybody was able to make their way in the world.

She often told Carmelita to put something aside for a rainy day. Abraham would have expected her to do that, she said. Carmelita never took the other woman's advice. She told me herself she should have done. The two met and talked often but never became really close until Martha took a turn for the worse.

At the end of 1950, in fact during a Christmas party to which all three went, she collapsed. She had become very sick and Abraham had her flown to Miami and checked by a doctor there. It was a very private trip; he did not even tell Chandler about it. They may have been at odds right then, as they often were, mostly because of Abraham's distasteful behaviour as a family man. Anyway, Carmelita went with them and a picture of them at Havana airport was later published in the papers.

It was in Miami, Carmelita told me, that she heard the doctor say that Martha was suffering from a weak heart. He recommended she move away from the tropics, and make her home somewhere cooler, like New York. At least during spring and early winter. But Martha wouldn't hear of it. Carmelita remembered that the doctor said something about a death wish, but when she mentioned this to Abraham he told her not to worry.

She was a little better when they returned to Cuba. She stopped doing the housework altogether and had the maid cook and clean for Alex instead. She hardly ate anything herself and became very frail. The only time she'd leave the house was when she went to visit her son or lay flowers on the Madeiros' grave.

For a few weeks, believe it or not, Carmelita stayed with her lover's wife and nursed her. That was when their friendship reached its peak. Martha told Carmelita not to waste her time on a lost cause. She told her she should think more of herself and never neglect her own career. She said Abraham might one day desert her too. There were no sour grapes, she said. She was not angry or bitter when she talked of her husband. She said he had saved her life and was a good man. It was simply his nature. Abraham, his wife told Carmelita, knew nothing of loyalty and expected none. But God would surely forgive him because he always meant well and never understood how much pain his habits had caused. He was a child who never wanted to stop playing, and that was all. He could never be close to anyone because he was afraid of losing them. At that time, when Martha was very ill and while Carmelita came to be with her every single day, Alex came too. But when Abraham was in the house the young man hid in the cane fields until he was gone. Sometimes he stayed there for many hours.

Alex loved his mother more than life. He was always good to her. He'd save his pocket money and buy her presents. Sometimes he bought rare German books and Swiss chocolates and sometimes he bought gramophone records. He made her happy. Even the maids commented on that. He'd sit with her for hours and bring her cold drinks and wipe her lips and her forehead and read to her. He kept telling her he would teach his father a lesson. Martha would ask him to swear to her that he would never hurt Abraham, but that was one thing he always refused to do.

He still ignored his father's mistress. Even when he saw how helpful she had become. He was curt and short with her. He looked at her and through her as though she was dirt. He took to having a friend wait outside to take him back to the city to avoid accepting Carmelita's offer of a lift. It was his own mother who told him to be kind to her because she was a good woman whose only crime had been to have loved his father.

'You love my husband very much, Carmelita,' Martha said once.

'I would die for him.'

'I believe you.'

'I'm sorry I came along.'

'Don't be. He never loved me.'

'He is a very lucky man to have you as his wife.'

'He is not.'

'Why, Martha?'

'I'm his prison.'

'Why do you say that?'

'He imprisoned himself by marrying me.'

'I'm sure you're wrong. He must have loved you then. In his way he still does.'

'You're sweet to me, Carmelita. How you must suffer.'

'He is the sun and the moon and the stars for me. I so wish it did not have to be you, Martha. I've tried to leave him but I cannot. I would die without him.'

* * *

She did indeed try. Once, when he was away on business, she went on a concert tour of Latin America. She was gone for six months. He had written to her and cabled her asking her to come back. He went to see her in Brazil and in Venezuela, but she refused to see him. She told me she received many marriage proposals and had gone out a lot but not once was she able to sleep with another man then. There were flowers and dinners and hand kisses but never more than that. For her, sex was an inseparable part of love, and love came to her in the shape of one man, Abraham Moreno. Finally she could no longer be without him and came back.

Abraham soon forgot all about this episode. He continued to travel around and wheel and deal. And then came Martha's illness and the friendship between the two women in his life intensified. Abraham accepted this without comment, and then, while he was on an overseas trip, Martha died.

Later, when Carmelita went on trial for the murder of her lover's wife, help came from the most unexpected corner.

It was Alex who testified for her. It was not an easy thing for him to do. The accused was his father's mistress and the cause of much of his unhappiness. He was a retiring boy who was tongue-tied in company, but when he turned up at her trial he cast all his inhibitions aside. For a short while, there in the witness box, Alex was a star.

He could have paid me back for all that I'd done to him, Carmelita told me, but instead he shone. He, the young man who was described in the press as one of her victims, was assumed to be a witness for the prosecution. But he was not. He came of his own accord and he cut the reporters in the gallery to pieces for condemning her before she had had a chance to defend herself. He had two years of studying law behind him and he was brilliant. He said, 'Carmelita was my mother's only friend when she needed someone. She stayed with her and looked after her like a sister and would have saved her life if she could have. You should all be ashamed of yourselves.'

'Who killed your mother, young Moreno?' the prosecutor asked.

And then Alex came out with the most difficult admission any man could make. He told the court his mother had taken her own life. It must have been torture for him. He could hardly speak. In a broken, husky voice he said she had written him a note in which she apologized for what she was going to do.

The public gallery's sympathy swung sharply towards Alex.

'May we see that note?' the prosecutor asked, and a heavy hush descended on the assembly.

For the first time, Alex looked the man straight in the eye. He was a pale, thin youngster and the prosecutor was a robust middle-aged man of authority and experience. Alex had never taken part in a court case before but suddenly his insecurity was gone. An awesome expression contorted his face. He looked at the man for a long time and then, in a commanding voice that cut the silence, he roared:

'Are you not ashamed of yourself, Mr Prosecutor? Surely, you do not expect a man to keep a note like that. You are asking for blood, no less, Mr Prosecutor. How many times does my mother have to die before you clear this woman of a charge she is undeniably innocent of? Hasn't enough injustice been done here?'

The older man sat down, dumbfounded. His eyes dropped to the floor. The electrified silence soon turned into verbal commotion and applause. The public had loved the accused and now they loved her defender. His performance had saved her life.

No one dared question him or Carmelita after that, and the case was thrown out.

Whether or not there was such a note Alex never said.

Carmelita Rodriguez would forgive him everything after that.

He had lied for his father's mistress, Carmelita said. In front of the whole world he had lied about his mother's death. It takes a brave man to do this, Mr Lawyer. And as for me, if I had any bad vibrations about Alex Moreno before, I have none now.

You know, Mr Lawyer, I asked Carmelita what it was she saw in Abraham. She loved talking about that. It took her half the night to answer. I'll give you only some of what she said, just the way she said it.

'He was', she told me, 'so much like us Latins to look at and yet he was different. He was full of life and open and yet he always kept something back to surprise you with. He was a flirt but he never made a promise he did not intend to keep, even if circumstances made it impossible. His bearing was legendary. He would walk into a room and his eyes would move around slowly, like a searchlight. They emitted passion and curiosity and patience and generosity all at the same time. When he looked at you and when he put his arms around you you felt safe but never sure of him, and that made him exciting. He would ask you what you wanted to do and you believed you could ask him to take you to the moon. If there was a way, he would take you there.

'Once, walking down a small Havana street, he asked me where I would like to go for lunch. I jokingly mentioned a small place we knew on Miami beach. Abraham stopped a taxi, took me to the airport, chartered a plane and off we went. He was like that. In love he was ardent, as if this time was going to be the last time we were together.

'He never loved Martha. Not the way a man loves a woman. He loved her like a sister. He married her because he honestly thought he was saving her life. In those days many Jewish refugees were sent back to Europe. She knew that well. She told me that herself, many times she told me. But I felt sorry for her and always insisted he had a special place in his heart for her alone. Abraham was a child, but unlike a child he never wanted to hurt anyone, even if he had to lie.'

We talked all night, Mr Lawyer. I could listen to her for hours. Her black eyes drilled holes in me through the dark hollow of our corner. Maybe I'm falling in love with her. Yes. I can see what Abraham Moreno saw. How he needed her enthusiasm, her clarity of vision, her simplicity and modesty.

He needed her honesty. Underneath her fervent belief in God you can see the passionate woman stylishly enduring this long-overdue middle age. Passion never dies. Not for Carmelita, not for any woman. When I think of her I see her for what she is inside. Right now, not what she was. She is a beautiful, caring woman with music in her voice and smiles. A loyal woman, who knew disappointment and gratification, a faithful woman yet sensual. As sensual now as she was when her body was young.

Young people, you included, Mr Lawyer, think that there is no love at my age. You're wrong, all of you. I know an old people's home in Jerusalem. A friend of mine was dumped there by his children and he says there are more love stories and jealousies up there than in the whole of Peyton Place.

The first rays of daylight welcomed me to El Gran Tucan when I finally got back. I feel poetic, Mister Lawyer. If that puts a smile on your grim face I'm happy. I've a lot more to tell but I'm tired now. My heart is palpitating a little but it's just a mixture of tiredness and excitement. I'll have a little drink. I'll end this recording soon and I shall ask the concierge, who is the porter and also the telephonist, to take this and send it to you by messenger. I'll use the money I won on the horses the other day. It won't cost you a penny.

* * *

I'll say one more thing, Mr Lawyer, before I send this off to you. I want to tell you about something Carmelita said that shook even me. When we said goodbye at the door of her simple little flat, she turned to me and she said:

'You know, Señor Danny, Martha died for me. She knew I was, after a fashion, a God-fearing woman who believed in destiny and the next world. I am a Catholic and yet I had lived in sin and she knew that underneath it all I had marriage on my mind. She knew how much I loved Abraham. She knew how much he needed me and she wanted to be out of the way to give us a better chance. A sick person can turn to the wall and die if they really want to. It was a sacrifice and it made Martha a saint, Señor Danny.'

Chapter Twenty-Seven

My wife's lawyer called to say he had great news for me. He wouldn't say what it was and kept me in suspense by announcing he would only tell me about it face to face. We set up a date for dinner but he did not show. His secretary said he had been called up for reserve duty. I had been trying to locate Alex Moreno. His man Juan Miret who had sent the money needed sorting out. I had received fifty thousand dollars from him without rendering an invoice. I had spent a good part of it in payments to my wife and redeeming my debts at the bank. It wouldn't be long before someone found out. They would want to know where the money came from and why. The income tax authorities in this country are notorious. People worry more about the tax people than about all the wars. I needed to have some documentation to justify the payment and the way I had used it.

The Custodian of Absentees' Property had news too. It was now established that Abraham Moreno had purchased two plots of land in 1946. The girl who worked there was able to tell me where they were at: one on top of Mount Carmel in Haifa and the other in north Tel Aviv. Both were now prime locations and were still empty. A call to one of my estate agent friends established the value of Moreno's holdings at a little under eight million dollars in the event of a quick sale. At least another million if the vendor was able to wait. The agent said it would not be difficult at all. The builders would kill themselves outbidding each other if such properties were to come on to the market. He asked me to let him handle the sale. I said I would give it to him if the legal owner agreed.

What I needed now was to find the deeds and the bills of sale. As Abraham was a businessman he was sure to have kept these documents in a safe place.

Just as important was to establish Abraham Moreno's

place and date of death and prove that his son Alex was his only heir. The best route would have been to find a will, but I did not hold out much hope in that direction. Neither Danny nor his new love Carmelita were the sort of people who would understand the significance of a piece of paper. I still knew nothing about Abraham's death, and as long as Danny was in Florida I did not think it would be proper for me to contact Morton Chandler with that kind of enquiry.

The only person who could have helped me was Alex, and he had gone missing. I checked every small hotel in Tel Aviv, every pension and rooming house. He was a disturbed man, and I had my secretary make a few discreet calls to most of the mental hospitals in and around Tel Aviv. She found no trace of him. The immigration authorities and the police had only my own office as the address at which he could be contacted.

Danny had said Carmelita would know about Abraham's end and I was waiting for his next tape, but a week passed after our conversation and nothing came. His last recording had sounded like he was floating high in outer space and I was apprehensive about him. I had to stop myself from calling Chandler's house or the Gran Tucan in case my anxiety was obvious. With his mercurial temper Danny would feel pressurized and that would be the end of his co-operation.

My mother too was behaving in a most unusual fashion. She kept asking about Alex Moreno, and three times she reminded me to be sure and invite him over for a meal. Maybe her sudden interest was merely commercial. I had told her about the value of his father's property and she got quite excited about it. She suggested she could help me locate him. I forbade her to get involved.

That week the PLO carried out a series of bloody attacks on Jewish settlers. Five people died in a shooting incident on a bus on the way to Jerusalem. Two women were knifed in the Old City. The intifada was gaining momentum. Everybody was waiting for some hard-hitting retaliation on

Israel's part. These reactions were understandable but they did not bring the promised peace any closer. Personally, I am for dialogue. I am not a coward or a pacifist. I have served in a combat unit and am willing to go to war to defend this country, but not to be a policeman and die while separating fanatical Arabs from fanatical Jews. My wife's lawyer was doing his reserve duty in the occupied area of the West Bank, and on his first leave he came to see me at my office unannounced.

That night we went to a club in Old Jaffa. It was warm and we sat outside, under a canopy of old Phoenix palms. A long-legged, black-stockinged flamenco dancer pounded on the wooden stage with her high-heeled shoes. Her guitar player made music and I watched his tortured face and thought of Carmelita. The flat my father had bought when he came back to this country was near by. He had finished decorating it shortly before he died and had left it to Joan and my daughters. Even in death he wanted to remind me of his disapproval. Of how unimportant I was to him.

My friend said Joan was thinking of using the flat as a studio for immigrant artists. She would let them work there without paying rent. She proposed that they give her the exclusive right to sell their creations in return. She was going to become an art dealer after all.

'It's an interesting idea,' he said. 'I was working out a way of putting it in legal terms when I was called up.'

'Good luck to her. She needs to be kept busy.'

'That's a condescending, ugly thing to say.'

'You are right. Of course you are right… I am sorry.'

'She's a beautiful and talented woman.'

'I know. I said I'm sorry. I don't know what came over me.'

'You two should really try and make it up. Don't you love her?'

'I'm crazy about her.'

We had a quiet meal and watched the rest of the show. A so-so magician and an ageing pop singer. When I got back to my flat there was a message from Alex on my answering machine. He was angry and complained I was never there when he needed me. He said he'd be in my office first thing in the morning. He sounded harassed and his voice was loaded with melancholy anticipation. He spoke slowly and repeated himself three times and was going for a fourth when the final beep shut him up. I could not make him out. I had to down a few stiff whiskies before I could get to sleep.

Chapter Twenty-Eight

He stormed in just as my secretary handed me a cable. It was from Juan Miret.

'Why can't I reach you when I need you?' he shouted. He looked somewhat haggard. As if he had not slept all night. But something told me he was relieved to see me.

'Look, Alex, I don't know what you're playing at. I haven't seen or heard from you in weeks.'

'Are you working for me or aren't you?'

'I am, but I do have other things... other clients...'

'Where were you last night?'

'Out.'

He sat down. He took the glass of water that stood on the desk and emptied it. My secretary said:

'This man... er... Juan Miret from Miami? He would like you to call him. He left both his home and his office numbers.'

'Fine. I'll let you know when to get him.'

She nodded, took one cautious look at Alex and disappeared.

'What's the matter with her?' he asked.

'She's scared of you, Alex. You have a dark side to you. Women have intuition.'

He sat back. I thought he was agreeing with what I had said. I thought he might even have enjoyed it. He seemed to relax. He poured himself another glass of water. The colour had returned to his cheeks. I said:

'What would your friend Miret want with me?'

'Juan Miret is not my friend now.'

'If one of my enemies sent me fifty thousand dollars I'd give all my friends up. Seriously, I thought you and he were...'

'We used to be comrades-in-arms.'

'Used to be?'

'Used to be. He went through the people's struggle against Batista from the beginning. The government threw everything at us, planes and tanks and men, equipped with the latest Yanqui hardware. We held our own against great odds because the people on our side were dedicated. Juan Miret was a hero in those days. A simple fellow, you'd think. If you looked at him, at his square shape and his bushy hair and his big hands, you'd swear he was a labourer straight off some sugar estate. He didn't have much formal education because he never hid his political beliefs and was constantly being kicked out of university. But he was an avid reader and a born leader. He also had a great head for figures and, most of all, he was the best sniper I have ever met... there was a rumour he could slice a flying butterfly in two.

'I remember being with him once, at a small fortified hideout in the mountains. I was recovering from an injury and could not do any fighting. I was sent there on a sort of morale-boosting visit. There was not a lot of work for me to do. Miret's group were all former estate workers. They only had jobs during the cutting season. After that they were left to starve. They were staunch Fidel men from the start. He was reading one of those books he always carried with him when we saw a whole company of government troops coming up the mountainside. He looked at the pace at which they were advancing and calculated their arrival time to the last minute. He wet his finger and worked out the wind direction and speed. They were coming straight for us. A light plane that had circled the area that morning must have given them our position. There were only ten of us and Juan Miret was in command.

'The troops were still coming and you could almost touch the nervous eagerness among our men. Miret collected four rifles from the others, loaded them and carefully laid them down by his side. Another man was waiting behind him, ready to reload. There was a lot of excitement and the men were itching to open fire immediately but he ordered them to wait. It wasn't all that long but it seemed like an eternity before the action started. The enemy had been showering us with heavy mortar fire for a good hour and we had to keep our heads down. You never knew where the next explosion would be. When the shells stopped falling, the company had advanced almost half a mile. It was an eerie, lonely feeling lying there.The smell of gunpowder and dust filled the air. You could not hear a thing but you saw them coming closer and closer. Their new rifles shone in the sun and you knew they had plenty of good ammunition. The prolonged waiting made people nervous and then, unexpectedly, the silence exploded as Miret opened up. He lay there, motionless almost, and took his time and aimed and shot as if the soldiers were ducks. He started firing at the back of the column, while the others in the front kept on negotiating the rocky terrain. Within seven or ten minutes almost thirty of those at the rear were down. The rest continued to crawl up the winding path, not noticing what was happening behind them. Our boys got ready to open fire, but Miret kept ordering them to wait.

'He took one more aim and shot the man at the head of the column and two other officers. Perhaps that was when the rest of the enemy noticed the carnage. They lost their nerve. They threw down their guns and ammunition and turned back and started running downhill.

'"Fire," Miret barked, and with ten guns roaring we got a good few more of them before they disappeared.

'Later, when we went down to collect the equipment, we

noticed that some of their guns were so new they had hardly been fired before. Some still had grease on them.

'Yes, Juan Miret was a comrade-in-arms before he changed. He was a hero. Just before he left the cause he went with Che to Bolivia to train others in the art of sharpshooting. He could have gone far in the Cuban Army.'

'Why did he leave?'

'I don't want to talk about that right now.'

'You always say that.'

'You ask too many questions.'

'I'm a lawyer.'

'Yes, but I'm your client. I ask the questions.'

'I need to talk to Juan Miret.'

'What for?'

'To organize something about the money. I have books to keep. Accountants to explain things to. I'd like to send him an invoice and a receipt for the money. Besides, I need to pay him back some time.'

'He'll wait. He's got plenty of money. You can pay him once you've sold my father's stuff.'

'Talking of your father's stuff, you have no idea how rich you are. I tried to get hold of you as soon as I heard. The properties are indeed in your father's name. They're worth an absolute fortune.'

'I don't care. I told you, money doesn't interest me.'

'What do you want me to do about it?'

'Do whatever you like,' he snapped.

His reaction confused me. I decided to leave it for the time being. I said:

'My mother wants you over for dinner.'

'She does?'

'Will you come?'

'I'll let you know.'

'Alex, I need to have some documents... copies of the land deeds and some proof of your father's death. I suppose they have death certificates in Cuba?'

'I suppose so.'

'And something to prove you're his only son.'

'I don't want to talk about that right now.'

'You're crazy. We're talking about serious money here…'

'Leave me out of it.'

'How am I going to get all the information without you?'

'You'll manage. You're a clever little lawyer, aren't you?'

'If we wait a little over the sale of the land you'll make a killing.'

'All you think about is money.'

'It's your money, not mine.'

'Well, I don't care for money.'

'You keep saying that. What do you want out of life, Alex? Why did you make me dig for all this if you have no interest in money? You don't like this country. You don't like the system, you're not trying to settle. You're not even learning the language. Why did you come here at all?'

'I told you already. I have some unfinished business to attend to.'

'Here in Israel?'

'Yes. Here in Israel.'

'Not your father's money?'

'No.'

'What sort of unfinished business?'

'A lot of it has to do with you.'

'With me?'

'Yes.'

'Then tell me. If it's me you're interested in I'm entitled to know.'

He said nothing. He just looked at me with his sad eyes. Then he shrugged his shoulders and got up. The telephone rang as he reached the door, then he was gone. Something of him lingered on in my room. Something sweet and bitter. I wanted to identify it but the phone kept ringing. I picked it up. It was my secretary.

'What is it?' I shouted.

'You have a call from Miami.'

'Put it through.'

It was a voice I had not heard before. A deep masculine American voice that sounded somewhat bewildered. I looked at my watch. Automatically, the way you do when you get an overseas call. It must have been the middle of the night in Florida.

'Hello?'

'My name is Morton Chandler,' the voice said. 'I believe you were a friend of Mr Katz.'

'Mr who?'

'Daniel Katz. He was doing some legwork for you out here.'

'Oh yes. Danny. What can I do for you, Mr Chandler?'

'I have very bad news for you.'

'What is it?'

'Danny died last night.'

'He what?'

'He died last night. Hit by a massive heart attack. They called me from the hotel he was staying at. Some small place in Little Havana… you know, down in South Miami. I had just come back from Las Vegas. I had only been in the house for half an hour when they called. I had to go down there myself to identify him. I looked at his papers to find your telephone number. I'm sorry. So sorry. I was very fond of the guy. He was such a sweet old man… so young at heart and so understanding. He was very special.'

'He was.'

'What arrangements would you like me to make?'

'I'm coming out there on the next plane.'

'Give me the details of your flight and I'll have you picked up at the airport. We'll get you up here to Palm Beach to stay with us. Danny spoke of you a lot. You'll be welcome in this house.'

'I'd like to stay in Miami for a little, near to where Danny was… but I'll let you know. What happens to the… to Danny in the meantime?'

'Oh, they'll keep him in the morgue down there.'

'Where did he… where did it happen?'

'I have no details yet. Maybe they did tell me, but I can't think straight right now. I'll call and let you know as soon as I can.'

'Fine.'

I replaced the receiver. A huge void seemed to hang over me and the air was heavy. I felt I had known Danny for years. As if he had been a part of my private world for ever. Everything about him had reeked of life. He was from the past but he belonged in the present. He was the now. He was an old man who loved the future.

For once I was pleased Alex had gone. I needed to be alone to face this amputation. I leaned back and thought about the old boy. About how we had met and how he volunteered to go and do my job for me. I thought about his voice and his excitement and his last emotional recording. About how he had been taken with Carmelita Rodriguez. His schoolboy infatuation with her. He had said he was going to send me more information. The recording might be on its way to me. It would tell of his love of people and colour, and through the words I would feel his energy. It would all come to me through the vibrations of a dead man's voice. I felt abandoned and drained. I needed to disappear, to lose myself long enough to think this out, but there were things I had to do. I had Danny's daughter's telephone number in Tiberias and I dialled it. I was in a daze, feeling almost drugged, when Danny's daughter came on the line.

Chapter Twenty-Nine

Danny had never bragged about her although he had plenty of reason to do so. She was his daughter in more ways than one. She took the news with great calm and courage, and he would have been proud of her. It is an almost impossible task to tell a person that someone close to them has passed on. I had to do so on two or three occasions during my military service. You do it, but you can't ever do it right because there is no right way to hurt anyone.

After telling her that Danny had died my voice faltered, and she did not push me for more information. I burst into tears, and still she kept her dignified silence. When I recovered I added that, sadly, there was nothing good I could say to her except that anyone who had known him would feel this same pain we were feeling. There was not much I could tell her by way of detail. All I could do was repeat what Morton Chandler had tried to tell me. She asked what was to be done next.

I told her I was going out there as soon as possible, and then I fell into an embarrassed silence.

'It was a good way for him to go,' she said. 'He called me just two days ago and he sounded ecstatic. He said he had just met some very special woman. You know, he had been on his own for many years. He talked to everybody but he was always alone. Maybe he was falling in love. He was a great romantic, my father, and you gave him a canvas to paint on. You gave him a new lease of life. A purpose. It was strange to hear from him so often. As if he knew there was not much time. While he was in Florida he wrote to me almost every day. Each time his letter sounded happier. Before you sent him to Miami I only saw him five or six times a year, when my mother and I came up to the village. He was a beautiful person, you know, and I am not saying that because he was my father. I have always known it, but these past few weeks he confirmed it for me again. Do you know what I mean?'

'Yes.'

'We once went to Spain on holiday, my husband and I. Oh, six or seven years ago. My father gave me the names of a few people he used to know in some village in C?. Near where one of the most decisive battles of the Civil War was fought. He said if his comrades in arms were still alive, and if they remembered him, they would be happy to see me.'

'Did you find the village?'

'Yes I did, and his old friends...they were all alive. Two Spaniards and a German who met my father in Paris and went to Spain with him and stayed. All through the Franco years they hid him in the village where he married and raised a family. A big, white haired man with a kindly broad face and the palest blue eyes you ever saw. His name used to be Hans and he'd been an art student but now he was a retired Spanish farmer and his name was Juan. The three still lived in that same village and they kept us there for nearly a week. None of them could drive a car so we hired one, and with them in the back we travelled all over. They talked about the battles and the dead and where my father slept and where he sang and what he did.

'Did they remember him? They worshipped him. They had attached a stone plaque with his name on it on the outside wall of the village church. "Compañero Daniel", it read. I took pictures of it and when I showed it to my father he made out it meant nothing. He grumbled, I remember, because no one called him Daniel. He pretended it did not matter, but I knew from the look in his eyes how proud it had made him...how much he appreciated it. They've buried me before my time, my father said, and they did it on the wall of a so-called house of God. At least they had the decency to put my name on the outside because God would never let me into one of those places.

'And then my father said something that made me realize he was a philosopher. He said you must never go back. Not to a place you have left for good or to people who were once close to you and are no longer part of your life. Not ever. Places change. Where there was once an orange grove there is now an apartment block or a shopping center. Or something else that wrecks what was left in your memory. People, he added sadly, people change too, because their circumstances change. And once you have parted from them it is best to leave things as they were.'

'I'd go along with that.'

'Yes...I was going to ask you something...tell me, did Danny help you in any way?'

'Did he help me? I don't think Sherlock Holmes himself could have done better. I couldn't have done without his help. It was a complicated assignment. He was nearly finished. He'd promised me another tape. I hope it comes.'

'Would you do me a favour?'

'Of course. Anything.'

'When you're through with everything, could you let me have his tapes? It would be nice to listen to him again... I mean, unless what he says is legally sensitive.'

'It isn't. And even if it were, I'd give the tapes to you. In any case, once this affair is over someone will get wind of it and write about it. This is an incredible story, and people should hear about it. You know, Abraham Schwartz, Cuba, the dancer, the money, and the way Danny entered the story and became a part of it... irresistible. Of course I'll give them to you.'

'Thank you. You're a kind man.'

I listened to her and the more she talked the better she made me feel.

* * *

I called my mother's travel agency. They were very efficient. They gave me all the alternative routes. They said I could get to Miami via either London or New York. They said they'd be pleased to make all the arrangements. I still had visas and traveller's cheques to see to and I said I'd let them know.

An hour later my mother called. She had only just heard I was going to Florida.

'They report to you on everything, don't they.'

'What's so unusual about that?'

'I thought you had retired.'

'I have, but I still own the place. I wouldn't go the whole stretch... it's far too long. I'd stop in London if I were you. Stay a couple of days. You love it so.'

'I'll see.'

'What are you going for?'

'My man in Miami has had a heart attack. He's dead. I have some loose ends to tie up.'

'Have you found out when Abraham died?'

'Not yet. I'll tell you when I do.'

'Have you seen Alex?'

'Yes. He was here this morning.'

'Did you tell him I'd like him to come to dinner?'

'I mentioned it.'

'What did he say?'

'Not much. He was not in a dinner mood.'

'When are you leaving?'

'I'm not sure yet. I have things to do here first.'

'Alex can come by himself if he wants to.'

'I'll tell him if I see him.'

I called Joan to tell her I would be away for a week.

'Where are you going?'

'Miami.'

'You're in a hurry to finish something, aren't you?'

'I need to go. There are things I have to handle myself. I must watch this case carefully.'

'You're a greedy bastard.'

'I love you too,' I said, and I heard her laugh.

'Would you like to see the girls before you leave?'

'Yes, of course. Would this evening be all right?'

'Yes.'

'Will you be there?'

'I'm always here.'

There was something different in her voice. In spite of all the emotions that were running through me, I could tell something was new. Her irritation seemed to have subsided. Perhaps she felt sorry for me. Perhaps this was the beginning of a new road for us. Or then again, perhaps her lawyer had said something good about me.

Chapter Thirty

I had booked myself a room at Danny's hotel, El Gran Tucan. I wanted to start where he had ended. The Cuban taxi driver knew immediately where the place was.

It was a small building covered with an enormous red bougainvillea that imbued the walls with a great deal of warmth. There were palmetto plants and hibiscus bushes in full bloom, stone benches and an ornamented concrete fountain. There were Mediterranean shutters and coloured tiles all over. I could have been in Spain.

The porter was waiting for me by the door. He greeted me like a long-lost brother and reminded me of our telephone conversation. He said he had never had a call from the Holy Land but when Señor Danny moved in he received one such call almost every day. He was sorry about Señor Danny. He was a perfect gentleman and spoke beautiful Spanish. He was familiar with everybody, even with the maids. This was a small hotel but a homely and friendly one. He was sure I would be as happy there as Señor Danny had been. The porter was well past his youth, but he insisted on carrying my suitcase up to the room. He climbed the one flight of stairs with me, handed me the keys and refused a tip. He said I would be sleeping right next to where Señor Danny had slept when he was alive.

The room was bright and cheerful. There was a picture of a flamenco dancer and a framed poster announcing a bullfight. By the bedside lamp there was a earthenware jar with fresh flowers. The dark wooden double bed contrasted with the whitewashed walls. It was early afternoon and I had been up for more hours than I could remember, but I did not feel tired any more. My mother always tells me that jet lag is no more than a stomach clock. If you do not eat anything at all during the flight and drink only water you will adjust to the local time immediately. I had followed her prescription and was starving.

I had planned to make the necessary arrangements for sending Danny back to Israel and to meet Carmelita Rodriguez. I was so close to Cuba, where Abraham had made his life and his fortune. Where Alex had been born and from where, I did not know why, he had escaped. I had heard so much about the island and its grand colonial capital I would have liked to have seen it for myself. But I could not get there from Florida. Not on a scheduled flight. I would have to go to Mexico for that, and so Havana would have to wait. This part of Miami, the taxi driver had told me, was as close as I could get to the real thing. I would not see the mountains or the sugar cane, he said. Nor the old buildings or the boulevards or the famous port. But Eighth Street would allow me to sample the true Cuban atmosphere. I decided to wait a while before contacting Morton Chandler. Give myself a chance to walk the streets of Little Havana first. Get the feel of the place and catch the colour and smell the local scene, the way Danny had.

I asked the porter to direct me to Eighth Street. I asked him whether he knew where Carmelita Rodriguez was working, and he smiled and shrugged his shoulders and said everybody knew that. Eighth Street, or Calle Ocho, was walking distance from the hotel. Along the way there were small food stores selling fish and Caribbean fruit and vegetables. There were second-hand jewellery shops and pharmacies and busy dry cleaners. Merengue and salsa music blared out of record shops and tailoring establishments alike. I passed more hairdressing salons than in the whole of north Tel Aviv. I saw women, young and old, walking about with their children. I saw hair curlers on every head. People strolled in family groups. They talked and they gesticulated and I could not help noticing the warm, secure atmosphere that permeated the area. On terraces and under the trees sat groups of elderly men, playing leisurely games of dominoes. I had been warned about drug pushers and muggers, but the place seemed friendly and safe enough.

Soon I got to the eating house. The place was a human beehive. It was exactly as Danny had described it, and I can add nothing to what he said. He could have been a great travel writer. A pale-blue-clad waitress asked me to wait by the cash register while my table was cleared.

'Is Carmelita Rodriguez here?' I asked, and she said she thought Carmelita was working the late shift that day. That meant she would arrive within the hour. Would I like a cup of coffee while I waited? I nodded. Behind the cash desk there were Spanish magazines and newspapers and cigars and a telephone. I rang Juan Miret in the hope that he was still in his office.

He answered the phone himself.

'I have been expecting you,' he said as soon as I introduced myself.

'How come?'

'Alex Moreno told me you were coming. He called me last night. It was a big surprise.'

'I bet it was.'

'When can I see you?'

'Any time you like.'

'Have you eaten yet?'

'I'm just about to. I'm waiting for a table.'

'Where are you?'

I told him. He sounded anxious to see me. I was not sure whether I should encourage him. I might not get a chance to speak to Carmelita at any length with him there.

'I'm just around the corner,' he said. 'I'll be with you in ten minutes.'

'How will I know you?'

'I will know you,' Juan Miret said. 'Alex has given me a full description. What are you wearing?'

'Denim pants and a dark blue blazer.'

'No tie?'

'No tie.'

* * *

By the time they had sat me at the table the pungent smells that were floating out of the kitchen had blown my appetite out of all proportion. The waitresses seemed to labour as they carried five or six dishes on their trays. The portions were enormous. Soups, salads, piles and piles of rice, black beans, roasted half-chickens, pork and beef. I looked at the faces. Mediterranean types, swarthy, smiling and brightly dressed in colourful shirts. They all looked so familiar I might have been sitting somewhere in Jaffa. They dug straight into the food as soon as it was put before them. There were painted women and beautifully turned-out children ran around. Cigar smoke drifted in circles around the ventilators and everybody talked at the same time. I wished Joan was there with me.

* * *

When I was a student in England we used to go out a lot. We tried every different type of food available. This was in the seventies, when many new restaurants started to appear all over London. We went dancing in discos and sat around in coffee bars and the world was carefree and young. Later, when our first daughter was born, we'd go out for lunch on Saturday. I used to look forward to it because in the afternoon, especially when my father took my daughter for a walk, we'd stay in and sometimes we'd make love until it hurt. I would gladly have given a chunk of my life to have the clock turned back.

Perhaps there was a chance. She had been very sweet the night before I left, when I went over to see the girls. She had prepared a light dinner, salad and scrambled egg and toast and smoked fish. There was a bottle of wine and she handed it to me with the opener. We sat at the table with our daughters and it seemed like the old days were back.

'You look very tired,' she said. 'I hear your client is giving you a hard time.'

'Yes.'

‘My lawyer said you’ve just lost a good friend.’
‘I have.’
‘I’m truly sorry.’
‘Thank you.’
‘Is that why you have to go away?’
‘Yes.’

I complimented her again on her idea of using my father’s flat as a studio for new artists. I said she could use the ground floor as a gallery and open it to the public; she was sure to succeed.

‘You’ll soon make enough money to support us all,’ I added, and she laughed.

We talked in that vein for a long time. The girls did not comment. Nothing in their conversation betrayed surprise at my being back with them there. It was as though I had never been away. When they were put to bed we finished the wine and had coffee, and although I wanted to stay I said I had better go. Maybe I hoped she would ask me, but she remained silent. I said I had to be at the airport very early. The security checks on Israeli flights take for ever.

At the door I badly wanted to kiss her. For one moment I thought she expected me to, but I could not be sure. I had yearned for her for so long it might all have been wishful thinking.

‘Call and let me know you’ve arrived,’ she said before she shut the door.

* * *

A hand patted my shoulder and my reverie was over. The sounds and scents of the Cuban eating house were back. I turned my head.

‘Juan Miret,’ the man said. He had a Hispano-American accent. He was perfectly dressed in a beige suit, white shirt and a flowery tie. His shoes were polished to a mirror finish. He looked like a wrestler. He was broad and short and powerful and his tanned face was clean-shaven. His teeth were white, his hair was grey and combed back close to his skull, and his black eyes smiled at me. I got up and he gave me his enormous hand and squeezed mine and looked at me and said:

'Nice to meet you.'

'And you, Mr Miret.'

'Juan, please. Call me Juan. By the way, how long has Alex been in Israel?'

'I'm not sure.'

'How did you two meet?'

'He wanted me to find things out for him. About his father.'

'Ah, yes. His father was born in your country.'

'Did you know Abraham Moreno?'

'I saw him many times.'

'Did you ever speak to him?'

'No. I knew who he was, of course, but I did not speak to him. When Alex was living on his own in downtown Havana he hardly spoke to his father himself, but he would sometimes point him out to me in the street. You know, from a distance, like pointing out someone famous you don't know in person. I saw him at the casinos. I used to gamble a little. I had a system to beat the roulette.'

'Were you successful?'

'Most of the time I was. For a while I was making quite a bit of money, but like all good things it had to come to an end.'

'What happened? You reformed?'

'Not at all. When they found out about the system they all got together and had me barred from all the casinos in town. But for a while I lived on my winnings. I even bought a motor car. It's funny, if a man is too successful when he's young he starts thinking the world is his oyster. He believes he can never fail, and that's when his troubles begin. I can't complain, though. I've been lucky… with money, anyway.'

'Alex said you had a good head for figures.'

'I suppose I do.'

He smiled and motioned me to sit, and then took his place

opposite me.

'You must be tired. You've had a long flight.'

'Not tired. I'm hungry, though.'

'We'll cure that right away. We're in the right place. What would you like?'

'Would you mind ordering for me?'

'I'll get a small selection, shall I?'

'I'll leave it to you.'

The meal we had was a feast. I sampled everything that was put on the table and the dishes kept coming. I ate like a pig. By the time the coffee appeared I could hardly move. He suggested we went for a walk to digest the food. He called for the bill and, in spite of my protestations, settled it. By the cash register I saw the waitress who had welcomed me and I asked her about Carmelita.

'Oh, yes. I forgot to tell you. I found out she won't be coming in today. I was told someone close to her has died. Maybe family.'

'Could you give me her address?'

'We're not allowed to do that, señor. But I can pass her a message.'

'That'll be fine. Would you please tell her a friend of Señor Danny is staying at the Hotel El Gran Tucan and would like to hear from her.'

I gave her five dollars and told her my name and she curtsied in the old-fashioned way.

'I'll do that right away,' she said.

When we walked out of the air-conditioned restaurant the hot afternoon air hit my face.

'I have to talk to you about money,' I said as soon as we were in the street.

'What money?'

'The fifty thousand loan you sent me.'

'I do not consider it a loan. More like...I don't know. I owe Alex more than I could ever repay. I would do anything for him. This is… well, call it his money. He saved my life. He got into a lot of trouble because of me.'

'He's a difficult man to understand.'

'He is fiercely loyal to his friends.'

'He had a bad relationship with his father, didn't he?'

'You can't blame him for that. His father was a playboy. He had no morals. It was obvious his son would turn against everything he represented. He rebelled against his father's class. The attraction of socialism for Alex was probably just that. At least he didn't turn on him as a person. He was very bitter, you know.'

'Still, it's a shame.'

'They got to know each other in the end.'

'They did? How?'

'Didn't Alex tell you? They were in jail together for a time. Each for a different reason. I'm afraid I am to blame for Alex's downfall and prison sentence, but true to his nature he told me he was grateful. I know about prison, you see. When people are incarcerated they are forced to give each other space. Tolerate each other's existence. That is what happened to Abraham and Alex Moreno, late as it was.'

'Did his father die in jail?'

'Oh, no. He survived it. He was a strong man, a born survivor. He never let anything affect him. He died later.'

'In Cuba?'

'Yes.'

'I need his death certificate to clear Alex's right to inherit.'

'That should be easy.'

I did not want to tell him just how difficult it was likely to be. He was a kind man, although Alex had said he was simple. He could not have been too well versed in legal matters.

'Here I am talking shop with you on our first meeting. I don't really want to bother you with my problems.'

'I assure you, it is a pleasure.'

'We can talk about this another time.'

'Yes, of course. You must be tired.'

I was. Suddenly, as I watched Juan Miret's smiling eyes, all my strength ebbed away. I was dead tired. It had been one hell of a long day and I had never been any good at sleeping on a plane.The hours finally caught up with me right there, outside that Cuban eating house. I could have fallen asleep on the spot.

'We had better go back to your hotel,' I heard him say. He suggested we take his car, but I needed to get some fresh air before locking myself in for the night. I said I preferred to walk. He walked with me.

We got back to the hotel at around five o'clock, and by the door we agreed to meet again the next day. I said I would call him as soon as I awoke.

I made a call to Israel from reception. My wife did not answer and I left her a message on the answering machine. I forget what it was I said.

I remember there was a plate of tropical fruit in my room, compliments of the management, and a note in Spanish asking me to call Carmelita Rodriguez at her home number. It said call any time, day or night.

I was certainly going to get in touch with her, but I had to clear up other matters first.

A distant hint of suspicion was itching to penetrate the pall of grey exhaustion that had taken me over. I tried to make it out, but as soon as I fell into bed it was gone.

Chapter Thirty-One

It was midday when I finally came down. The porter, having watched me descend the stairs, handed me a cup of coffee as I reached his desk. I gulped it down and walked into the sun. Juan Miret's driver was parked outside the main entrance. He sprinted to open the door and as soon as we were on our way he said the boss was waiting for me at the Versailles.

This, he said, was a famous Cuban restaurant where Señor Miret had his lunch every day.

It was an elegant establishment farther down Eighth Street with its own carpark and a porter. The tuxedo-clad maître d' who welcomed me inside said I was expected. He took my arm and guided me to the bar, where I saw Juan Miret looking my way. He jumped off his stool and rushed over with the agility of a teenager. He pumped my hand and smiled. He was wearing a slim-fitting blue suit and a red polka-dot tie. He was brushed and combed and shaved to perfection and made me feel quite sloppy .

He led me towards a quiet corner table and motioned me to sit down.

'Did you sleep well?'

'Like a log.'

'A what?'

'I slept very well.'

'Alex called me again this morning. He said I am to make sure you have anything you want. See anything you want to see. Nothing should be hidden from you.'

'Is there anything to hide?'

'Not from you, it seems. He likes you a lot, you know.'

'Tell me everything you can about him.'

'There is such a lot… I don't know where to start.'

'Start at the beginning.'

He ordered the food and I sat back. I am not a storyteller or a writer, and I wished my father had been there with me. With his insight and style and sensitivity he could have written a beautiful piece about this tale.

The more I heard, the more I became convinced that Alex Moreno, drab and laconic as he was, had a great sense of occasion. Throughout his life, he had managed to surround himself with the most exciting characters anyone ever met. I could not, for the life of me, understand how. Perhaps it was not his doing at all. Perhaps it was simply his fate to live his life the way he did. To encounter people and know instinctively whether he was meant to love them, hate them, help them or do them damage.

And what of me? Why did Alex pick me? What possible value could my own insignificance have added to his life in view of the road that was chosen for him by destiny?

I only got to grips with it at the end of our acquaintance.

* * *

'Alex Moreno and I were both born in the same year and the same city but we first met at university. We came from very different social backgrounds. My father was an accountant who worked for an American sugar-broking firm. Alex was the envy of most other classmates because he had lived in a flat of his own and had money to burn. No one bothered to find out more about him because he was not a very sociable kind of person. He did not talk much about his family, or anything else. That didn't make any difference because in spite of his silence, everybody knew the most important thing about him: his father was Carmelita Rodriguez's lover.

'He was teased to death about having Carmelita as a kind of stepmother. I imagine he was hurting inside but I never did a thing to stop the others. You must understand she was not a mere mortal. She was then at the height of her career and the dream woman of any full-blooded youngster. She was beautiful and talented. She was loved and admired by everyone. She was an institution. In this country, today, Carmelita would have been what they call a superstar.

'To know her in person, to have her in your circle the way Alex did, was virtual stardom. The joke was, of course, that Alex refused to talk about her, and that only served to increase the mystery surrounding him and his life outside school hours. He was never very friendly or exciting as a person unless the conversation turned to politics.

'One time we got to talking about the economic conditions of people on the plantations. He seemed to know a lot about the countryside and its problems and as he spoke he became animated. I asked him how, with his particular background, he had become involved in social problems. His father, by his own admission, was a *bon vivant* who was interested only in women, adventure and money. My question clearly embarrassed him. He blushed, then mumbled something banal about the need to help the underdog in our society. He did not sound particularly inspiring. The conversation would have ended there had he not mentioned Gustavo Madeiros.

'He wasn't bragging. Alex was not a show-off. It only came out by accident, and as Madeiros was a man I admired immensely, I thought there must be more to him than met the eye. To be able to quote things that great man had said in person, you needed to be someone special. I belonged to a secret cell of the Communist Party. To me and my friends Madeiros was a hero, a saint, a modern-day revolutionary, like Jose Marti. To Alex, although he never said so, Madeiros was a family friend. He knew, of course, that Madeiros had led a double life. That in spite of moving in the most fashionable circles, he was a member of the Communist Party.

'The government, when it suited them, recognized and used Party leaders to its advantage. They often encouraged known members to go around the plantations and the canneries. To talk to the masses and convince them to stay put when there were rumours of an impending strike. People knew that the legitimacy the communists enjoyed could not last. In the early forties the Russians were heroes, but at the beginning of the Cold War the Party went into hiding again. It was best never to admit you were a part of it, and I never did. Alex, although he hated it, was safe because of his father's connections. He played the part of an *enfant terrible* and made a nuisance of himself in every direction. Stole cars and borrowed money and sold underground newspapers just to be thrown into jail. It was never long before his father's friends intervened and he was let out again.

'As is often the case with delinquents, Alex became very daring. Especially later, during his last year at university. He participated in many raids on army camps around the country and ambushes on units in the field. He once walked into an air force base and blew up two of Batista's planes. After that his identity became known and his father could no longer help him. He went into the mountains.

'All that was before the open rebellion that finally brought the government down. When that started, Alex demonstrated new, very different talents. It was in the political and psychological conversion of soldiers that he really made his name. He would interrogate Batista prisoners and convince them of the justice of Castro's struggle and the impending victory. He excelled at that. When the prisoners were released they were returned to their units and successfully talked many other soldiers over to our cause. People said that half an hour with Alex Moreno would turn any fascist into a Red. They even joked about his ability. They said he could have converted Batista himself to Fidel's cause and avoided the all-out war that came later. After the victory people became too nervous about him to poke fun.

'I did a little bit of fighting in the mountains. I was naive and enthusiastic and along with lots of people I was enthralled by the spirit of the bearded heroes. They were young and brave and fought against a huge, organized army. It was exciting and romantic. You did not have to be a communist to admire what they seemed to stand for. To start with, Castro was backed by many members of the middle and upper middle classes. There was plenty wrong with our social order and corruption was everywhere. They promised to make Cuba a true, free and just democracy. They promised work for all, food for all and education for all.

They represented hope, but of course they did not deliver. I am not sure when exactly I became disenchanted with the new regime. Or perhaps I do. I think it was when they started executing people all over the place. Sometimes without trial, and sometimes with. But those sham courts meant nothing at all… had nothing to do with justice because very few of the accused ever got a chance to say anything, let alone fight their case. One of my own friends, a man who had fought at my side, was tried for treason and was never heard of again. I learned later he was shot. Yes, that was when I began to have serious doubts about where the country was going. I began to notice the mistake they were making. I mean, after all, the greatest task of any regime is to provide the man in the street with freedom,the dignity of a job and a fair crack at personal happiness. In this, the new Cuba was to fail completely, and I saw that quite soon. With the execution of my friend, my involvement with politics and the revolution was over, but Alex… Alex never changed. He was totally sincere, the way fanatics often are. He believed the speeches, he believed the slogans… and he was a first-class organizer. During the first few years of Castro's government they recognized his value and he was flying high.

'He gained a hell of a lot of experience and they trusted him completely and that gave him power. He travelled as a roving commissar with Che. I used to run into him in those days because I had spent time with Che myself, training South American guerrillas in sniping. I was a field man and not a bad shot, but I did not want a military career.

'Alex was not a field man at all. He was much more political. Later they seconded him to some of our embassies in a couple of South American countries. He worked with the local communist parties and helped them plan the overthrow of their military regimes. He organized clandestine training and shipments of arms for would-be revolutionaries. The operation, although it did produce a tough opposition to the rulers, was not a success. Not one revolution ensued. Alex was declared *persona non grata* in seven countries for abusing his diplomatic immunity. Within a few years his name became mud in Latin America. He was a wanted man and there was a price on his head. But back in Cuba he was a hero of the revolution. He never wanted publicity and only people up top knew who he was. With his cover blown, he went to eastern Europe, where he served as ambassador in at least two countries. He was in Angola, too, some months before Cuba got involved in the war there. After that he went to Europe again and then he came back.

'The Bay of Pigs invasion took place while he was out of Cuba. By then I'd had enough and wanted to leave the country and was collecting American dollars for that purpose. I had built up a small but thriving shirt-making business. At that time there were hardly any private companies left in Cuba, and the government made a real mess of things. You could always sell products on the black market but the Cuban currency had no value outside our borders. I used to have a friend in the central bank who exchanged the black money I was earning for greenbacks. This went on for a good few months and then my friend was caught and among his papers the police found my name. It was not a great offence then but they took all my dollars and I was thrown into jail. Perhaps they forgot about me. Perhaps the people who arrested me kept the dollars for themselves and never reported me. I sat in a cell with twenty other people who were there for a variety of reasons. They came and went. Some returned and others disappeared. No one asked for me and not once did anyone tell me why they were keeping me there for so long. No charges, no trial, no nothing. Rumours spread like wildfire, and as the months passed I began to lose hope. I thought I was going to die there. It was a frightening experience. You heard all sorts of stories of the outside. You watched your countrymen harden into seasoned oppressors and killers. You could be taken out and shot at any time, and never be missed.

'When Alex came back from his second tour of eastern Europe he was put in charge of the Bay of Pigs aftermath.

When this fiasco was over the Americans demanded the return of the exile prisoners we were holding and Alex handled these negotiations. There were interrogations and blackmail and maybe torture. The prisoners were finally allowed to go back to the States, on condition that were not known to the public at large.

'During the week that agreement was concluded, there was a commotion and demonstrations all over town. There was a riot on the other side of the prison. Most of our guards were sent to help quash the uprising and the rest of the place was understaffed. That night a group of hard-core criminals blew a hole in the wall, and when the smoke dispersed it appeared that something had gone wrong. They either used too much dynamite or maybe it was put in the wrong place. A whole section of the building was gone. Two guards as well as a few convicts were killed and in the confusion I slipped out. I walked the streets for a couple of days, and then I thought of Alex. He was the only man I could approach, even if it meant going back to prison. I was tired and hungry and confused enough to take the risk. I hoped he would remember me from the old days and I went to his flat.

'I did not know what to expect or whether he was even on the island. I needed to see him alone, and in his position he was always surrounded by security people, but I was lucky. That evening he came home early and by himself. He must have known what had happened because he was not surprised to see me. Could be he expected me. I don't know. I did not have to ask for his help. He saw me waiting there in the dark and he called my name and pushed me in and said I needed to get away. I never found out why he did it because I never asked him. Perhaps he was more compassionate than I knew. Perhaps he just wanted me to be in his debt, but that is being cynical.

'Perhaps I was his only friend.

'His plan was to get me out of the country by using the identity and papers of someone else. They always use such stuff when they mount a security operation somewhere.

Working as he was, on the darker side of government, I suppose he had a whole lot of blank documents at his disposal. I did not know what he had in mind until the second or third day, when I summoned the courage to ask him. He looked straight at me and smiled and said I would assume the identity of someone who had been killed in the Bay of Pigs.

'It was a brilliant idea. The man I was to impersonate was a Cuban exile who had undergone training in the United States. By bringing him back to life I would be able to leave with the other prisoners and get to the States without causing a stir either on departure or on arrival. I suppose you know that most of the participants in the Bay of Pigs invasion were poorly trained exiles who were hoping to wrestle Cuba away from Castro with the aid of popular support.

'Of course, they were wrong. At that time the love affair between the people and Castro was all-powerful. He managed to blow the affair up in the minds of the population. It was a battle for their right to live as free men. It was a battle for their very lives, and it was being fought on the sacred ground of Cuba itself. *Patria o muerte*. The rhetoric worked wonders and the people mobilized with great enthusiasm and fought like tigers. The invasion was a flop. It never did have a chance. Not when it happened. I don't know why they chose that time and place. The Americans had not done their homework properly. Their backing was half hearted at best. A lot of good people died for nothing. There is a statue for them in this town, just a little way up this very street.

'Anyway, Alex told me he would arrange for me to have the documents of one of the dead. He was, without a doubt, putting his head on the block. As long as I was on the island the truth could come out at any time. But he was as good as his word and made the arrangements all by himself and in secret.

'I stayed in Alex's flat until the prisoners were made ready to leave. I do not remember how long I lived there but it was a lonely time. During my stay Alex gave me every bit of information I was going to need. He briefed me about what I was to say. He gave me the date on which I had supposedly arrived in Florida and where I had lived and what job I had done there. Who I was and who my family were and why I'd volunteered to go with the invasion and where we trained. What sort of weapons we had and who our instructors were. He knew everything and he prepared me well.

'While I was waiting I could not be seen anywhere because the police were still looking for me. Alex did not spend much time in his place. It was like being in solitary confinement and I became quite depressed, I can tell you. And then one night, not a minute too soon, the time came. He walked in and without much ado he said we were leaving. He handed me a large brown paper bag that contained an old torn uniform and a pair of boots. He told me to change right were I stood and led me out of there. He drove the car himself, and during the entire journey we did not exchange one word. He took me to an old camp where the column of returnees was being assembled. I hid in the back of the car, and when he showed up at the gate no one dared stop him. Alex drove straight up to one of the tents and then he handed me the papers of the dead man and I slipped out of the car and watched him disappear into the night. There was no one around and I crawled into the tent and found myself an empty bed. The next morning we all left for Florida. He did not send me off empty-handed. Into my tunic he had sewn twelve one-hundred-dollar bills. That money came in useful when I started off.

'I did not see him again for many years after that night. Then we met in Mexico. He was on some official visit there and called me at my office and asked me to fly out and meet him. How he knew where to find me I could only guess. It was all cloak-and-dagger stuff. He did not tell me where he was staying but he knew where I was and he came to my hotel room. He did not say he thought he was being followed but I think he was. He was rather nervous then. We talked about this and that and we reminisced about our youth and the revolution. I think he was pleased to see how successful I had become. To tell you the truth, I do not know why he wanted to see me. Maybe it was sentimental. He did not ask for anything. We just had that one dinner and we talked. And yet, all through that evening, he had not one bad word to say about the deteriorating state of Cuba. The people were starving while Fidel was spending a fortune on sending troops to Angola and God knows where else. But for Alex Moreno nothing changed. Fidel and his revolution were still as great as Jesus himself. Alex, despite all they have done to him, all he has suffered, is as staunch a Castro man today as he was when we were young.

'I think he helped Carmelita to escape too. I will never know how he managed to do it, but at that time Alex wielded an enormous amount of power, all behind the scenes. Even ministers and army generals and other bigshots were wary of him. More than that. They were scared of him. He had a bad name, but no one dared say why. There were rumours of visits he'd paid to people in the night. Of perfectly innocent citizens disappearing. The stories were told in confidence, and although Alex's name was never mentioned, it was clear they were talking about him. He was not often seen and travelled about in that dark, windowless limousine of his. There were a lot of relieved officials, high and low, when he finally fell from grace. It was, as you have heard, because of his position that I managed to get out. I arrived in Florida a returning prisoner of war and on my first day there I found a job in an accountant's office. A couple of years after my arrival I changed my assumed name back to my own. Then I settled down to build a new life for myself here in Miami. Miami was good to me.

'A few years later they found out about my escape and Alex's part in it. The whole affair was discovered because the *Miami Herald* published a kind of 'missing persons' article about the man whose name I had stolen. There was his name and photograph and a copy of the list on which he was named as having survived. It said he was supposed to have returned to the States with other prisoners and had made no contact. His family had looked for him for years and finally, since nothing had been heard of him, they approached the newspapers. By the time I got to speak to the editor and the security people it was too late. A copy of the paper had found its way into the wrong hands back in Havana and Alex was apprehended. I feel sure someone had pointed a finger at him. Someone who knew about me and Alex's part in my escape. Someone who chose to wait with the information until he could do some real damage. And damage he did, whoever it was.

'There was some sort of a monkey trial behind closed doors and Alex went to jail. Rumour was they were going to shoot him but they did not. I suppose he had been too loyal and too well known at the top for that. Of course, that episode was not the only reason for his downfall. People who run dictatorships need more than one reason to get rid of their enemies, but his smuggling me out was the excuse. I am afraid I was entirely to blame for that because I should have looked for the dead man's family and told them what had happened right from the start. They would never have contacted the papers had they known. I would have saved them years of anguish...but you live and learn.

'Later, when Alex himself finally came out of Cuba, I confessed it had been down to me and, would you believe, he did not bat an eyelid. He did not blame me or reproach me or anything. He saw I was in great distress and he consoled me. He said it was an accident. Said he knew I did not mean to inform on him. He was, of course, right. I do not like to talk about this…not even now, after all this time. Alex understands that, and I am sure you do too. There is so much pain because I know he had a rough time while he was inside.

'One good thing came out of it. Abraham was himself in prison when Alex was arrested, and they met there and I believe they made up. I don't know too much about it because Alex did not tell me and I never saw Abraham again.'

I put my hand on his arm and asked:

'Talking of Abraham, did you not tell me yesterday it would be easy to get a copy of his death certificate?'

'Very easy. Especially for you.'

'What do you mean?'

'The certificate you need is in Israel already. Alex has got it. There are, in fact, two certificates there. Both his father's and his mother's. Hers says she suffered a fatal heart attack but actually she took rat poison. In the old days, if you had money, you could get the doctor to sign anything. Anyway, you'll have no problems there. Alex is in possession of his parents' death certificates. I kept them in my office safe for a few years at his request. I returned them to him the day he left Miami for the last time. You ask him.'

The shock waves of this revelation reverberated in my head. They were about to devour me, but I kept calm.

'Alex was living in Havana and you were here. How did the certificates get to you?'

'Alex had them both sent to me.'

My chest felt heavy. I said:

'I didn't think there was a postal service between Havana and Miami.'

'There is and there isn't. News and letters from Cuba usually arrive with refugees.'

'So he entrusted the papers to somebody. Surprising.'

'Why?'

'I didn't think he had many people in his confidence.'

'The person who brought the papers to me was not in his confidence. That person was in his debt, just like I am. Debt is sometimes a stronger obligation than friendship. Not as pleasant but infinitely more reliable. That was how I found out about the end of the feud.'

'Feud?'

'Yes. Alex's messenger told me about how Abraham and

his son had met in prison and how they had finally made their peace.'

'What happened to all those papers?'

'Nothing happened. I have already told you. I gave them to Alex before he left. I didn't know where he was going. You know how secretive he is. Until I heard from him the other day I had no idea he was in Israel. I thought he went to Mexico or eastern Europe or Angola or somewhere where people knew him… Somewhere…'

I thought I would choke. The charlatan had had the papers all the time. What did he need me for? Why did he involve me in all this? And why did Danny come all the way here only to die when all the time what we were looking for was right there in Israel with that sonofabitch Alex? I fought to hold my temper. Fortunately, just then Juan Miret called the waiter and did not see my face.

'Who was he, that messenger?'

'Not he. It was a she. Alex sent me his parents' death certificates with Carmelita Rodriguez. That was the time she came over to Miami for good. When there was nothing left in Cuba for her. And as I told you, I am sure it was Alex who helped her get out.'

I was on fire. The bastard did not help Carmelita. He did not help anyone. He just used her. Like he was using me. Only I did not know what he was using me for. I asked:

'Will you tell me about that?'

'No, my friend. I think you should hear it from Carmelita herself.'

I had lost the note with her address and was too confused to face her just then. I needed time to myself and I spent the next day seeing the sights.

Chapter Thirty-Two

Juan Miret called to say he had to go on an overseas business trip. He would be away for three or four days and would call me as soon as he was back. I told him I might well have finished my business in Miami by then but wanted to see him again. Just to thank him for all he had done for me. He said it was nothing in terms of what he owed Alex. I said I hoped he might come to Israel one day, and he replied he would only do that if Alex asked him to come. His wife was religious, and had asked him to take her on a visit to the Holy Land. But he did not want to embarrass Alex with his presence. I was not sure what he meant by that, but I said I would see what could be done. Would he mind if I asked him one more question?

'Not at all,' he said cheerfully.

'How long did Alex spend in prison?'

'Years… oh yes, years. Did he not tell you?'

'He hinted.'

'Well, that's our Alex. Never volunteer information.'

'Tell me about it. He's not an easy man to love.'

'Once you get to know him there will be little you wouldn't do for him.'

I knew what he meant, but I was still angry with Alex. Juan Miret owed him his life and was certainly not the man to talk to about my frustrations. I took a deep breath and said:

'I wish you a successful trip, Juan.'

'You are fond of Alex too, aren't you?'

I was silent for a moment, but what Juan had said and the way he had said it left me no option.

'I think I am,' I said. 'At least, I'm trying to be.'

'If you are lucky enough to get to be with him as long as I have, you will be.'

'There's something I want to know. Perhaps it's wrong to

ask you about this over the telephone, but…'

'What is it?'

'When and how did Alex arrive in Miami?'

'Oh, didn't you know?'

'No.'

'He was a Marielita. Came across at the time of the Mariel fiasco. You must have heard about that.'

'I'm afraid not.'

'It was the time Castro opened his gates and allowed thousands of Cubans to leave for the United States. I think there were more than a hundred and fifty thousand of them landing in the lap of the American government in a very short time. They all left from a Cuban port called Mariel, which gave this particular exodus its name. It was a flood. Many of them were criminals and drug addicts and homosexuals. The authorities here did not know what had hit them. Until then, Cubans who had managed to leave were given immediate permission to stay. It was more or less automatic, but with the sheer masses turning up, the immigration people changed their tack. Instead of the usual procedure, the Mariel people had to be processed differently. Some were kept in camps, behind barbed wire, while a thorough screening took place. There were riots…and later, when the facts and figures came out, it was said that Castro had emptied his jails to get rid of his social parasites and dumped them on the Yanquis. Most of the people who settled here are decent and hard working and the Mariel business did their reputation no good, believe me. It only goes to show you how cynical Castro is…how little he cares.'

'Wasn't Alex too well known to join up with these people? Didn't someone recognize…How did he get out?'

'He managed to change identities with a convicted murderer who was in the same cell as him. Got hold of his release papers, passport and photographs. That man was never seen again, but he killed four children and will not be missed by anyone. Alex might have had him finished off…or…I don't know the whole story. All I know is that Alex got his papers and boarded the ship with all the others. No one recognized him when he was let out and his absence was not discovered until the emigration tide created by the Mariel incident was over. Once he was in Miami, he assumed his own name again.'

'And then?'

'Well, it did not take the authorities long to find out that he was no run-of-the-mill thug or a drug addict. He did not even try to hide his real name or the nature of his career. They took him to CIA headquarters at Langley. They found out about him. How he used to be a big shot in Castro's early years and that he was still an unrepentant communist. They were not interested in keeping him here. Not unless he'd co-operate, and this he would certainly have refused to do. They had to get rid of him and they probably gave him two options: he could either go to Mexico or, being a Jew, he could go to Israel. You have a law of something or other. Enabling anyone who is Jewish to settle in Israel.'

'Yes, the law of return.'

'So he was back in Miami for a couple of weeks and then he left. He never told me where he was going…All I knew was he couldn't stay here.'

'Strange, that. He doesn't like it in Israel and made it very clear he had no intention of staying. Why did he not stick to his false papers? He could have remained in Miami then.'

'I cannot tell you that. I do not know. I was surprised to see him here in any case. For Castro and his followers Miami is the pits…a place only weaklings run to. Deserters who refuse to stand and fight and suffer for independence. To Alex coming here was necessary, but staying here would have been nothing less than treason. He would probably have preferred to stay in Cuba, jail or no jail. They were going to let him out one of these days anyway because he was not a threat to anyone. He was no crowd-puller and no leader, you see, and would never have gone into opposition. On the contrary, he was a loyal Cuban revolutionary and a socialist and would have followed Castro all the way to hell and back. Sometimes I feel he wanted to stay in jail for some reason, because he never wrote to anyone outside like the others did, never pleaded. But I have no right to question his intentions or what lies behind his actions. I agree with you. He did not need to come here and suffer the humiliation of being kicked out again. I must confess it made no sense to me. I don't understand any of it. I really don't. If he wanted to stay here he could have kept to his false papers. There was no way they could find out who he was that quickly. Sure, they would have discovered it in the end, but it would have taken time. Do you know what I think?'

'What?'

'I'm sure the Americans found out who he was because he wanted them to find out. I don't know why he came or why he left again but it is not my place to ask these questions. For me, Alex can do no wrong. He must have had his reasons and I respect them even if I don't understand them.'

'He must have had some other plan up his sleeve. In all my dealings and conversations with him I've found that nothing about Alex is ever what it seems. Do you think he is still working for the Cuban government? Do you think he is a spy?'

I must have touched a sore spot. In an instant, Juan Miret's affable demeanour was gone. He became remote and his tone became cool, his words to the point.

'Have you arranged to see Carmelita Rodriguez yet?' he asked.

'I thought I'd contact her today.'

I proceeded to talk about Miami and how exciting it was here. I talked about the food and the people and the atmosphere. I said nothing more about Alex or the Mariel business, and as I blabbered on he began to relax. He mentioned a few places of interest for me to see.

'Somehow,' he said, 'I have the feeling you'll still be here when I return. You just let my office know if there is anything we can do for you. My driver has instructions to be at your service while I'm gone.'

'Thank you. Can I tell you something?'

'Anything.'

'Your English is superb. Not just the language...the way you describe things.'

'I'm an American now. I told you, Miami was good to me. Besides, I read lots of books. Novels mostly. Always have. Didn't Alex tell you I was a bookworm?'

'No.'

'Adios,' he said, and hung up.

* * *

I went to Carmelita Rodriguez's workplace to ask for her address. They told me she had suffered a fall and had been taken to hospital with a mild concussion. I went to visit her there but was not allowed in. I left a bunch of flowers and a get-well note and went back to my hotel. I spent two days on arrangements for Danny and had all my meals in my room. I called my office every few hours. I needed to talk to Alex. He had gone missing again, and I instructed my secretary to ask him for Abraham's death certificate as soon as he made contact. I told her to make it clear to him that we knew he had it. After that I did not want to think of him. The whole affair was beginning to upset me. I wanted to bring the Moreno case to an end and forget I ever started it. I called Joan a number of times and she was sweet. Especially the last time.

'When are you coming back?' she asked.

'As soon as I have made contact with someone. One last person.'

'This business is taking a long time, isn't it?'

'I've more or less completed my part in it. There's a woman I must meet. She'd be sixty or sixty-five years old now. She used to be an entertainer. She was very famous. I hear she can still stir them with her voice and her dance. But I want to share some memories with her...memories that are bound to be tragic for her. Tragic because the man I want to talk about was the love of her life. One last meeting, Joan, an encounter as far from business as you can possibly get.'

'How unlike you to dig so deep under the skin.'

'Not unlike me at all. You've forgotten...or maybe I never gave you a chance to see it. Or maybe I've changed.'

'Show me. Tell me more.'

'I will when I get back. It's a long story. Not something we can talk about on the phone.'

'You're right. I'm sorry.'

'No, don't be. Right now it's just a question of finding the last strands of the drama I've got involved in. You know, what happened to the main actors, where they ended up and how and why. Sort of closing the circle of events, you might say.'

'Can you not finish the case otherwise?'

'I can, but this one is for me, myself. Not as a lawyer. As a person. Very little of it has to do with fact. I have most of the facts already. Whatever is missing can be found back home in Israel. No, this information is more than mere fact. It's to do with loves and hates and jealousy and revenge and, most of all, it's to do with passion.'

'Passion? Is that something in those law books of yours you kept to yourself? I thought they were exclusively about the codex of King Henry and the common law. Passion? You mean you got involved in a human interest story? You actually got involved with...with life?'

I did not react. I was afraid to. Deep within my insecurity there was an inexplicable glimmer of hope. A new element was entering our relationship and I was not sure what it was. It could not be bad, my gut feeling suggested. Her laughter was sincere. She was enjoying this...enjoying speaking to me. No. It could not be a bad thing.

'Look after yourself,' she said.

'I love you to death.'

'The girls miss you.'

I knew I had to hang up soon or burst into tears. Silence fell between us. I kept hoping Joan would say something more explicit but the words did not come. She had said nothing about missing me. Nothing about a possible change in her feelings or a reconciliation. Nothing about love. I told her I would let her know what my plans were and we said goodbye.

I felt the blues return. I needed to be with someone I was close to, or just hear a familiar voice to remind me that all was not bleak.

I tried to call my mother but she was not at home. At her travel agency they could not tell me where she was. She might have gone away on a trip, they said. To Eilat, perhaps. Or to the Dead Sea. She had certainly not gone abroad, her partner told me. They would have known about that. It was as if someone was trying to hide something from me, but I could not be sure who or what.

Paranoia is alarming, but it can be a great diversion. A self-defence mechanism almost. Did it descend on me then to shield me from the trauma that waited around the corner?

* * *

I had made all the necessary arrangements for shipping Danny's body back to Israel. I was going to return on the plane with him, but had yet to speak to Morton Chandler. Most important of all, I still had to see Carmelita Rodriguez.

Jewish tradition calls for the entombment of the dead as soon as possible. I felt confident that Danny would have forgiven me. He was not a religious man.

My staying on in Miami had nothing to do with business. This was for me. I was burning to know what had happened to Abraham and how and where he had met his end. I wanted to find out why Alex never told me what he knew. Why he had made it all so difficult and costly. He could have concluded his business in less than a week with all the evidence he had. He did not really need me at all.

I was certain that the answer was here in Miami, and so I stayed. I called Danny's daughter. I told her when her father would arrive. I asked her to try to delay the funeral until my return. She said she would do her best.

It was early afternoon. I had had no lunch and decided to walk over to Eighth Street and have a bite to eat. There was a lot to think about. I was preparing to leave the hotel when the phone rang. It was Morton Chandler.

'I hear you've been here for quite a while. Why have you made no contact?'

'I had to tie up some loose ends. I hope to be through by tomorrow.'

'I shall be in my house up here in Palm Springs all week. I trust you'll allow me to take care of you for a day or so.'

'We'll see. I'm very grateful for your help so far. For what you did for Danny. I hope you'll give me a chance to reciprocate one day.'

'Not unless you make sure we meet.'

'Of course we'll meet.'

'Promise?'

'Promise.'

'When?'

'You'll hear from me.'

I replaced the receiver and the phone rang again. This time it was the porter. He had a message. Carmelita Rodriguez had called to say she had recovered and was back at her flat. She was waiting to see me, he said. I could call her any time.

I asked him to get her on the line.

Chapter Thirty-Three

She was relieved I could speak Spanish. She said she could just about make herself understood in English but was too old now to learn it perfectly. In this part of Miami one did not need to. She had hardly any contact with Americans, either in her work or her private life. She was willing to meet me right away, said she had known Danny only a short time but when he died it was as if she had lost her closest friend. Dancers, she told me, have a good sense of balance and rarely fall. Danny's death had made her absent-minded and that was why she had not been watching her step. She was all right now, she insisted. Two more days off work and she'd be perfect.

She said she had hesitated before she called because there was something about the prospect of us meeting that frightened her. It might sound superstitious, but in all her life she had known only two people from the Holy Land and they were both dead now. She had caused unhappiness because of her relationship with one, and the other left this life before she got to know him. She hoped she would not bring me bad luck. If I did not want to see her she would understand.

I laughed. I said I was not superstitious and would be delighted to see her. I wanted to talk to her, I said. I needed to….She was one of the main reasons for my visit here. Could I come right away?

When I passed the porter on my way out, he winked.

* * *

She lived in a run-down duplex with a couple of doorless old cars parked on the overgrown lawn in front. A heap of discarded mattresses was stacked by the fence, held down by a huge wooden ladder. A rusty refrigerator leaned on the outside wall. In my mind's eye I saw the luxury she once knew. The marble floors, the chandeliers and the servants. Why is it, I thought, that one so often reads about how celebrities end up on the breadline? Unpaid income tax or scheming divorce lawyers are usually blamed, but these could not be the only reasons. Could it be because they lost all interest in self-preservation once the fame, the adulation the public had given them, was gone for ever?

On the roof, a long line of washing fluttered in the wind.

Sheets and pillow cases and towels and children's clothes. The afternoon sun was edging towards the horizon. From the direction of the airport I heard the jets taking off and landing.

Everything I had ever heard about her was true. She was taller than I had expected and did not look a lot over forty. Her black hair was pulled back and tied at the back of her neck ballerina-fashion. Her skin was white and her curved body swelled against her blue polyester dress.

She looked at me and held her hand over her heart.

'*Dios mio*,' she whispered. '*Dios mio*. My old eyes are playing tricks on me.'

'What do you mean?' I asked.

'You'd better come inside.'

It was a small, well-ordered flat. Sparse, if anything. There was a television set and a radio and everywhere there were photographs of people. Yellowing black-and-white ones in wooden frames, other more recent ones in colour stuck along the edges of the mirror. I looked around carefully. I noticed one marked absence. There were none of the posters I had expected. Posters that would tell of her glorious past. Brochures from great hotels. Menus. Theatre notices from all over the South American continent. Announcements and printed sheets of music. So-and-so presents the great Carmelita Rodriguez. But there were no programmes, no publicity pictures. Not a thing. I asked her about it as soon as we sat down.

'I don't want to live in the past,' she said. 'I don't want to look at myself the way I was. I am a different person now, and live a different life. It has so little...no, it has nothing to do with the old days. You keep such mementoes if you are still in the business, or if you have given up on life. In my case it's no to both.'

'But other people...'

'Other people must not dictate to you. Not once you've retired. You would become a curiosity and then they'd start feeling sorry for you. It would all be too depressing. I have my memories and only reality rules over me. It tells me I have another life now.'

She was right, of course. I said:

'I understand, and I admire that. It takes a lot of strength.'

'Not at all. Not if you know you have never really changed. Carmelita Rodriguez is here still. I don't need any evidence, any documents, to remind me of her, because I know her well. I am she.'

There was such vivacity, such power and, yes, such sensuality oozing from every inch of her. I could well imagine what she had been like all those years ago, and why Abraham had lost his head over her. And Danny. She looked at me with great intensity. For a few seconds I read suspicion in her face but the feeling did not last. On top of the television there was a silver-framed picture. She got up and walked towards it. Her walk was sex in motion. Her hips shook as if to music. She picked the frame up and came back. She showed it to me. There was a young man on a horse, his black hair falling over his smiling face. He seemed tall, and he held a white straw hat in his hand. His powerful legs squeezed the animal's torso.

'This was Abraham Moreno,' she said, 'when I first knew him long, long ago. Can you see the resemblance? Even Danny commented on it.'

I looked again. All right, he was about my height and had a large nose as I have. His hair was unruly like mine used to be, but that was all.

'Not really.'

'Amazing. I would have said you were brothers. Didn't Danny tell you?'

'Yes. On the day we first met he said something to that effect.'

'Well, he knew him when he was young. Even before I did. Didn't Alex say the same thing?'

'He may have, but I still don't see what the fuss is all about. I should imagine Alex was referring more to my character. I'm not shy or polite or sophisticated. I talk a lot,

I like money. So, apparently, did Abraham. So what? There are others like us all along the Mediterranean coast.'

'Are you romantic?'

'I can't answer that.'

'No matter. It is incredible how things are always in the eye of the beholder. Beauty, ugliness, even similarities. I'm sure you've often heard someone, a woman, say, telling you about some friend of hers. She describes this friend in minute detail. The way she looks, the way she walks and talks and dresses. Soon you realize she is talking of someone just like herself, but she would never know it. People do that sometimes, when they want to talk about themselves. We have no idea what we are like, even though we can look at ourselves in the mirror. You, my dear young man, look exactly like him, but you wouldn't see that. You can't. You're too close to yourself.'

'I see a vague similarity, that's all. I told you, there are plenty like me back home in Israel...in Italy, in Spain.'

'I must admit it is difficult for me to sit here with you. Perhaps it's wishful thinking, but even your voice sounds like his. Can you sing?'

'Not at all. I'm tone deaf.'

'So was he, you know. Didn't Danny tell you that?'

'No. I don't think he knew him all that well.'

I took the wooden crucifix out of my pocket and handed it to her.

'A present from Danny's daughter,' I said. 'She went to Jerusalem herself to get it when she heard I was going to meet you.'

She took the crucifix in her hand and kissed it.

'How wonderful,' she whispered. 'How kind of her. May the good Lord bless her with a long and happy life.'

'You made Danny's last days very beautiful, very...exciting. Yes, exciting.'

'He did the same for me. I was falling in love with him. Or maybe I thought I was because I wanted to be in love again.' She looked at me and then her voice cracked and she wiped her eye. 'It would have been easy, falling in love with him. They don't make men like that any more.'

'They sure don't,' I said.

We sat there in the silence of the room and she looked at me closely. Our thoughts and our feelings were floating about us. At times the intimacy that was building between us was almost embarrassing. I had to remind myself that I wanted something of her. There was a power behind the silence of her incredible eyes, and there was a secret there. It was as if she wanted to share it with me, but was holding back. I can be quite sensitive to people's moods. It is important for a lawyer to know whether he is being told the truth. I always knew when my mother was hiding things from me. Here sat a woman who wanted to tell me something. Whatever it was, it was clamouring to get out.

And then, instead of coming out with what we both expected her to say, she started talking of the past. She talked of Cuba and how life there began to change, but all through her monologue I felt she was acting. She used big words and political clichés. Not the sort of words that came naturally. Her lips said one thing, her heart ached to say another.

Life was not that bad for her when Castro first came to power. She was not from a landowning family and the people, including the freedom fighters, loved her. She was an institution. She made a few films after the revolution and was still in demand overseas. The government had nominated an agent for her and she continued to tour and earn foreign currency for Cuba. Everything was centralized and private ownership was phased out. Like many Cuban businessmen, Abraham was put in charge of the company he had started. The country house where Martha had lived and the estate on which he bred his horses were confiscated. They still had his Havana flat and were able to stay there until they caught him dealing dollars on the black market. He had a source, she did not know where, of American medicines and spare parts for cars, and he sold them under the counter in exchange for other goods, mainly cigars. There was a great demand for Cuban cigars in the United States, and Abraham had found a way of getting them there. He still ran a car and there was always food to eat. He had surrendered his American passport during the old regime and now he did not want to leave the island because she was there and he had nowhere else to go.

At the beginning no one stopped people from leaving. On the contrary, Castro eliminated much of his opposition by allowing them to leave. He was not interested in what was said about him. After all, he was putting little Cuba on the map. Until Castro came to power, no one really knew about Cuba. By the end of the seventies, everybody did. Cuban soldiers fought battles far away from home. The country had managed to play the two superpowers one against the other. The little island that was almost annexed by the United States on more than one occasion over the years was now making Capitol Hill nervous.

I think she was bored with the conversation. It was all too factual, like an election manifesto. I had the feeling she wanted to end it but did not know how. I thought I'd give her a hand.

'Why did he not leave Cuba while there was time?' I asked.

'He never thought Castro would last. Not once he started nationalizing all these American companies. Cuba had always depended on the United States and Abraham thought the rift between the two would mend as soon as the economy dictated it. The Americans, he said, wouldn't just be sitting by, watching their enormous investments disappear. And as far as Cuban society was concerned, they wouldn't stand for Fidel for ever and the old order would come back. In this part of the would it always did.

'But Abraham was wrong because this was not the way it happened. He had been living in Cuba most of his life, but he did not understand the enthusiasm, the support Castro had. Even within the middle classes, from where Castro himself had come. Most of his lieutenants, too, came from the middle classes. He was young and attractive and he knew how to ignite the imagination of his listeners. Of course, the middle classes were soon disappointed with him but the masses loved him like a god. Castro did something no one ever succeeded in doing in a Latin country. He managed to break the back of the people who had ruled for centuries...the people who owned everything. And still do in Latin America. Castro broke the back of the oligarchy. That was big news in local politics.'

'Maybe he didn't understand politics, but Abraham was not stupid. Not as far as self-preservation was concerned. Surely he knew he was a marked man?'

'That is where you are wrong. Abraham was not the best of judges...not as far as his own safety was concerned. He always fell into dangerous situations, but when he was younger he was able to survive. He always thought the revolution would run out of steam, but Abraham ran out of time instead. Besides, I was there and could not leave. You see, I was an important part of the cultural life of the country and earned foreign currency. I was given a diplomatic passport when I travelled, but the minders that came along made sure I always returned. Abraham could have left any time. He knew how to arrange things. But he knew, too, how I loved my profession, and he said that as long as I had my career I would have to stay and he was not going to leave me behind. I protested. I said my singing would always take second place to him. I said I'd follow him anywhere and I meant it, even if he did not believe me.

'But that was not the only reason. I think he was afraid to leave. His failure to foresee events had taken his confidence away. Maybe he felt he was too old to start again, and he would never allow me to support him.'

'He could have gone to Miami,' I ventured. 'His old friend Chandler would have helped.'

'Yes. He would have helped, but he and Morton Chandler had fallen out and Abraham was too proud a man to beg.'

'He could have gone to Israel. That was where he was born. And he had made some good investments there... enough to retire on even then. Any Jew can immigrate to Israel. It's the law of return. A right. That's how Alex came. It's an integral part of the constitution. It's...'

'No,' she interrupted. 'No. Abraham could never go there. Never. Never.'

'Why?'

'I'm going to tell you, but not yet.'

She said this quietly and very definitely. With all the firmness she could convey without suggesting anger. She said it as though it were the ultimate truth, the last statement to be made about the man she had loved for so long. I had to respect that.

* * *

'Did he ever make his peace with Alex?'

'Yes. When he was arrested the second time.'

'The second time?'

'Yes. The first time he managed to escape. He never told me how. I was living in a small apartment in town after they took his flat away. Someone sent me his personal effects. Perhaps it was his son Alex...I don't know, I never discovered who it was, but it made me think Abraham had died in prison. I tried to get over my worry and depression by working harder than ever, but I wasn't very good at it. And then, one night, he appeared. He had grown old and grey and thin and his exuberance was gone. I looked after him all by myself. I had lost the maid we had and for almost a month he stayed indoors. *Dios mio*, how he suffered. He loved the open spaces and the bustle and he loved people and freedom. It was difficult for me, but it was hell for him. He went down and down and down until there was no more of his old self left. At times I was afraid to leave him alone there because I thought he would kill himself. And yet...and yet these were happy days. He talked to me about everything. He made some confessions. About places and people and deals and relationships I knew nothing about. That was when I realized he could never go back to his country of birth. There was too much for him to face there. Things that were buried in the past. Things that had taken their own course and were far from his reality here in Cuba after the revolution. Most of the people he had known were either in exile or dead or imprisoned. He had no money. His health had suffered and now he had lost his freedom of movement.

'Anyway, I had to work, you understand. I went on my tours while he was a non-person. He was outlawed and the rest of what he had was confiscated. He remained in my flat, hiding. I had left him enough food to eat. Cans and long-lasting vegetables and rice. He stayed there until someone decided to have the flat searched. They broke the lock and fell on him one night. He was taken back to prison. That was the second time.'

'How could he have survived all that?'

'Oh, Abraham was a strong man. I think he preferred to be in prison than alone at my place. He had made new friends even there. And there was the ex-police chief and other former captains of industry, wheeler-dealers and ageing former playboys. He had fun there because in jail he was with exciting people. Oh, you would never believe it, but it was during his second term in prison that he recovered. The old Abraham, his zest for life and optimistic energy, his charm and his ability to plan, came back, and only because he had an audience…because people flattered him and he needed that like air. More than air. Besides, soon after that Alex was put in prison too. That was when they made their peace. After that I knew he would never go. It became the most important thing to him. He was going to stay and find a way to make it up to his son…'

She stopped there and gave me that look again.

'Are you friendly with Alex?'

'As friendly as he will allow me to be.'

'Ask him about his time with his father in prison. He'll

tell you.'

'I'm not sure he will. He's a secretive man. He won't tell me a thing if it touches any sentiment in him.'

'You should try and get to know him.'

'I would like to. I don't know how. In any case, my business with him is almost over. He will probably disappear from my life for ever.'

'I doubt that very much.'

'Why do you say that?'

'Because blood is thicker than water.'

I took a deep breath.

'I don't understand you, Carmelita,' I said, but I knew something terrible was about to be said. I knew it was going to shock me. Explode in my face. Maybe I had suspected it all afternoon. Maybe I had begun to suspect it even earlier. Then she came out with it:

'You are Abraham's son, Mr Lawyer. Alex is your brother. There, I said it. I was going to tell you from the beginning but I was afraid. Afraid even to meet you in person before you knew. Maybe I was hoping you had worked it out for yourself. Alex is your brother. You are Abraham Moreno's son.'

* * *

I thought I was dying. That room, the whole world, was closing in on me, and the shrinking space was pressing against my chest. I was drowning. I could not breathe. I looked around for an open window. There was none. I needed to be by myself. To think. But my brain was misty and out of control. Pictures flew past. Places, faces and voices. It was a shock, but surely I must have suspected something. Not because of the way I looked, but because of what Danny and Alex had said to me. Or had tried to say to me. I strained to think of details. Of innuendoes and expressions and patterns of behaviour in Alex. I searched for fragments of conversation but my brain was congested. All sorts of emotions ran through me at speed. Warmth, love, hate and anger. The anger brought my mother into my mind and there she stayed. A much-needed target for all that fury. I thought of how she had lied to me all these years. And then I thought of my father and how he must have known the truth and yet had managed to be kind to me. I thought I heard Alex say something, thought I heard Joan crying. I thought it was surely a good time to die.

I looked at Carmelita. There was pain and compassion in her eyes. There was much she wanted to say and I could see she was fighting to keep the words inside. The room was silent for an eternity. Then, suddenly, she got up and put her hand on my shoulder. A bottle of Scotch appeared from nowhere. I took a long swig and then another. My head felt light. The room assumed its former dimensions and then I felt the stab of new doubts. What now? Who was I? What did my father's identity matter now that I had my own? What did anything matter? Had I suspected this all the time? Was that what Danny had tried to say that night? Was that the reason for my mother's strange interest in the Moreno affair? Carmelita handed me the bottle again. I took another swig and a warm feeling of carelessness engulfed me.

'I needed to tell you. I was too abrupt, too brutal. Maybe I hoped...maybe I thought...that you knew.'

'I did not.'

'I'm sorry.'

'Don't be. It had to be said. I'm pleased it was you who told me. Does Alex know?'

'Of course he does. His father told him all about it when they were in prison together. But I'm sure Alex had known about it long before that.'

'How long have you known, Carmelita?'

'I always knew. Ever since it happened. Ever since he came back from Palestine. We had no secrets from each other, Abraham and I. Painful as it was, there was only truth between us.'

'Was he in love with my mother?'

'Yes,' Carmelita said quickly. 'I am sure he was.'

'Don't tell me that to make me feel better. Please don't. There was, you said, only truth between Abraham and you. I want it to be the same for us too. I want the truth about him and my mother.'

'The truth? The truth is subjective…it depends on what a person believes.'

'Then tell me the truth of what you believe, please. Do you believe he was in love with my mother?'

'He was in lust, maybe…or maybe more. Yes, he loved your mother. Abraham loved all women. When your mother told him she was expecting his child he wanted her to come out here. She would not hear of it, and then Abraham did what he always did. You want me to tell you the truth. Well, God forgive me but I am. She told him she would not come and he made arrangements for her and for you and then…and then he forgot all about her. Or pretended to because he wanted to spare me the pain of it. After that life went on as before. He was like that in business. He always discharged his responsibilities. Always paid his debts. But with people and their emotions it was different. He knew little of relationships. Maybe Alex has inherited that from him. But not you. You know how to maintain a relationship, I'm sure you do.'

'Not always. I'm so confused. I wish I could speak to Alex now. There is so much to say. You know, I think he was trying to protect me from something. And then there is my mother. In all the years that have passed since my father – I mean her husband – left her, I…I wanted to know why. I know now. He was an English gentleman. He knew but he never said. I suppose he understood that I needed to have respect for her in order to grow up with some substance under my feet. He was a good man, selfless and strong. He had to be. Watching me and walking with me and talking to me must have been torture for him. My mother's betrayal, in the shape of my person, stared him in the eye every day, all the years we spent together when I lived in England. But he understood that I was not to blame. He could not love me but he tried to steer me in the right direction. I didn't always give him a chance and we didn't part company on good terms. He deserved better.'

I felt the blood leave my face. My throat hurt. I wiped my eyes and Carmelita looked at me and said:

'It wasn't your doing, my boy. Not your choice. Don't blame yourself. How can you? You didn't know.'

'But my mother...She never said a thing. Even adopted children are told they were adopted once they reach a certain age.'

'Don't be too hard on her.'

'What do you mean?'

'You would have to be a woman to understand how irresistible Abraham was. How kind, how considerate, how funny and understanding. He'd recognize a vulnerability and form an instant friendship with women. No, not just a friendship. Within minutes of meeting a woman he'd form a...yes, he'd form an instant intimacy with her. A closeness that would make her forget her inhibitions. A woman could ask him for anything, advice or help, and he'd come through with the right response without ever making her feel insignificant. He made a woman feel important. She could confide in him and feel she'd known him for years.'

'Did you forgive him?'

'Of course I forgave him. I loved him and I wanted him back. He was a child. You can't be angry with a child for ever.'

Just then my eyelids became unbearably heavy. My knees felt weak. I had been hungry and thirsty but now I was just tired. I stood up.

'I've got to leave now. I must think. I'm so tired.'

'You can stay here. I have a spare room. Use the telephone if you want. Call anywhere.'

'I have nothing to say to anyone right now. Thank you.'

'If there is anything you need, just call me. I will wake you up for some food at midnight. Your father liked his food best at that time, just before we went out. Havana was a gay place then.'

Chapter Thirty-Four

I slept like it was going to be the last time I was allowed to sleep. I lay on the wide soft bed and I thought I saw people come by and look down at me and whisper, and then the scenery changed. I thought I saw Abraham and my father and they were fighting a duel. Abraham and my other father, the English writer who had married my mother. It took place in a valley below Rosh Pina. To the east I could clearly see the Sea of Galilee while to the west there was a palm-lined tropical beach. Abraham was sitting on his horse and my English father was standing on his desk dressed in full uniform, with his service pistol in his hand. Across his chest, with the medals, there was a large picture of my wife. The two men looked at each other and they smiled. Then the wind started blowing and the place became dusty and I could not see them. The dust dispersed but still I could not see them. I strained my eyes but they were both surrounded by people. Danny was there, and Morton Chandler. I could not see his face but his name was written in gold letters on his T-shirt. There were about fifty Arab boys carrying a large placard that read 'Do not harm the man who saved our sister'. I could hear Abraham's horse's hoofs scrape the ground and hit something. Again there was dust everywhere.

Alex was there, wearing a Castro-like cap and khaki fatigues. He was standing on a little wooden stage with a microphone in one hand. In the other he held a long rolled leather whip. He seemed to be running the show. He looked at me and blew me a kiss and then he started counting to ten. In Hebrew.

'At last you're learning,' I heard my own voice say.

'Because you're my brother,' he said.

'Why didn't you tell me?'

'I don't want to talk about this now.'

'It's easy, you see?'

He looked at me and I thought he smiled. A new, cool, dustless wind blew at his hair and beard and his figure grew and grew until he became a giant and his image obliterated the scene.

'I can't see a thing,' I said.

'I'll fix it,' he said with a smile.

He lifted a large screen-like cloth into the air and shouted in my direction. The cloth was blood red. He waved it like a flag and went on shouting. I was not sure what language he was using, but his words were magic words and the wind stopped and the dust settled. My two fathers were back in view.

'You can see them now,' he said softly.

In front of him, lying down and tied to her glass-topped coffee table, was my mother.

Abraham and my father were making threatening noises at each other.

'She's not worth dying for,' I heard myself scream. 'She denied you. She denied him. She denied everybody. If she hadn't existed they would have been friends. Now look at them, killing each other over her.'

'They're not fighting over her,' Alex shouted.

'What are they fighting over?'

'I don't want to talk about that now.'

'Oh yes you do, brother dear,' I said. 'I will not stand for that shit any more. You will tell me. You will talk. Oh yes you will. You will talk about it right now.'

'I can't hear you,' Alex said.

I felt someone's arm on my shoulder shaking me gently.

'Wake up. You're having a bad dream,' Carmelita said.

'Just let me sleep five minutes more. One minute. That's all I need. I must get back there. I want Alex to tell me why they're fighting. I want to see what happens next. Please let me go back there. It won't take any time at all.'

'No one is fighting, my poor boy,' she said. 'You had a bad dream and you're hungry. You can go back to sleep later.

You'll have a better dream on a full stomach.'

I sat up and rubbed my eyes. Slowly, I began to observe things around me, and the more I saw the more relieved I felt, as though the dream had exorcized me. It was dark outside. The room was cool and I heard the air-conditioner humming in the corner. Then I noticed I had someone's pyjamas on.

'Your father's,' she said. 'That is all I have left of him. When I die I'll leave them for you. I know you will keep them because you're not bitter about me the way poor Alex was. I've washed and ironed your things. I love doing that. We always had maids, but when the revolution came and when your father stayed with me after he escaped I did everything for him myself. Maybe it was the happiest period. I loved it.'

'What's the time?'

'Midnight.'

I was fully awake. I said:

'I smell like a pig. I've been sweating.'

'I have run the bath for you.'

'Carmelita, you're an angel.'

'Not yet, I hope. Go have your bath. The rice is nearly done.'

'Did Danny know?'

'He suspected. I think he suspected. As soon as we met he tried to sound me out. He went about it in a roundabout way, you know, saying how alike you and Abraham were and everything…but I cut him short. He did not expect me to tell him the truth right away. But I did tell him. On our second evening I told him.'

'I think I know when that was. During one of our telephone conversations I thought he was trying to hint at something.'

'Maybe he wanted you to find out by yourself. It's always easier that way. He said Alex should be the one to tell you. Frankly, I would agree with that.'

'He didn't know Alex. He never met him.'

'I know, but he understood him. Danny was a man with great powers of intuition. When we discussed it…I mean after I had told him that Abraham was your father…I said I thought he should have written to you about it, told you the truth. But he said you were not ready for it. He said he had tried to tell you but that you were in a bad mood.'

'I was. I was rude to him and he told me off. How I wish I could talk to him one more time.'

'I do too. Danny was not a believer, but I know God will take him into his arms. After all, he died quickly without suffering. Maybe he didn't even wake up. He had what we Latins call *la muerte de un angel*…the death of an angel.'

I soaked in the softness of the bath water and sensed the sweet scent of the salts through the steam. The relaxing feel of the water induced a sense of optimism. I should really feel good about the way things had turned out. I had Alex. And Alex had a large family now. He might forget the loneliness of his childhood. My daughters had an uncle. They would love him and he would love them. I sank deeper into the water. The comfort of it would soon put me to sleep again. I must not sleep now. Carmelita was waiting. I lingered and somehow, in the safe warmth that surrounded me, I could feel my fears roll down my cheeks and my shoulders and my chest and disappear into the water.

* * *

Later we ate at her table. She drank cold water and I had beer. The food was delicious. Rice and peas, fried bananas, roasted chicken, mashed avocado in garlic and lime and boiled shrimps. A huge salad and white Cuban bread. In the centre of the table there was a lemon meringue pie.

'You made all this?'

'I could tell you a lie and say that I did. But I am too old to lie. No. I cannot cook. I was never a real housewife. In my youth my mother despaired of me. She said I'd never find a husband. I ordered it from the restaurant. You know, the place where I work. I will make the coffee all by myself, though, I promise you.'

'You shouldn't spend money on me.'

'If you understood us Cubans you wouldn't mention that. Hospitality is a way of life for us, a pleasure, not an obligation.'

'I'm sorry...I just thought you could not afford to spend money on me.'

'If you must look at it that way, remember your father spent plenty on me. He was a generous man. Even towards the end, when he had very little, he sold his watch and bought me a diamond ring. He said he had nothing but time and did not need a watch any more.'

'Did he ever talk about me?'

'Yes. He knew when you were born and he knew you were a boy. After your mother wrote to say her husband was coming back it was over for him. He thought the best he could do for you was to leave you alone. Your mother refused to come here. She wrote and said she was going back to her husband. There was no room for him there with the other man.'

'But the other man left her. As soon as he was back from the war, he left her.'

'Your father never knew that. I know he sent her money, but I don't know what she used it for. That was between the two of them. You'd have to ask your mother.'

I could just imagine what my mother would say. I could hear it.

I don't want to talk about that right now, she'd say.

Maybe I actually said it out loud for Carmelita looked at me with her big kind eyes and she spoke softly, almost in a whisper.

'Forgive me. I had no right to tell you what to say to your mother. You know, I could have been your mother. I have been thinking of that all evening, while you slept. I came over and I looked at you. I wanted Abraham's child but I am a barren woman. That is a great curse in this part of the world. It is a legal ground for divorce. I would have made a bad housewife and because I could have no children things could have been disastrous. But God has been generous with me. He gave me a voice and a talent to amuse, and he gave me Abraham to love. Do you have children?'

'Yes. Two daughters.'

'You love your wife a lot.'

'I do. Very much.'

'Danny said so.'

'Danny had insight.'

All of a sudden the heavy food and the beer were taking their toll. I strained to think. Abraham Moreno was my father. Where was the shock? How come I had taken the news so lightly? Had I expected something like this all the time? What was I going to say to my mother? To Joan? What was I going to tell my daughters? How were things going to be with Alex, now that he was my brother? Not once did I think of Abraham's property and its value. Or how it was going to make me a rich man. I had worked on this issue almost exclusively, but now it seemed to have lost all importance as the people involved assumed centre stage. As though what had started me on that road was no longer valid or viable or significant. The deal itself was cancelled out that night because it was no longer a deal. It had become a drama and I was a part of it. My eyes were heavy. I was going to call Joan but my head kept falling onto my chest. Maybe I wanted to run somewhere and get lost. To escape what was waiting for me in that new reality.

And yet, I thought, none of it really mattered any more. None of it could possibly make any difference to my life. Both Abraham and my father were dead and I was a grown man. I could not blame anyone. I must take responsibility. The last thing I remember was Carmelita pulling me to my feet and leading me back to bed. The room was cool and she tucked me in. I had a dreamless night.

Chapter Thirty-Five

I awoke and found myself in a strange room and I thought perhaps the whole thing had been a fantasy. Then I recognized where I was. It had not been a fantasy at all. It was the truth. I was Abraham's son and I had slept in his mistress's bed.

I felt rested. The nagging jet lag had gone and I sat up and thought about the situation and tried to see it in perspective. The man I believed had fathered me was not my father, but I was still the same man. The faults and the talents I possessed had not changed, my hopes had not changed. Most importantly, my desire to get my own family back was as strong as ever.

I had yet to give the news to Joan. During our last conversation she had been kind to me, but that did not mean she had forgiven me. Alex, who would now become an important part of both our lives, would not change just because I now knew the truth. He would still be a difficult man. It would be hard for him to become the loving brother I might have dreamed of in my drunken stupor.

I heard the main door slam. I got up and went into the bathroom.

Carmelita had laid out some shaving gear by the basin and on the mirror there was a note: 'Called the hotel to say you were here. Otherwise they might think you were kidnapped. Will be back soon. Fresh coffee in thermos flask.' What a woman. I called Joan.

'I was worried about you,' she said as soon as she heard my voice. 'We haven't heard from you in two days. Your secretary had no idea where you were. Don't you ever think of others?'

She was angry, but I could hear the relief in her voice.

'It's a long story,' I said, and regretted it. It was an unfortunate choice of words. It was precisely what I had said when she had demanded to know about my affair. The day I confessed and was kicked out. The day my troubles started.

She must have remembered this too because there was silence at her end of the line. Our truce was still fresh and shaky.

'You're not starting that again.'

'No, Joan, nothing of the kind. I've just come out of one shock. I wouldn't knowingly fall into another.'

'What happened? We called your hotel and they said you were staying with some woman...I didn't get the name. Who is she? Where are you staying?'

'In my father's mistress's place.'

'Your father's mistress? Have you gone mad?'

'Maybe I have. At the very least, I am someone else...I've changed. I'm not who you thought I was. Not even who I thought I was...'

'Have you been drinking? What are you saying to me?'

'You heard me, Joan. I'm not who I thought I was.'

'What do you mean?'

'I've just discovered that my father was not my father.'

'What do you mean?'

'You know the case I'm on...the Cuban immigrant whose father's property we're trying to find? Alex Moreno? I told you about him.'

'Yes.'

'Well, my client's father was my father too. We are brothers. Isn't that a scream? I thought it changed nothing but it seems to have affected me. I got truly drunk last night. I've been dreaming...I mean dreaming real nonsense. I feel confused. I need some time to sort myself out. I wish you were here.'

'Good God.'

'You can say that again. There's so much to think about...so much to tell. I wish...'

Again there was silence. For one moment I thought she'd suggest coming to join me. Then she said 'Good God' again and I mumbled something.

'You poor soul...I had no idea. I am so sorry I blew up. You must be going through hell. You must take a rest...take as much time as you need. Do whatever you think you must do.'

'That's just the trouble. I don't know what I must do.'

'When do you think you might be back?' she asked softly.

'In a day or so. I'm not thinking very clearly right now. Would you do something for me?'

'Anything.'

'Would you please ask my secretary to give Alex my client...no, not my client, ask her to give Alex my brother your telephone number. Ask her to tell him to contact you and arrange to meet you. As soon as possible. Ask her to tell him I'm begging him to do this for me. I would like you two to meet before I get back. I would like him to meet the girls. He has a family now and should get to know them as soon as possible. But don't tell him the last bit.'

'Why not?'

'He might run. He's a shy man. You'll understand when you meet him.'

'Why don't I call him myself?'

'I don't know where to find him.'

'You're not serious.'

'I don't know where he lives or where he goes. I never knew. He's a man of mystery, my brother. There will be a lot of adjustments for all of us to face. Especially him. Be gentle with him, Joan.'

At that moment I heard the door open. Carmelita came in. We waved at each other and she motioned me to take my time.

'Are you sure you want me to do this? Why me?'

'Because you're the only permanent, the only true person in my life. The only person in the world who can bring my brother and me close together.'

I heard Joan's breathing down the line. Could what I had said have hit home, or would she think I was lying? I looked at Carmelita and I saw her cross herself and mumble *Dios mio*. Then she smiled at me and touched her lips with her hand and blew me a kiss.

'Thank you for your trust,' Joan said softly, and I wanted to end the conversation right then. Maybe I was afraid she'd remember how much pain I had caused her.

'I have to go now. We'll talk again. I'll be back at my hotel later this evening.'

'Look after yourself.'

'I'll call you tonight…no, with the time difference it'll be too late. I'll call you tomorrow.'

'You can call me any time.'

'Thank you, but you need your sleep. Kiss the girls for me.'

'Do you want me to put them on?'

'Not now. Better not. You understand.'

She did not answer. She did not have to. I knew she understood. Maybe she understood even better than I did. We hung up. Carmelita came over to me and we hugged in silence. Maybe we cried a little.Then she spoke.

'Beautiful,' she said. 'It was a beautiful and rare thing you said to your wife. Better than all the flowers and all the diamonds in the world. You are a true romantic. You make your wife feel important. You know the words to say, those sincere words that can only come out of one heart if they are to touch another. Like my Abraham.'

'Thank you,' I said, and she nodded.

We sat down and she poured me some coffee.

'What made Abraham…my father…what made him go back to Palestine…after so long?'

'He had to get out of Havana.'

'Why?'

'He got involved with a couple of troublemakers. They were students at the university.'

'Students? I don't understand. How...'

'It's a long story.'

'Could you tell me about it?'

'There was trouble in Cuba at that time. Not in the streets

but at the university. The University of Havana was always a law unto itself. Political trouble there invariably spread to the rest of the city later. Even the Spaniards, during colonial times, experienced it...and they often tried to kill the problem before it became widespread. They once executed several medical students for suspected rebellion. But the dissent continued. Later, after the Spaniards had left, the newly independent Cuban government continued to have their share of trouble with the students. Traditionally, you see, every faction in the country had their representation at the university. The communists had a strong following there, as well as the right-wingers.

'In the mid-forties, just after the war, more people were able to enter higher education. With the new, wider span of different opinions, the university was almost like a parliament, but much more aggressive. The opposing sides formed groups that resembled street gangs in their violence, their secrecy and the fierce loyalty they held among themselves. Students or not, politics or not, members of these gangs openly assassinated each other's leaders.

'It was round about that time that Abraham needed to get away. He had to go quickly. Miami was not safe, and you will soon hear why. So he said he would visit his old country. He wanted me to go with him. You'll never know how much I wanted to go, but I had a concert tour planned and he went on his own. I never saw the Holy Land.'

'I'll make sure you see it soon. You'll be my guest.'

'You know, today I'm so very happy I did not go with him then.'

'Why?'

'If I had gone he would never have met your mother. Do you find this strange? I promise you it's not. Everything happens for the best, believe me. If Abraham had not met your mother there would have been no you. I'm happy you came into the world and into my life. Abraham lives through you.'

I looked into her eyes and I believed her and we hugged

again.

'We are friends, no? You're all I have from him now.'

'We are friends for ever,' I said.

'It was a good thing he went to the Holy Land...that he did not run to Miami. He would have been in serious trouble there.'

'What happened? '

'He killed someone.'

'Killed someone? Who?'

'One of the gangs at the university specialized in extortion. Of course, they all claimed they were using the money for poorer students and for the good of the country. They always do, don't they? Anyway, this particular gang would look for and find all sorts of dirt about certain people in high places. They would then offer it to anyone who could make political or business use of it. Sometimes they auctioned the information to the highest bidder. One of the companies they approached was Abraham's. They said they had some evidence to prove that his American friend Chandler was cheating the United States tax authorities. They were going to denounce him through the American embassy and demanded the sum of twenty-five thousand dollars to drop the matter. In 1946 this was a fortune. The speed with which Abraham was willing to pay up convinced them they were on to a long and profitable association. Within days, they demanded the same payment again and Abraham complied.

'After paying out fifty thousand dollars, Abraham realized they were never going to leave him alone. I'm sure he never told his friend Chandler about it. He simply did not want to worry him, but that was the way your father was. When the students demanded a third payment, Abraham invited the two leaders to his office. It was late in the evening and the three men were the only people there. Abraham laid the money on the table and apologized for it being in small denominations. He asked them to count it so that there would be no misunderstanding. While the two young men were hunched over the pile of notes, Abraham pulled a pistol out of his drawer and shot them both. One of the two was an American citizen. A communist history student whose father was a big wheel with the United Fruit Company. The other was a law student who was addicted to gambling and had run up enormous debts. It turned out they had gone into business for themselves. No one else knew about the money, and Abraham told me that most of it was still on them when he looked through their bags. None of it ever reached any of the so-called charitable causes it was meant for.

'The police chief was Abraham's friend. They managed to cover the whole thing up and the bodies were never found, but it was suggested he should go away for a while. The Americans made their own enquiries and the boy's father sent a private detective to Havana to find out what had happened. That was why he could not go to Miami. Instead, Abraham went to New York and from there to Palestine. The Foreign Office said he was already out of the country when the boys disappeared and that he couldn't have had anything to do with it. That is how it was.'

'How long was he gone for?'

'In all he was away for three months. A long, lonely three months. Then he came back, and as soon as I saw him I knew something had changed. We women have an intuition about such things. Oh, he loved me and he brought me beautiful presents, a Dior dress from Paris and a gold watch and much more, but I knew something had happened to him.'

'Do you believe in confessions, Carmelita? Do you think when someone has an affair he should tell his partner about it?'

'You have a reason for asking me that, and I do not know what the reason is, but I'll tell you what I think. Yes. You must confess. You must take your wife in your arms and tell her you love her and then confess. Tell her it is all over and never meant anything. Tell her it was a mistake. She may react badly. You might have to go through a lot of pain and humiliation, but so will she. Honesty is the only way to keep a relationship going. Honesty shows trust and respect and it takes much courage. These things always come out and I think it is best you tell her yourself.'

'I'm not so sure you're right.'

'If a relationship is strong it can survive anything, even betrayal. Anyway, your father and I had no secrets from one another. On the second or third day he told me about how he met your mother and what happened.'

'Why did he wait so long?'

'He wanted us to be together again. Maybe he wanted to reassure himself about his feelings for me or mine for him. He wanted me to know how much I meant to him. When he came back we stayed in a hotel and we did not leave the room. It was flowers and music and champagne and love. On the third morning he told me about your mother. About her being married. About her husband having been away in the British Army for years. As things turned out, it would have come out anyway after she wrote to say she was expecting his baby. Expecting you. He showed me the letter and he told me he was going to ask her to come over. He was not going to marry her, but he was going to do all he could to help her.'

'Tell me how they met, Carmelita.'

'Why do you want to know?'

'It will teach me something about my mother. I can never imagine her as...You know what I mean. She always seemed such a cold woman.'

'I am sure she is not cold. We women are strange sometimes. Talking about this with her might change your mind. Maybe you will see a side of her you have not seen before. Maybe it will bring you closer to her.'

'You tell me, Carmelita. Tell me how my father met my mother.'

'It is a personal story. Something that happened between

two people neither of whom is present here now. One of them was my man, your father Abraham. He told me about it...the way he saw it. There are two sides to every tale and I only know Abraham's. It would not be fair of me to tell you his side alone.'

'You don't understand, Carmelita. I just want a few details. Nothing of importance...the place, the occasion, the time of day.'

'Oh, but I do understand. The place, the occasion and the time of day are not details at all. These are vital elements in any meeting...as important as the state of mind of the individuals concerned. Were they happy at the time they met or were they sad? Was it a windy day, did it rain or was it night? Places, too, can have a profound effect on us women. Atmosphere...the position of the sun, the scent in the air. All these things joined together have their own life...their own vibrations. They can make all the difference.'

'Places have nothing to do with it. Only people matter...animal attraction.'

'For a man, maybe.'

'For my mother certainly.'

'You're wrong. I am sure of it. I am sorry you feel that way about her. You probably don't know what motivates her. I only heard your father's side of it. If you want to know more you must ask your mother and look beyond the words.'

'But what if...'

'Do not speak to me of this again.'

The resolution in her voice was unmistakable. Of course, she was a kind woman, and while I was with her she did everything for me. She always knew what was needed without being asked. But she flatly refused to talk about that subject any more, and I knew no amount of cajoling would change her mind.

Perhaps she refused to talk about it because the memory of it was painful still.

Chapter Thirty-Six

We parted company in her flat the day I went up to Palm Beach to meet Morton Chandler. It was a short, sad parting. I held Carmelita in my arms and felt her body shudder as she wept. There were tears in my eyes too. I wanted to talk but she put her hand over my lips and silenced me.

'Have a good life,' she said. 'Try and form some roots. That was your father's greatest weakness. He carried his roots with him and never let them take hold in any one place, with any one person. That was his tragedy.'

'But he had you. You were…'

'I was his love, I was his mother and his sister. I could not be his roots. Maybe because I could not have his child. We were so different and yet…'

It was my turn to put my hand on her lips.

'Hush,' I whispered.

'I will see you again,' she said.

'Of course. Maybe you'll come to Israel.'

'I think not. You come here. There is so much for your daughters to enjoy here. Disneyworld, the Seaquarium…you know.'

'I know. But most of all I'd like them to meet you…I'd like Joan to…'

'You'd better go. Do you have everything?'

'Yes. It's all packed safely in the car. I haven't taken Abraham's pyjamas.'

'They will be yours one day. I wish I had something else of his…'

'You have me.'

She crossed herself and looked at the ceiling and then she said:

'Yes. God is great. I have you.'

She was going back to work that day and I dropped her on the corner of Eighth Street. She did not want us to go as far as the restaurant. She stepped out of the car and I saw her walk down the road, her beautiful figure swaying like that of a young girl. I followed her with my eyes until she was lost among the people on the pavement.

The thought of her and the revelations that had cemented the short friendship between us sustained me through the long drive to Palm Beach.

* * *

The sight of Chandler's estate reminded me of Danny's first letter. He had described it down to the last detail and every bit of what he had said unfolded in full colour. It was the kind of place you see in programmes about the rich and famous. The security man at the gate lifted the barrier with a knowing smile as soon as I mentioned my name. I drove in and heard the humming of the tires on the pebbled driveway across the lawns. There were exotic plants and miniature lakes and close to the house I saw a couple of pink-necked flamingoes which moved gracefully out of my way. Morton Chandler was waiting by the door. He came towards me, his arms outstretched.

'Christ,' he whispered, 'you look just like him.'

I was going to have to get used to it, I thought to myself, and I smiled. Morton Chandler hugged me, slapped my back, pumped my hand and said:

'You don't just look like him...you move like him, you smile like him. You are an apparition. You are Abraham Moreno come back to life. You are...'

'I am his son.'

'You know about it, then.'

'I know about it.'

'When did you find out?'

'The day before yesterday.'

'Must have been quite a shock for you.'

'It was.'

'Danny knew. He guessed, although he only found out for sure after he met Abraham's mistress.'

'The lady has a name. Carmelita. You mean Carmelita.'

'Yeah, Carmelita. She told him or he wormed it out of her. Danny was the kind of guy you wanted to tell things to...to confide in.'

'When did you speak to him last?'

'The day before he died. I was still in Las Vegas. My last day. I go there, sometimes, to relax. It's decadent, I know, and one should not gamble when other people are starving. I was losing a fortune. Anyway, he called the house and said he wanted to talk. I don't know why they didn't give him the number. I usually stay at Caesar's Palace. My housekeeper passed the message on and I called him.'

'How did he sound?'

'Like a bar mitzvah kid before opening his presents. He was in a hurry. Told me he was going out with Carmelita. Told me what a great woman she was. How she made him feel young. How he thought he was falling in love. How he wished he could spend more time with her. What a lucky guy Abraham Moreno was. Anyway, that was when he told me he had found out about you being Abraham's son and stuff. When I asked him what you thought of it he said you didn't know yet. He figured it was going to be one hell of a surprise for you and wondered how he was going to tell you about it. He was going to take a few days off and spend some time with Carmelita. After that he was coming up here one more time, to stay with me and talk. But that was not to be. The funny thing was, after my conversation with Danny I went back to the tables. I won all I had lost and came out with more. I'm going to give it all away. He brought me luck before he died.'

'I think he might have brought some luck to us all.'

'God sure wants his own in a hurry up there, by his side.'

'When did you hear of his death?'

'I told you when I called you in Tel Aviv, remember? I had just come in from Las Vegas. Danny's hotel called. I had to go down to Miami myself to...you know, identify...'

'Yes. I'm sorry. I remember now. So much has happened

since.'

'I understand.'

'Do you know how it happened?'

'Yes. The porter told me. And the police. Danny had been out until late. They said he came back some time after midnight. Maybe one or two in the morning. He looked fantastic. The porter…you know, the old guy there…said he was as happy as a groom. Maybe he was even a little drunk. Anyway, he talked a lot that night. He told the porter he had met the love of his life and was going to become a Cuban. He couldn't promise he would stay a Cuban for long because he was an old man and his time was running out. He said if Carmelita would have him he'd marry her, and if she did not want to follow him back to his village, like women did in the Bible, he'd stay right here in Miami with her. He'd wait for her every day and play dominoes in the sunshine. The porter asked him if Carmelita knew this, and Danny winked and said he was going to break the good news to her the next day. He even did a little dance routine at reception and won an ovation.

'The lift was out of order. Danny had to walk up the stairs and the porter said he could hear him singing. He sang an old Spanish song. From the Civil War. About someone called Carmela. Then the singing stopped and the porter heard a thump from the first floor. He ran upstairs and he found Danny lying there. Right in front of his door. He said there was a smile on his face.

'"*La muerte de un angel*," the porter said to me. An angel's death, given only to saints. I said Danny did not believe in God, but the porter replied that it didn't matter. Maybe God believed in Danny. I can tell you he still had that smile on his face when I went to the morgue to identify him.'

Morton's eyes were moist. I thought about what he had told me and I nodded, and then I put my hand on his shoulder and said:

'I've arranged for Danny to go home. He should be

arriving today. Round about now.'

'Will his family be waiting?'

'Yes. I spoke to his daughter last night. They'll try and delay the funeral until I get there. I hope to leave tomorrow.'

'It would have been great to have had you here for longer, but I understand. Do you mind if I come along too?'

'You don't need to ask. I'd love you to. His daughter would love you to. And most of all, Danny would have loved you to.'

'Thank you. I'm going to charter a plane. You'll be my guest.'

'Isn't that hellishly expensive?'

He looked at me and then his eyes roamed over the wealth that surrounded us and he shrugged his shoulders as his lips formed an apologetic, sheepish smile.

'This is one time having dough comes in useful. It isn't that bad, though. I have a friend who owns a neat little jet. I get to use it at cost.'

He led me into the hall. There were tiled floors and white marble statues and indoor plants that made you feel you were in some old Roman garden. There was a liveried servant with a tray of cold drinks. Sombre classical piped music descended softly from somewhere. There were large paintings on the walls. Prowling state-of-the-art cameras recorded every movement we made. I asked if I could call Danny's daughter, and when she came on the line I told her about the arrangements I had made. She thanked me for my help and said the airline had informed her that the body was arriving that day. They were going to the airport in the afternoon. The funeral would take place in two days' time, up at the village. Would that be long enough for me to get back?

I said I'd see her there, and put her on to Morton Chandler. They chatted for a few minutes. He had tears in his eyes.

All the while I thought about Danny. How we met and how we were going to part in the same place, the old cemetery in the village of Rosh Pina in upper Galilee.

* * *

While Chandler and I were having a leisurely lunch my secretary called to say Alex Moreno was at the office. She said he was demanding I get back immediately and would not leave until I was there in person. He would stay the night on my couch if need be. I asked her to put me through to him. She said he refused to talk to me now. He was going to talk to me face to face or not at all. Not ever. He was in a bad way, she said. I asked her to suggest he stay the night in my flat. She came back on the line and said he had refused. He was, he had insisted, going to wait for me right where he was. If I wasn't coming, I would never see him again.

She said he had made enquiries and he knew there was a flight to New York that very afternoon. It would be leaving in two hours. I could make a British Airways connection to London that evening, and that would give me plenty of time to catch the morning El Al flight to Tel Aviv. I knew from my secretary's tone that I had no option but to comply with what Alex demanded. I told her I would arrive in Israel at lunch-time and come straight to the office. I asked her to find out the flight number and tell my wife. She said she was going to see my wife in person very soon because she was on her way to the office. She had arranged for her to meet Alex there. Wasn't that what I had asked her to do? Did I want her to call me when she got there? I said there was no point because I had to leave right away if I was to make the flight.

Chandler must have been a mind-reader. Perhaps he did have the mysterious gift of reading the stars. I did not need to explain to him why I was not able to accept any more of his lavish hospitality. He got straight to work. First he ordered a helicopter to take me to the airport, and then he proceeded to book all the seats for me. The woman at the other end of the line recognized his name. She told him she read his every word and that it was a privilege for her to serve him. I think that pleased him no end. When all the arrangements had been made I said I would pick him up as soon as he landed in Israel. He said he would fax the details to my office. We could catch up on anything else then.

* * *

The helicopter arrived quickly and I ran to the open door. Chandler waved. We took off and I looked down at the marvel of his compound and saw the tennis courts and the swimming pool. I thought if there was a heaven Danny would surely be there and see what I was looking at. He would be surprised, I thought, and remembered what the porter at El Gran Tucan had said. How God would recognize Danny even if Danny did not recognize God. I chuckled to myself, and I saw Chandler's diminishing figure still waving as he stood on his giant green lawn like a miniature king.

Chapter Thirty-Seven

When I stepped out of the customs hall I saw Alex. He had shaved his beard and his long pale face stood out among the tanned multitude. He was there with Joan and my daughters. Their eyes fished me out of the crowd and they cut loose and raced towards me and screamed and clambered all over me. It was heavenly. As I held the two wriggling bodies close to me I looked at him. He seemed taller than I remembered. Joan remained by his side, as if to let me have a private moment with the girls. She was wearing a light blue dress we had bought when we were in Rome the year before last. It was a favourite of mine and showed off her marvellous figure. That day she looked more beautiful than ever. I carried the girls in my arms while the porter followed behind.

Alex gave me his hand. I held it while my younger daughter clung to my neck. His face was gaunt and handsome. I felt as if it was the first time I had seen it. He had combed his hair and was wearing a suit. I looked at my wife and she winked, but she did not make a move towards me. Perhaps she wanted to stay in the background while I wrestled with facing this man for the first time as a brother. I walked towards her and her eyes shone.

'Hello,' I said.

'Hello, you,' Joan said. I stood there and wanted to hold her but it was the wrong moment for any intimacy. Her smile was one of those public smiles, there were people around and my arms were full.

'I see you two have met,' I said quietly. Joan nodded and Alex grunted something.

'We have a new uncle,' my elder girl chanted, 'but he can't talk.'

'He can't talk,' the little one repeated.

'Of course he can talk,' Joan said. 'It's just that he talks in another language.'

'Then how come he is our uncle?'

'Because he's your father's brother.'

'Is he, Daddy? Is he really our uncle?'

'Of course he is. Mummy told you so.'

'Is that why he had supper with us yesterday?'

'Yes. That's why.'

Alex stood there stiffly. I thought he looked embarrassed.

'Do you want my car?' Joan asked. 'We can take a taxi back to the house.'

'Can't we all fit in?'

'It's not that. Alex says you have to go to the office first.'

I did not want to go to the office first. I did not want to go anywhere first. Not with Alex or anybody. I wanted to go home with Joan. Take her in my arms and make love to her. As soon as we walked in. Untamed love. On the floor. Like we used to do when I came back from a trip or from the military. I wanted her then because all of a sudden she had that look on her face. The look she had all those years ago in Florence when she told me how she lusted after me.

'We can go to the office later,' I said.

'Come over for dinner tonight. You should spend some time alone. I think you have a lot to say to each other.'

She was right, of course. I said we'd take a cab. The girls hugged me and Joan smiled and said she'd catch up with me later and then they were gone.

I flagged down a taxi and Alex got in first. All the way into town we did not say a word. He looked sad, dejected. I put my arm around him, but he jerked away stiffly. Had I known then what I know now I would have persisted.

When we got to the office his expression changed. He even smiled at my secretary as we passed her paper-laden desk. From his pocket he took a box of chocolates and put it by her phone. He spoke quietly to her and in a still-tense voice he asked her how she was and thanked her for all her help. She was too shocked to answer, but she mustered a nervous smile.

We went into my room. He seemed happier there. More relaxed. I sat down behind my desk and leafed through the correspondence that had collected there. It was stacked in an unusually tidy heap. He sat on the table, a casual look in his eyes.

'Here we are,' I said in Spanish.

'You look tired,' he said.

'It was a traumatic trip.'

'You picked up a Cuban accent,' he said, and he smiled.

'I suppose I did. I lived around Eighth Street...and there was Carmelita. What a woman.'

He cleared his throat and I realized I had been insensitive. Whatever her character, Carmelita was the woman his father had preferred to his mother. The woman who had made his mother lonely. I was going to tell him she would rather have died than hurt anyone. I wanted to remind him how she had looked after Martha when she was ill, but he did not need reminding and this was not the time. We had all our lives for that, and much else had to be said first.

'I'll be posting some papers to this address,' Alex said.

'You'll have them in a few days.'

His attitude agitated me. Papers meant legal work and at that moment I was no lawyer. I was someone's newly discovered brother. I was bubbling with emotion and I shouted at him.

'Papers? What papers? What are you talking about?'

'You'll see. They're to do with Abraham's land.'

Of course. Abraham's land. I had forgotten about that. I had forgotten what he had come to see me for in the first place. Somehow, since Danny's death and my new awareness of Alex as a kinsman, the case of Abraham and his plots of land had paled into insignificance. I said I didn't want to talk about that now.

He looked at me sternly and slammed his fist down on the table. Clearly he did want to talk about it. I asked, almost in a whisper:

'What do you want me to do about all that?'

'What do you mean?'

'Do you want me to put the land on the market or what?'

'You can make any arrangements you like. As soon as you get the papers.'

'What sort of papers are they, Alex?'

'Wait a few days and you'll know.'

'Come on, Alex.'

'I don't want to discuss it now.'

'All right…but there is something I want to know.'

'What?'

'How was it between the two of you, Abraham and you, when you met again in the prison in Havana? Did you really make up?'

'I don't want to talk about it right now.'

'What do you want to talk about?'

'Nothing.'

'What are we doing here, then?'

'I wanted to be with you…just be.'

* * *

We sat there for a long time. I thought about how we would get on together. How we would never separate. How I would make him part of my life and family and business. He was, after all, a qualified lawyer, and we could soon get him to study and sit for the local exams. He'd join my firm. He could handle Latin American clients. Moreno Brothers, I thought. That was the first time it dawned on me. My name was not my father's name or my mother's. My name was Moreno. The same as Alex's. It was Joan's name and my daughters' too. I thought about changing it by deed poll.

If Joan took me back I would give him my flat until we found him something to buy. I would sell the land and with what we were going to get he could live anywhere he wanted. He would be a rich man and he was still young. He could get married. My mind was racing and I realized I knew so little about him. I didn't even know if he had ever married or if there was a woman in his life somewhere. Or children. I didn't know a thing. All I could hope for was that he'd stay. It was good having an older brother.

I saw him feel inside his jacket pockets and then he looked at me. A strange, uncomfortable expression emerged on his face then settled there. I knew what the reason for this expression was, and what would come next. This would be humiliating for him and I swore to myself that it would never happen again. I should offer before he asks, I thought. I was going to say something but he beat me to it.

'Can you give me a few shekels? I'm right out. I had to get some…'

I handed him all I had, but he took three hundred out and gave the rest back.

'You'll never need to worry about money again, Alex,' I said. I thought I saw a flash of pride in his eyes. He got up.

'I don't care for money.'

'But that was what you came here for.'

'No, it wasn't.'

'Why did you come here, then?'

'To meet you.'

'What are you going to do?'

'What do you mean?'

'Will you study Hebrew, will you go into law…?'

'I don't want to talk about that now.'

'Would you like to stay in the flat with me tonight?'

'No.'

'Will you, at least, come and join Joan and me and the girls for dinner?'

'No. I can't.'

'Why not?'

'I have made other arrangements. I have to see someone tonight.'

'Who?'

'You'll find out in good time.'

'Come on, Alex, surely we are beyond secrets now.'

'You'll find out. I'll not see you tonight. I have work to do. I've booked into a small hotel. That was why I asked for the money. Sorry.'

'Don't apologize. What's mine is yours. You are my brother.'

'Be nice to Joan. She's a wonderful person.'

'I know that.'

'You've been a silly boy, brother.'

'I know that too.'

'Women like that are rare.'

'How did you find that out in such a short time?'

'I have my ways.'

'Yes, I'm sure you do. Tell me, how did you two converse?'

'We managed.'

'Oh yes. I heard you at my mother's. You speak perfect English. I forgot.'

'You must have done.'

'What do you think of your nieces?'

'I haven't had time to think about that. I'm bad with children. I'm bad with family. I was an only child until Abraham came back from Palestine, and even then it took for ever until I met you. I've known about you for a long time, and for most of that time I hated you. You were not a real person to me then. More like a ghost. But I had other things on my mind. I was living through an exciting time in my country. I was fighting in the mountains along with the others. We were chasing Batista out of Cuba…the casinos, the whores, the exploiters. We were living in an exhilarating time. The whole world was watching us. We were fighting on the side of justice and progress. Up there I never thought of my father or of what he had done to my mother and to me…and to you, and to you too. But when you sail through wonderfully stormy waves into the calm of the rising sun you don't think about such things. There's no room for depressing thoughts then. And later…and later, when I was in jail, I had time to think about everything and I learned to accept you. Perhaps it was easy because I didn't imagine we'd ever meet, and yet…and yet my curiosity about you may have started then, when I had so much time on my hands. It was a curiosity that kept on growing and I came to the conclusion that you could not be blamed for what Abraham did. That curiosity took all these years to satisfy. I could perhaps have come here earlier, made an effort, but I suppose I was afraid…I don't feel comfortable with family. Not in theory and not in practice. To me it is a sad, lonely institution. A dimension full of empty rooms and silence over the dining table…of arguments and cruelty and illness. The only family I knew was unhappy.'

'All this will change.'

'We'll see,' he said, and then he walked round the desk towards me. I kept looking at him.

His eyes were soft. He stood by my side and his fingers ploughed through my hair.

'You need a haircut, little brother,' he said. 'My little brother.' He opened his arms to me. I fought back the tears as I got up and we hugged for the first time.

It was warm and wonderful and too short.

He tapped my shoulder, playfully pushed me back onto

my chair, and looked down at me. He pinched my cheek and smiled, and before I managed to tell him how much I liked that he was gone. My secretary came in.

'What's wrong with Mr Moreno?'

'What do you mean?'

'He smiled at me on the way out…but I could have sworn he was crying.'

'Is that what you came in to tell me?'

'Not just that. Here, you have a fax from Chandler.'

'You tell me what it says. I couldn't possibly concentrate on anything just now.'

'It says he couldn't get the private plane before next week. He's arriving today on a scheduled flight. I have all the details and have checked the estimated time of arrival. It's on time. It should land in an hour.'

'You'd better get me a car. And make hotel bookings for Mr Chandler.'

'I'm not finished. The fax says he's done all that already. He'll be staying at the Dan Carmel in Haifa. I took the liberty of booking you in there too. He wants to go up there straight from the airport. Meet you for dinner and then drive to Rosh Pina tomorrow.'

'Tomorrow? Why tomorrow?'

'With all the excitement of your return and the new Mr Moreno I forgot to tell you that Danny's sister called to say she couldn't delay the funeral any further. Religious reasons, she said. She did explain but I didn't understand. I'm sorry. Anyway, it'll take place tomorrow afternoon.'

'Does Chandler know?'

'Yes, he knows. That's what I am trying to tell you. Danny's sister said she'd told him about it over the phone. That's why he's flying in today.'

'I'm sorry. I'm a little slow right now.'

My secretary shook her head.

'You're going to need a rest,' she said, and left the room.

I called Joan. I did not expect her to be in. She was probably having her hair done or shopping for food. It was going to be one of those evenings of old. She wanted everything to be perfect for us. I was going to leave a message on her machine but I could not speak and hung up without saying a word.

A heavy anxiety entered me and took hold, like an anchor. I was Abraham's son and bore his name but Joan had adored my other father. Had she known all about Abraham Moreno she would have hated him. Would she take my accepting Abraham's place in my life as a betrayal of the man who had adopted her as his own, who loved her and always took her side? Would that make her change her mind about me? Would she see me as a reincarnation of Abraham?

I must be mad, I told myself. I could not be blamed for what had happened. It was my mother's sin. My mother's betrayal. There was no question of divided loyalties here. Both my fathers were dead and gone now, and the man she would live with henceforth was me and I had not changed. Or had I?

I needed to tell Joan that I could not see her that night and I dialled the number again. Soon her voice came on the line and I forced myself to think straight for a moment.

I started by saying that I was truly sorry and that it would be the last time. My voice was hoarse and weak and I stopped talking for a few seconds. What did I mean, the last time? The last time for what? But I had to speak or else she'd think I had been cut off. It would be the last time I wouldn't be able to accept a dinner invitation from her, I said. The last time she would cook for nothing. I said Danny's funeral was in Rosh Pina the following day and I had to be there. I said there were plans for me to stay over, but if I could I'd get back at some point, however late it was.

I was still talking to Joan's machine when my secretary came in and whispered that my mother was on the line. I motioned her to wait. I finished my message and apologized for the confusion and asked her to give my love to the girls. I put the phone down and asked my secretary to say I was busy and would call my mother later. She came back within two seconds.

'Your mother insists.'

'What do you mean?'

'She insists on talking to you now.'

'She can insist all she likes. Tell her I've just this minute arrived after a hellishly long flight. Tell her I've so much work to do I've no time even to go to the toilet. Tell her anything you want…just keep her off my back until I get back from the funeral. And don't tell her where I'm going or why. This has nothing to do with her…nothing. She doesn't run this office or my life, you understand?'

As I was about to leave I heard the phone ring. I looked at my secretary. She said my wife's lawyer was on the line.

I went back to my desk and picked the receiver up.

'You're back from your travels, I hear. You've been a long way this time. Country too small for you, is it?'

'I've no time for a chat, old friend. I'm in a tearing hurry.'

'I won't keep you. Just thought you ought to know.'

'What? Ought to know what?'

'Your client Alex has asked to see me. We're meeting for dinner tonight. This is strictly off the record, of course.'

'Of course.'

'You've put your cynical voice on again. What's eating you now?'

'Where do you know him from?'

'Your mother introduced him. She suggested he come to see me.'

'My mother…? What are you meeting him for?'

'I haven't the slightest idea. When he called I asked him the same question. I told him you were his lawyer. I told him we were friends and he said he knew that well. He said that was why he had called me. I agreed to meet for an informal dinner. Well, you told me a bit about him and how he's a strange sort of guy. I thought you might know what he wants to see me about.'

I said I didn't and hung up.

My anger at this new turn died as soon as I got to the car. I drove carefully and I cried.

Chapter Thirty-Eight

There were many people at the cemetery that day. Young and old, the villagers came to pay their respects to a man who had lived among them for most of their lives. Some left little stones or flowers on tombs of loved ones. Some whispered reminiscences; others held on to their grief in silence.

Danny's darkly clad son-in-law said the kaddish prayer for our friend's soul. The ancient Aramaic words rang out like the plangent notes of a bugle and my mind sailed. The speeches and laments passed over my head and flew away with the wind.

For miles around, as far as the eye could see, the land was dressed in the full bloom of spring. The Sea of Galilee spread below us and beyond was the breathtaking spectacle of the Golan Heights. Closer, rocky hills and pylons and freshly ploughed fields were gracefully flattened by distance. Trees and roads and plantations and animals and flowers and villages old and new. All converging on the violin-shaped, blue marvel of the ancient sea. I felt Carmelita's presence. I could almost hear myself telling her that this was the land Jesus had walked on.

Danny's sister and daughter looked into the dark hole into which he was being lowered. Their eyes were dry. As though they were thinking that it was not really Danny who was being buried, only his body. His soul was somewhere among us, and would live on and continue to make us laugh. The only sobbing came from Chandler, who held on to my arm.

'He was a hero,' he kept saying. 'He was a hero.'

His whole body was trembling and I took him for a stroll. I had to steady his faltering step. We looked at the gravestones and my eyes searched for Abraham's family but I could not find them. Danny would have known exactly where they were. I would come back, I promised myself.

With Joan and my daughters and Alex, once peace was restored to the family. We would make a day of it.

We went to Danny's house for the customary coffee and cake. Some of the village elders sitting in the corner chatted about him among themselves. They were laughing as they talked, and I thought Danny would have been pleased had he been there.

I took Chandler's arm again as we left the house. We sent his car back to Haifa and he got into the passenger seat beside me. Danny's sister waved from her verandah.

* * *

The day had begun the long process of dying by the time we reached the shores of the lake. The orange sun was beginning to dip behind the mountains to the west. Soon, the lights of settlements across the water would quiver under the stars. I knew the area well from the time of my military service.

'You must be dog tired,' he said.

'No more than you. I'm still on US time. My body thinks it's lunch-time.'

'Will you stay in Haifa tonight?'

'I'm afraid not. I have to see my mother. And later on we're having dinner at my wife's house. It was meant to happen yesterday but had to be cancelled. Alex and I and…'

'Things are looking up between you and your wife, eh?'

'I hope so. Look, Chandler, would you like to join us?'

'No thanks. I could use an early night. I'll catch up with you guys later in the week.'

'How did Abraham die?'

He was silent for a moment. I was watching the traffic and could not see his face, but I had the feeling he was embarrassed. Maybe the abrupt question had startled him. We were entering Tiberias. He pointed at one of the lakeside cafés and said something about a lunch he had had there twenty years before.

I was negotiating the curving road that was taking us up

the hill towards Haifa. 'How did Abraham die?' I repeated.

'Maybe you should talk about that with your brother.'

'No. I want you to tell me.'

'I'm through talking for a while. When Danny was in the States that's all I did. I talked for days into that machine. I told him all about Abraham's life. I'd prefer not to talk about his death just now. You'll understand.'

'I think I ought to know. It's just one more favour...for me. How did Abraham die, Chandler?'

'We've just buried Danny, for Pete's sake. Do we need to...isn't one piece of bad news enough?'

'I need to know...I really do. I mean, he was my father too.'

He made no comment as I fought the traffic, and then we reached the top of the hill. With the last moments of daylight the Sea of Galilee flashed brightly one more time and then it went grey. Shortly it would become black, and I knew it would remain so until the moon came out. The last thing we saw before we hit the wide Haifa road were the magical lights of Tiberias twinkling on. Chandler sighed deeply and said:

'You did know that Abraham came to Miami before he died, didn't you?'

'I know nothing. How did he manage to get out of Cuba?'

'Alex arranged that.'

'But how? I mean, wasn't Alex out of favour at that time? Wasn't he in jail?'

'Yes, but they have ways of doing things in Cuba. It's still a Latin island, left or right...people never change, whatever their politics. Alex had enemies, plenty of enemies. But then, like anyone else, he had friends too. Maybe they weren't friends, but they owed him. When you're down, there's always someone who owes you for something you did for him when you were up.'

'How? Who?'

'I think you'd better ask Alex about it.'

'He doesn't like to talk about his career.'

'I'm not surprised. With what he's got on his conscience, anyone else would lose all power of speech, I can tell you.'

'All right, Chandler, you've made your point.'

'I didn't mean to upset you.'

'You're not upsetting me. So Abraham came to Miami…never mind how. He came to call on you, did he?'

'Yes. He contacted me.'

'Did he ask you for money?'

'No, not money. I would have given him all he wanted, but he didn't need money, or if he did he didn't say so. At his stage of life and in his state of mind he was not interested in money. He wanted something else, but he took his time asking for it. It wasn't like him to keep things bottled up, but Abraham Moreno had changed beyond recognition. Oh, his looks had not altered much beyond what is normal for a man of his age, but his manner…boy, his manner was something else. There was another soul inside his body and that soul was a ruin. I'm happy my father did not live to see it. He admired him you know. Oh yes, Abraham was a changed man when I saw him last.'

'In what way?'

'I'm not sure I can tell you exactly. He went kind of quiet…he was no longer the wild, enthusiastic guy he used to be. He seemed…well, he seemed kind of spent, kind of scared even. And this was a man who used to be absolutely fearless. He'd go anywhere and talk to anyone. At the beginning, years before, when he first followed my father to Miami, he worked in collection for a couple of months…you know, calling in bad debts and stuff. He'd give them one look and they'd capitulate because they knew he wouldn't hesitate to take hostile action. Even if there was more than one of them there. Abraham Moreno never needed to rough anyone up or make threats. He'd go in there asking for what was due and before you knew it there'd be laughter in the place and he'd become a buddy. The other guy would pay up and they'd go have a beer or something. People liked his looks, his self-confidence, and they respected his strength. He was always at his best, always riveting, when there were people around. He was a very sociable man and the life and soul of any party.

'But when he came to see me that last time there was not a sign of that charisma. He didn't want to see anybody...he wanted to be on his own and booked himself into some creepy little hotel. A far cry from the crowded parties, the marble luxury of beachside suites and room service that were his trademark before. He never moved out of his room and he took to drinking on his own and I started to worry about him, so I got him to stay with us. He came up to the house but you wouldn't have known he was there. We hardly talked. He'd sit on the porch for hours staring at nothing. I figured there was something medically wrong with him. He had lost a lot of weight and was pale and his hair had gone all grey. The old elegance of white linen suits and panama he was famous for had vanished. He wore the same shabby jacket over the same pair of creased, ancient slacks, and kept himself to himself. He seemed to be mourning someone or something but I couldn't think who or what. I even got a shrink to come and check on him but Abraham refused to see him. I tried to talk to him myself, many times I tried, and in the end I concluded he had simply lost interest. And then, two or three weeks into his visit, I found out what it was he wanted.'

'And what was that?'

'He wanted to get hold of some stuff he had stored over here years ago. Papers he had kept in a safe deposit box in downtown Miami. Some kind of documents. I didn't know what they were, but from the expression on his face and the sense of urgency you would've thought they were a question of life and death. Suddenly he was in one hell of a rush. What I'm trying to say, I guess, is that Abraham had lost control. He went into a panic. No sooner had he told me about the stuff than he insisted we go down there right away and collect it. He was not sure he was ever coming back again and before picking anything up he needed to have someone reliable to look after it. I suggested myself.

'As soon as I said I'd do that for him the crisis was over and he told me to forget it. For a couple of days he relaxed and said no more about it. I began to think he'd made the whole thing up, and then one morning he slipped out, took a cab to Flagler Street all by himself and got the papers out. That evening after dinner he asked me to come out to the garden with him. There was no one around, but he insisted he wouldn't talk indoors, so we went outside. He kept looking over his shoulder and spoke quietly, like we were talking military secrets. That's what happens when you live in a dictatorship. He took this envelope from under his arm. You know the kind...big and official-looking with plenty of stamps and signatures all over. He handed it to me, gave me a serene look and said:

'"When you hear of my death you give this only to one of my sons."

'I had forgotten about you by then, and I assumed it was a slip of the tongue. I thought he meant to say "my one and only son" or some such thing.

'His English was never as good as his Spanish and it was late. He was tired and so was I, so I let it go. It was weird, though. Even the way he had said "When you hear of my death" sounded weird, but I didn't comment and I took the papers from him and put them in my safe. He seemed at ease after that. His expression was kind of tired...no, resigned. You know, as though he had come to the end of the road.

'The next day he came down to breakfast clean shaven, wearing a new blazer and it looked like some of his animated manner had come back. He spoke about Alex. Spoke softly and said nice things about him, like a man speaking of his favourite grandson. What he should have done for him and what he was going to do and so forth. There was an odd expression of relief on his face. Of deliverance. As though he had completed some last task he'd set himself. The last obligation of his life. He loosened up. More than that, he...well, his eyes looked like they'd just died and I witnessed one final change in him. I saw Abraham Moreno's passion for life being severed.

'He took off the next day and I figure he went to Cancun or Merida or Mexico City, where they've got flights to Havana every day.

'I guess I'll never know why he went, knowing they were going to throw him back into jail as soon as he landed. Maybe that was what he wanted. Maybe the tranquillity that seized him during our last breakfast came to him because he finally decided to set the record straight and pay his debts. Alex was still inside, and it could be he wanted to join him behind bars. Either to be punished for what he'd done to Martha or to compensate for the way he had treated Alex when he was a kid. Maybe he'd gone back because his woman Carmelita was still there. Everything is possible but I can't be sure. I never saw him again.'

'What happened to those documents?'

'I kept them for him and later I gave them to Alex when he came out of Cuba. I hadn't seen him in years. Not since he was a teenager, and I didn't recognize his voice on the phone until he said who he was and asked to come and see me. He was there in no time, as though he had called from some place around the corner expecting me to invite him over right away. Which, of course, I did.

'He came over with some other guy. Some Cuban who lived in Miami.'

'Juan Miret?'

'Maybe. Yeah, Juan Miret, that's him. Alex was leaving the next day. I don't know why, but I was positive he'd been out of Cuba for quite a while and I couldn't understand why he waited until the very last moment to come visit with me. Maybe he didn't like me very much, and I don't mind telling you the feeling was mutual. I think he went to Mexico first or maybe somewhere else, but now he was leaving and he came to collect the papers his father had left with me for safe-keeping. He never said where he was going but I figured it had to be Israel because that was the only place that would have him. I mean, they wouldn't let him stay in the States or anywhere else on account of who and what he was. On top of that, the papers he came to collect had to do with Israel, so I reckoned he was going there.'

'What sort of papers were they?'

'They were the deeds and documents relating to the land Abraham had bought here in this country after the war. When it was still Palestine. Maps and bills and receipts. The works. They weren't much in '46 but today they could solve all Alex's problems...and yours too, being his brother. That land must be worth a bundle now.'

'Yes,' I said quietly. 'It must be.'

That was all I said. I did not feel any anger or anxiety, nor was I surprised. For the rest of the journey Chandler talked of this and that and I watched the road and nodded or said 'yes' or 'really' whenever it appeared appropriate. Nothing important was said. No more than small-talk. I still knew nothing about Abraham's death.

It was pitch dark when we reached the outskirts of Haifa. The car climbed the curving road and we passed the golden-capped Bahai temple. Down below, by the quay, a few ships were arriving and others were departing and the world was going about its business. As we drove up towards the top of Mount Carmel, surrounded by the magnificent lights of the city and the bay, I thought of my brother Alex, and thinking of him made me feel wanted and needed and warm.

The calm manner in which I had accepted what Chandler had just said came as a surprise to me. Why hadn't I exploded? Why hadn't I thought of the months Alex had made me waste searching for evidence of Abraham's purchases? Was I tired of getting upset by my brother's strange ways, or had I simply got used to it?

They say a man gets a big shock when he hears bad news, and then the blow softens each time it happens again until finally there are no more surprises and all pain ceases. But that was not the reason for my calm.

Somehow I could no longer harbour any animosity

towards Alex. Not even for a few minutes. Somewhere in the complicated labyrinth that was his mind there had to be some explanation. Soon I was going to understand the reason for all the difficulties he had put me through. I was going to recognize the noble, selfless soul that he was, and my only regret is that I did not become aware of it earlier.

* * *

I am not really prone to mood changes. Israelis are known to be a loud and vivacious people. By local standards I might even say I am considered a rather quiet sort of man. My mother always said I had learned to keep cool during all the years I lived in England. I would have maintained this calm state but then, just as we pulled up in front of the Dan Carmel, I remembered Joan's lawyer and his call and the mystery of his meeting with Alex.

With this frustration my tranquillity was gone. I could have driven all the way to Mars and not once thought of my bed. The sudden energy that seized me threw me. It was not anger. It was not even curiosity. Maybe it was a desire to prevent Alex making any legal decisions that might harm him. Or maybe I was jealous because Alex had decided to confide in someone else. I was angry, but not with my brother. I was angry with the other lawyer. He was an old and trusted friend of mine, but he did not know Alex as well as I did. He could not possibly understand the vulnerability that lay behind the nonchalant attitude Alex projected. I would call my friend as soon as I got home and find out what the meeting was all about, and once that mystery was resolved I would sleep for a year.

When Morton Chandler said goodnight I got back into the car. My dormant anxiety was back with a vengeance. There was very little traffic on the coastal road to Tel Aviv and I put my foot down. The car flew.

When I got back to the apartment it was empty. I had hoped Alex would change his mind and stay with me but there was no sign of him. There was a short message on my answering machine. It was from my mother. She commanded me to call her as soon as I got back.

But I had to do that other thing first.

Chapter Thirty-Nine

'Is this the old Soviet Union?' Joan's lawyer said. 'Why are you calling in the middle of the night? I was asleep and you're frightening my wife.'

'I'm in no mood for jokes,' I said.

'And I'm in no mood to talk,' he said angrily, and hung up. I rang again.

'Is that you again?'

'Yes. It's me.'

'You've got a nerve, you know. Some of us are family men. Some of us keep normal hours.'

'Some of us forget what friendship is about.'

'It's not about waking people up at all hours...I wouldn't do that to you.'

'And I wouldn't steal any clients from you.'

'So that's what you're on about...'

'I need to know what Alex said and what was agreed and what was...'

'Are you asking me to break a client-lawyer confidence?'

'If there is such a break it was committed by you. Alex Moreno is my client.'

'"Was" is the operative word. He's my client now. There's a fax on your machine to that effect.'

'You're a fast worker.'

'On the insistence of your former client. At the end of dinner he made me go to my office and type the fax out myself. He went with me to make sure. Didn't leave until it was actually sent.'

'You're supposed to be my friend. You should never have

accepted.'

'When you understand what this is all about you'll agree I had no choice.'

'Give me a hint.'

'It's all being prepared. You'll soon know.'

'What does the fax say?'

'The usual. Alex Moreno no longer wishes to be represented by your firm…that sort of thing.'

'I still don't understand what's going on.'

'All the relevant documents are in my office now. You'll be in possession of everything by midday tomorrow. Your legal dealings with Alex are over.'

'He told you that?'

'You don't need to shout. Of course he told me that. I wouldn't act on his behalf otherwise. From now on you two are family, period. The land Abraham Moreno bought is safe. You'll be pleased to know we have all the documents now, deeds and all…well, all except for Abraham's will, but we have his death certificate and that of his wife and except for you two there are no surviving relatives.'

'Are you sure Alex doesn't have his father's will? He had all the rest.'

'I'm sure. You can forget all about that side of things. You can discuss commercial matters, but you'll no longer represent him legally. Not that there are any legal matters left between you.'

'This is outrageous.'

'Believe me, it's all for the best. How are things with Joan?'

'Why do you ask?'

'Because I care. You know I care. How is it?'

'I don't know. I've only just returned from the Galilee. I haven't spoken to her yet.'

'I hope…no, better than that, I'm sure it will work out for you.'

I hung up. I hadn't slept for many hours but I was wide awake. I thought of waiting until the morning before calling my mother but I was in no mood to wait. I was good and mad. I sat on the edge of the couch and dialled her number. She picked the phone up immediately. From the sound of her voice I could tell she had been expecting me to call. She was as alert as ever and she spoke first:

'How was the funeral?'

'That's not what you want us to talk about, is it?'

'No.'

'Why bother to ask, then? You don't believe in small-talk, do you? You always said people should get straight to the point. All the rest is a waste of time.'

'What is this I'm hearing?'

'You're hearing your own words, Mother.'

'What's the matter with you?'

'You know perfectly well what the matter is.'

'Perhaps we should postpone this conversation...'

'No way. This conversation is so overdue the words are burning in my throat. You've made me believe a lie. All my life you made me believe it. Worse, you made me live a lie.'

'We can't have this kind of discussion on the telephone. Maybe we should...'

'Good to see we agree on something...I'm on my way.'

I slammed the phone down and shot out of the flat. I did not wait for the lift but ran down the stairs. As soon as I got into the car I realized I should have called Joan first. She would have known how to calm me down. But perhaps I did not want to be calmed down. Perhaps I needed this anger to face up to my mother.

* * *

It must have been two o'clock in the morning. The streets were empty. The traffic lights kept changing colour but I ignored them and listened only to my screaming tyres as I took the corners. All I had on my mind was how I was going to deal with my mother. I would make her talk even if I had to force the words out of her. There would be no more excuses or double talk. It couldn't have taken me more than four or five minutes to get to her house. I parked in front of her entrance and rocketed up the stairs.

Like a ghost, her face lit by the yellow lamp on the wall, she stood by her open door. She was dressed in a white summer dress that was blown up around her by the air streaming out of the apartment, revealing her beautiful legs. She pressed the thin cotton down. Without smiling, she pushed her cheek in my direction for the habitual kiss, but I darted past her. The lights were all on and from the open window I could see the black void of the Mediterranean as it spread towards the star-studded horizon. The late spring night carried a warm, gentle wind that crept silently into the room. I sat down. I did not wait to catch my breath. I said:

'I've been waiting for this moment for over a week.'

'I've been waiting longer…years maybe.'

'Amazing…mother and son waiting that long for something as important and as natural as the truth.'

She sat down and we looked at each other. Her face was pale but she was ready for me.

'Not so amazing,' she said. 'The truth is often difficult.'

'Surely not between you and me. I'm your closest relative, for God's sake.'

'Especially between you and me. The truth can hurt.'

'You're damn right it can hurt, but it hurts less when you're a child. Children accept…they forget. That's why people tell children about these things when they're young. You should have told me.'

'I was going to.'

'Going to? What made you wait?'

'I don't know. Circumstances probably.'

'Were you hoping I would find out by myself?'

'Maybe I was. You have, anyway.'

'You're not getting away with it. I want to hear everything, and I want to hear it now, from you. I'm not going to go into all the problems your silence has caused…all the years I let that poor guy treat me like a son. I thought he was my father and I used him shamelessly. I let him give me a place to live and money and support and take me on holidays and be a grandfather to my girls and a confidant to my wife and all the time he knew he was not my…He did know, didn't he?'

She nodded, a model of restrained self-control, and said: 'Yes. He knew.'

'Poor bastard. What a homecoming he must have had. Imagine finding someone else's brat in your wife's arms.'

'That's not how it happened. He knew about you long before you were born. I wrote and told him what had happened.'

'You wrote? You wrote? Were you already that cruel then? The poor bastard.'

'Why poor bastard? He got the best of you in the end. He had you close to him for years, during the important years of your life. All the time you lived in England. He loved your wife and your daughters. You gave him a family. He always wanted a family and you gave him one and he followed his family back to this country…stayed here. Something I couldn't make him do.'

'You don't understand a thing. Other people's pain means nothing to you. You'll never know what torture you've put him through…and me. Of course he wanted a family, but he wanted his own family…his own flesh and blood, not some bastard son of an adventurer.'

'In his way he loved you like his own son.'

'What would you know about his feelings…about anyone's feelings?'

'You've become cynical.'

'Are you surprised? A man wakes up one morning to find his father is not his father…his name is not his name. He wakes up to find his mother has been lying to him…denying him the knowledge of his own birth. I don't know you at all. You're a stranger. A woman of mystery. I've no idea who and what you are. Tell me, what other lies are there in store for me? Are you Alex Moreno's mother too? Go on, tell me. I'd believe anything. Am I your son?'

'Yes, of course you're my son.'

'He was a decent man, your husband…much more decent than you. He trusted you like I did, and you went and whored with that renegade. How many others did you whore with while he was away fighting?'

'I won't have you talk to me like that. You'd better leave.'

'How many others?'

'Only once. Just that one time. Never before, while I was married. Only that once.'

'You expect me to believe this? Believe anything you have to say? If you were the good loyal wife you say you were before Abraham Moreno turned up, why that time? Why him?'

'You don't know what happened.'

'You're damn right I don't. You've never told me, but you'll tell me tonight. You'll tell me now.'

'I don't much like your tone of voice.'

'I don't care. Tell me.'

'Those were difficult days.'

'Spare me all that crap. I know there was a war. What happened to you happened to hundreds of women all over the world. But they didn't lie to their sons…they didn't make them live with this terrible denial. At some stage in their lives they were told.'

'We agreed to keep it from you.'

'We? Who is we?'

'My husband and I. We agreed that before he left.'

'Bullshit. It was your idea.'

'It was, but your father…my husband agreed. We were going to tell you about it later.'

'How long is later?'

'When you were little I had to work hard to build my agency. Then you went into the army and later to London to study law. There was always something, always something. I wanted to sit with you and tell you everything, but somehow I never got the chance.'

'Did you love Abraham?'

'I don't know if I loved him. I couldn't resist him.'

'That's it?'

'That's it.'

'Did he love you?'

'He never said he did.'

'You're not making any sense to me.'

'It didn't make much sense to me, either. Look, it happened over forty years ago. It was like in a dream...a mad dream. A mad, romantic, passionate two weeks that swept me off my feet. It was the only time in my life I lost control. There, now you know that too.'

'Not enough.'

'Not enough?'

'No. I want to know how it happened.'

* * *

She was no great talker at the best of times. Maybe I kept pressing her because I knew I was putting her through hell. Maybe I was being cruel. Maybe I wanted to humiliate her. I wanted her to apologize, but I knew she would never do that. And yet that night something about her was different. Even from what she had said so far I could see that a crack had appeared in the ice.

It was agony for her to tell any story. Especially a story as personal as this. She was strictly a staccato, two-line merchant who never went beyond recounting the bare facts in as brief a manner as possible. I did not expect her to rise above her usual where, when and how. But she was about to surprise me, and perhaps even herself.

* * *

Something else was missing that night. I did not think about it then, but all through her ordeal she never once pointed her finger at me. She said nothing about my own indiscretion, the brief affair that could still cost me my marriage. Could that have been because some of my English father's gentility had rubbed off on her? Could it be that, until that night was over, I did not know her at all?

We sat there and looked at each other and slowly, as the night wore on and the mist hovering over the sea started to dance upwards with the light, she talked. It was embarrassing for her because she was talking about her own betrayal, but she was open about it and did not hide a thing. Not even the most intimate feelings that had made her succumb. The woman who was my mother unfolded the circumstances of my conception with descriptive powers I never knew she had. And as I sat across the table and listened, it seemed to me that all she told me had happened to someone else. Some other man and woman I did not know and had no feelings about. I became someone else, a stranger, and I was listening to the confession of another stranger. A monologue. A novel that was being read to me the way novels are read to the blind.

I choose to remember it just as a tale.

Chapter Forty

My mother said:

'I met Abraham Moreno for the first time at the Café Piltz. It is still there but it has been refurbished and the atmosphere and what it stood for then are no more. There are many places in this town now, but once the Piltz was special. In the old days it was a popular meeting place where you could have a quiet drink or a dance in an elegant room overlooking the sea. They served good coffee and marvellous cakes and people came there to get away from the news of the war and the shortages. It was frequented by British Army officers on leave and affluent members of local society.

'I went there that Friday afternoon on my way back from the office. In those days I was considered a...well, a pretty woman. I was young then, in my mid-twenties. I had come to meet one of my husband's brother officers who was passing through town on his way back to England. My husband had written to me about him, and in his letter he enclosed a photograph of the man, to help me recognize him. With transport being very restricted just after the war he was not sure when his friend would arrive. He was not going to stay long, but while he was there, my husband wrote, he'd appreciate it if I'd take care of him.

'That Friday morning the man called me at the travel agency, and after a short, very polite conversation we arranged to meet at the Café Piltz. It was the only place we both knew. He had spent a few evenings there two years before, while stationed in Cairo, and I had been there a few times with my husband and once with a girlfriend.

'My husband's friend was not there when I arrived so I sat at the bar and ordered a gin and tonic and looked around. I felt very mature and sophisticated with the drink in my hand, because I was not used to going out by myself in those days. Business at the office had recently picked up and we were very busy and I was tired. I was wondering how long the man was going to stay and what he wanted to see and how much time it would all take, and then Abraham Moreno walked in. I noticed him immediately. I suppose everybody did.

'You should remember that we had just been through five long years of war. We had the Free Polish Army and the British and Australian troops and Italian prisoners of war. It had been a nerve-racking time, because everybody knew what would happen to us if Rommel crushed Egypt. Palestine was a melting-pot of immigrants and locals and black markets and, above all, there were shock waves about those horrible developments in Europe. The truth about the concentration camps had only just come out. You did not see too many well-dressed people around and most of the men who came into the Piltz were in uniform or locals, who never had much of a sense of dress, and the women they were chasing or hoping to chase. Nothing prepared me or anybody else for the kind of ostentatious elegance Abraham Moreno flaunted. And one more thing...nothing, but nothing, about him or his demeanour had any connection with the war we so badly wanted to forget, with the military or any other part of our own lives.

'He was then in his early forties. He was tall and tanned and a little hint of silver had started showing at the temple-edge of his coal-black hair. He was wearing a perfectly pressed white linen suit and a red bow tie and matching handkerchief. He had a panama hat in his hand and on his face he had a smile that made you forget where you were and why, because it made you feel instantly happy. He was a very handsome man. Almost, perhaps, too beautiful for a man, but his shoulders were broad and powerful and he walked with the agility of a tiger. There was an air of unmistakable, masculine opulence and pride in the way he carried himself, and at first I thought he must be some famous American film star.

'The waiters must have thought so too. As soon as he walked in and took his hat off, two of them raced towards him and showed him to the best table in the place. Friday was usually a very busy time, but they did not even ask him if he had a reservation.

'He stood there for a moment, and then he looked at me and handed them his hat and pointed at the bar. You would have thought he owned the place the way these two fussed over him. They more or less led him straight to me. He thanked them in Spanish and pulled out the stool next to me and sat down and ordered a Scotch, and all that time his eyes were glued to me as though I was the only person there. His eyes were pale blue and they gazed at me with such intensity I could hardly breathe. He really was stunning and the scent of his eau de Cologne reached me as soon as he opened his mouth to speak.

'I cannot recall what it was he said. He was conceited, I remember thinking, because he spoke in Spanish, taking it for granted that I understood the language and that I did not mind him talking to me. He had his hands on the bar. He had beautiful, well-manicured fingers, and in spite of the heat outside there was not one drop of sweat on his forehead.

'He said something more and then I looked at him and said in English:

'"I don't understand what you're saying."

'That wild, charming smile appeared again. It was not the greasy, cheap sort of smile you saw in films, spread over the faces of those so-called Latin lovers. It was assertive, yet at the same time it was helpless and gentle. His eyes, too, for all their strength and assurance, seemed to contain the sadness and sensitivity of the whole world.

'"I am new to this café," he said in English, and I heard his strong Hebrew accent and asked him if he spoke our language.

'"I was born in this country," he said in perfect, if old-fashioned, Hebrew, "a very long time ago. Long before you. I am probably the oldest man in the place. Maybe in the whole town. Yes, I speak the language, but it sounds much better coming from you. You must be a very educated girl."

'"What makes you say that?"

'"Oh, I know. I know because I was born a peasant. Long ago and far away in the upper Galilee. A sophisticated girl like you would never have been there, I bet."

'I asked him the name of his village and when he told me it was Rosh Pina I admitted I had not been there.

'"You see," he said, "this is a very small country and yet there are places no one but the locals know. When I was a boy, I did not travel much. Most of the people in my village lived and worked there all their lives. A few square miles of fields and walled gardens and a house, and maybe some hills and the distant shores of the lake, were their entire universe. Those who did travel far travelled very far indeed. The rest might have visited Jerusalem once, or Tiberias, but that was all. I only came here to Tel Aviv after I left the village."

'"Where have you been living?"

'"Cuba. It is an island in the Caribbean."

'"Are you in entertainment?"
'"Funny how everybody asks me that. Even at the hotel."
'"You look like an actor. Are you in that business?"
'"In a way I suppose I am. I have shares in a few nightclubs. I wheel and deal. I am in agriculture and canned fruits and a few other little things. Nothing that would interest you."
'"How long have you been away?"
'"Sixteen or seventeen years."
'"Why did you leave?"
'A shadow crossed his face then and he fell silent. That was when I caught my breath. Here I was, talking to a total stranger and asking him questions I had no business with as though I had known him all my life. You know I can't make small-talk. I never made friends easily and yet talking to him seemed the most natural thing in the world. The music stopped just then and I asked myself what I was doing and why, but then he spoke again and I was caught up in what he was saying.
'"I ran away."
'"Did you kill someone?"
'"In a way I did."
'"Who?"
'"Oh, he was an old Scottish doctor."
'"What did he do to you?"
'"Nothing. He was my lover's husband."
'"How…how did you kill him?"
'"I did not kill him, but it was I who caused his death. He had been kind to me. As kind as a father would be. So kind you wouldn't believe. I don't know why I'm telling you all this. Maybe because we might never see each other again. Or maybe because I feel we have known and trusted each other for many years. You have this quality, you know, the quality to understand others, and you have the ability to listen to them. Anyway, I was a very young man then and had never been out of our area before he came into my life. He took me out of the village and we travelled together. I

drove the car and acted as a bodyguard for him along the lonely routes we took. We travelled all over the Middle East – Cairo, Beirut, Damascus and Amman. I helped him with the language. Arabic, Hebrew…you know. He was a very religious man."

'"What was his wife like?"

'"What can I say? Had I met you then I would have felt exactly the same about you. How does a young farm boy see a beautiful woman, a woman of the world, who lures him away from his village, his family and friends? I wanted her from the first moment. She was an apparition, someone from Hollywood. The women I knew before were farmers' wives and daughters, who sweated in the sun and whose hands were hard…who cooked and cleaned and worked the fields and with time seemed all to look the same. Don't misunderstand me. They were, as human beings, far more valuable than I will ever be. They achieved something and believed in what they did while I did little more than spread misery. Anyway, she entered my limited dimension, like a being from another world. She was foreign. She was twenty-eight years old, she wore city clothes and jewellery and silken underwear, stuff you only saw in your dreams, and her perfume drove me mad. I don't need to go on in this vein. You are a woman of the world yourself and you understand all too well. On top of that, I have always had a restless soul. I would have left anyway…maybe she was only an excuse."

'He went on to tell me the whole tale. Of how she taught him about the world and the big cities and about clothes and table manners and, mostly, how she taught him about sex. About how sex was much more than sharing the grass with someone for a few moments before running home or back to the field.

'He told me the Scottish doctor and his wife took him away from his village and he stayed with them for two or three years and then he tried to escape.

'"Why?" I asked Abraham. "Why did you want to

escape?"

"'Maybe it was because I felt sorry for the old boy. He read the scriptures and prayed every minute of his spare time. He went to church but mostly he cured people. He was an eye specialist and there was plenty of work for him all over the place. He was the son of a rich landowner and he had a private income and never charged for his services. The villagers loved him and they offered him produce and chickens and eggs but he never accepted any more than a glass of water or a bitter cup of coffee. He was a legend and stories were told of him and his kindness, of his obsession with curing people's sight. There wasn't a town too far, a village too inaccessible for him to go to. The Scots are like that, because they are proud mountain people who have not forgotten what hardship is. Abu Eini, they called him, father of my eye. He was probably a saint."

"'She wasn't, was she…I mean, his wife?"

"'No. She was not a saint. If he was Jesus she was the Antichrist. She was the reason I went away. She became obsessed with me. She was jealous…even of her husband's affection for me. He wanted to adopt me and send me to school in England. He knew what was going on between us because she never tried to hide it, but it didn't seem to bother him at all. I think he saw me as her victim. Of course, he was most probably right. After she killed him I had to get away…"

"'How did she kill him?"

"'Oh, she injected him with something…I don't know what it was. Maybe it was insulin or maybe he was made to think it was insulin. Maybe it was some other concoction, but the name insulin has stuck with me for some reason. You probably know more about medicine than I do. He used to suffer from something and he was used to her giving him injections. She started off as his nurse and then he married her.

"'He died in a small village not far from the town of Gaza and the police came and she found some official she knew and he gave her the necessary papers and they shipped him to the shores of the Sea of Galilee. He was buried in Tiberias. That was where he wanted to be buried because there is a Scottish church there. At least she did that for him. No one knew about what had happened and to start with I thought it was the heat or old age or something else that had killed him, but she told me she had done it and said it was because of me. She did not want to share me with anyone. I could not report her, but after that there was no way I was going to stay with her. I dearly loved this man and now that he was gone I no longer wanted to be with her. That was why I left. Maybe I left because I was a coward, but then I don't think of myself as a coward. I don't know. I could not live with a woman who could do what she had done. I could never share a bed with her again, and as soon as the funeral was over I left her in Tiberias and started roaming the countryside. I worked in many places but did not settle.

'"She looked for me everywhere and then she found me in Haifa and she threatened me. She said if I did not stay with her she would tell the police I had killed her husband. She said that being a nurse she knew how to produce enough evidence to hang me. In British Palestine no one would accept my word against hers. I had no choice but to accept her offer and we travelled about for a while. I pretended all was well between us. It is easy to do that when you are young and your body still takes orders from your brain. We stayed in big hotels in Cairo and Beirut and she spent money like it was going out of fashion. She bought me clothes and a gold watch and anything she thought I wanted to have. I was pretending this would go on for ever, but all the time I was planning my escape. I realized I would have to go to the other side of the world to get away from her. That was how I left the country, but as I said before, with my itchy feet I would have gone anyway. The village was too small for me maybe. At least, that was what my father had always said."

'Again he stopped to think. By that time I had forgotten where we were and what I had come there for. Here was an older, most attractive man who looked up to me. Who talked to me as though I was his confessor. As though I was the one person who understood him. He did not try to hide his faults. His doubts. His vulnerability. In a way, his eyes were begging for forgiveness for all the wrong he had done without actually telling me what wrong it was. No, not forgiveness, more than that…he was asking for absolution. I was young in those days and always felt my well-read, educated husband knew so much more…was so much more than I was…and right here by my side was a mature man who looked to me, yes… to me… for answers, who took me seriously, and most of all, a man who seemed to place all his trust in me.

'I was too flattered, too pleased with myself to notice the attraction, the animal passion for this man which was getting a slow but impossibly firm hold on me. He was about to say something when the music stopped, a gong went, and then I heard my name being called and I looked up. There was a telephone call for me.

'"You don't come here much," Abraham said.

'"No. How do you know?"

'"They would have known who to call. They would not have needed to page you."

'I nodded and went over to the entrance. I picked the phone up. It was my husband's army friend.

'"I am still stuck in Jerusalem,' he said. "I am terribly sorry. Have I taken you much out of your way?"

'"Not at all. I live near here."

'"I won't be able to make it before tomorrow morning. And then I'll have very little time because they've got me on an RAF flight to London. Perhaps I ought to stick around here until I have the tickets in my hand. It will be some surprise for my wife. The last time I wrote was from India, and she expected me to travel by boat."

'"You'd better stay in Jerusalem…then go direct to Lydda airport. If you come here you might miss your chance to get on the flight."

'I don't know why I said that, or maybe I do, but he went on apologizing while my mind was elsewhere. All I wanted to do was get back to the bar and hear Abraham's story. Be with him. Watch him and smell him and absolve him of the crimes he was going to tell me about. I suppose I was looking for my own release, but I couldn't face that. My husband's friend was still talking, but I didn't hear what he said. Then there was a pause, and I thought he was waiting for me to say something.

'"How long is it since you've been in England?" I asked.

'"Same as your husband. Four years."

'"You stay put and get your ticket and don't miss the plane. Give my love to your wife."

'I didn't ask him when my husband would be back. He was stationed in Burma then, and it was likely to be many months before I saw him again. He didn't volunteer any information. He thanked me for my patience and my understanding and said he would be sure to contact me if he was ever in this neck of the woods again, and then we hung up. I had to stop myself from running. I must have looked pensive when I got back to the bar. Abraham got off his stool and waited for me to sit.

'He asked:

'"Bad news?"

'"No. The man I was supposed to meet here phoned to say he can't make it."

'"Someone stood up a girl like you? Stupid man."

'"It's not like that. He is a friend of my husband's. Just passing through."

'"Where is your husband?"

'"In the Orient. Where is your wife?"

'"You are assuming I have a wife."

'"Yes."

'"Why do you assume that?"

'"I don't know. I just do."

'"Well, you are right. I have a wife. I have a son, too. He is twelve years old."

'"Are they here with you?"
'"No. They are in Havana."
'"Is your wife from here?"
'"No. I met her in Cuba. She was a refugee from Germany."
'His answers seemed curt. He didn't speak of his wife with any great longing or affection, and I apologized for asking him such personal questions.
'"You have the right. I have been opening up to you...why shouldn't you ask personal questions? I feel I can talk to you. I feel we have known each other for ever. I am bad, but not all bad, and people tend to judge one another too quickly. You are not judging me at all, are you?"
'"No. But that is because we will probably never see one another again. Are you going to stay in this country now that you are back? Are you going to bring your..."
'"No. I am going back to Cuba. My life is there. I left here a long time ago. There are too many memories..."
'"Do you not have any family up there in the village?"
'"I do. I think my father is still alive. I have a brother..."
'"And you are not going up there?"
'"No."
'"You are not interested in them?"
'"We live in different worlds now. We have not been in touch since I left. They'd prefer it this way. I told you, I left under a cloud."
'"What kind of a cloud was that?"
'"Maybe I'll tell you and maybe I won't. I don't wish to wreck all you believe in."
'"You must do what you want to do. Tell me what you want to tell me."
'"Do you want to know?"
'"Yes."
'"Fine. You see, up in the village they always believed I killed the old doctor. Some said it openly and others didn't. After I left his wife I came home to the village, but all my father did was accuse me of murder and threaten me with

exposure. Day and night he taunted me with it. He said he was ashamed of what I was and what I did. He said I was not fit to live among honest and hard-working people. He said I was nothing more than an ungrateful parasite and a criminal. And so I left the village and never went back. These accusations were misguided, and after all these years I have no desire to exonerate myself of a crime I did not commit. I have done many bad things since. Yes. Bad things. Anyway, I didn't come here to look up relatives. I came here for something else."

"'What?"

"'Well, you see, my wife may want to emigrate here. Or my son perhaps. I want to make some investments here. In my line of business, and the way politics are in Cuba, you never know what will happen. I was thinking of buying some land."

"'This is a good time. There will be a boom here when peace comes, when all the Jews come to settle here...when Israel is an independent state. Yes, it's a good time."

"'You have a good head for business. Do you work for yourself?"

"'No. But I would like to one day."

"'You should. What is stopping you?"

"'I must learn all I can about the travel business, then make some capital. I don't know what my husband will want to do. He may not even want to come and live here. He never did get used to life in this country."

"'What about you?"

"'Oh, I would prefer to...I am staying here."

"'You are surrounded by nomads."

"'No. My husband is not a nomad. He just likes his own country better. He came from England."

"'You mean you might join him there?"

"'I might."

"'I suppose you are too young to have any children."

"'No. Not too young, but we have no children yet."

"'Too interested in your career?"

'"No. Maybe...I don't know. My husband has been away for a very long time. We've had a war here, Mr Moreno."

'"Call me Abraham."

'He gave me his hand and bent towards me and kissed me on the cheek. I felt the softness of his faultless skin and my face lingered close to his and then he kissed my lips. It was as though I had been waiting for that moment all my life. Waiting to be caught, if only once, in an exciting, uncontrollable whirlwind of passion. I did not even look around to see if anyone was watching. I was flying. I did not care. I had forgotten about my reputation and what people would say and everything. The world just ceased to exist, but within me, within every bone and every muscle, there was irresistible electricity. I was a mare on heat and lost control. There was nothing I could do about it. My heart palpitated...like in those novels you read, it palpitated...and we went to the dance-floor and embraced and that was how it started. I have talked enough. Maybe I have talked too much. I do not want to talk any more.'

* * *

The sun had sneaked up on us without warning. The night had been there one minute and suddenly it capitulated to an irrepressible onslaught of light. The world basked in day and the blue and green colours of the sea sparkled through the open window. My mother looked burned out. Her eyes were cold, and I knew I would never hear her speak to me like that again. My sense of calm had returned.

'So he loved you and left you,' I said. I got up and walked across to her and tried to hug her, but she lifted her arm and stopped me.

'You don't need to feel sorry for me.'

'He didn't just fuck you. He fucked up your marriage...your life...'

'Do you have to use such words?'

'He did, though. He had his fun and ran. What a shit my father was.'

'It wasn't like that.'

'What do you mean?'

'He wanted me to come to him as soon as he heard about you...about my pregnancy. He sent me money. A lot of money. I was able to buy this apartment and a share in the business. Later I bought it all. He did all he could do for me. All I let him do. What are you going to do about Alex?'

'What am I going to do? He's my brother. I'm going to take him into my business. He's a lawyer, and a clever one too. We won't exactly be poor, with Abraham's land.'

'You have all the documents now?'

'Yes. All except the will. But we'll find a way round that.'

My mother looked up at me and then she smiled. She said:

'I have Abraham's will. It was legalized before the Israeli consul in Miami. It deals with his property in this country. He left it to both of you. I didn't get a chance to tell you.'

'Why not?'

'We had to have this conversation first.'

'When did you get his will?'

'Oh, nine or ten years ago...Abraham sent it here. Of course, I couldn't tell you about it because you...well, because we had not had this conversation yet. I kept it at the office all those years, until last week.'

'What happened last week?'

'I gave Abraham's will to your brother Alex. We've spent some time together while you were away.'

'Why didn't you give it to me?'

'Because he asked me to let him do it. It seemed like a good idea.'

* * *

There was nothing more to say. I read a short story once. By Luigi Pirandello. I think it was called 'The Other Son'. In the story a woman is raped, and the child resulting from that rape grows up with her and every day he looks more and more like his father, the cruel man who violated her. Her son is a soft, considerate and caring man, but she cannot bring herself to get close to him. Even when all her other children leave her and go away to America, and he alone remains behind to shelter, feed and clothe her, still she cannot face him.

They all said I looked like Abraham. Danny, Carmelita and Morton Chandler. Was that why my mother had always kept me at arm's length? Was that why she never hugged me and never showed me any affection? Was that why she never kissed me goodnight? Did she hate me for what Abraham had done?

No. She was just a cold woman who had found real passion and had spent it all just once in her life. She herself had admitted it was the only time she dropped her guard. She was afraid to show her emotions after that. Would she change now? Would she allow herself to get closer to me now that we had come clean? Now that the secret was out?

My mother and her emotions and her love were not my concern at that moment. Suddenly I was tired. So tired I could have fallen asleep right there.

I got up and my mother picked up the phone and motioned me to sit. Her face had slammed shut on the past and on me and assumed its usual efficient expression. She dialled a number and listened and then I heard her tell Joan to come and take me home.

Chapter Forty-One

I awoke late that afternoon. I heard my daughters come in and out and I heard the television, but I could not open my eyes. It was only when I felt my wife's hand on my forehead that I realized where I was. I looked at her out of the corner of my eye. She smiled and I saw the compassion in her expression and heard it in her voice and with it I felt her forgiveness. She sat down and I longed to take hold of her but I feigned sleep until she said I might as well look at her.

'You've done it,' she said softly.

'Yes.'

'It can't have been easy for you.'

'It was. I was angry enough to tell her what was on my mind. I might have been a little rude but I have no regrets. She was magnificent. But I don't really want to talk about it now. I sound like my brother Alex...By the way, have you heard from him?'

'No.'

I sat up and we hugged in silence. I heard the sound of a cartoon the girls were watching next door. The room was filled with packages and cartons and I noticed two of my suitcases by the door. I was going to ask her something but she put her finger to my lips.

'I took the liberty of packing your stuff and moving it back here,' she whispered. I touched her chin and held her head and I kissed her. That way.

'Not now,' she said.

'I want you.'

'We have plenty of time.'

'I hope so. God, how I hope so.'

I felt a heaviness descend on my chest and creep upwards. My breathing came heavily and I fought to keep the tears out of my eyes.

'Has my secretary called?'

'Yes. She wants you at the office. There are some urgent documents you must look at.'

'I'd better go, then. Are we dining in?'

'You call and let me know how things stand,' she said, and she got up. 'You'd better get dressed. Your things are there on the hanger.'

I went into the bathroom and showered. The stinging water seemed to wash the previous months away. The lonely evenings, the regrets, the fights and the nasty telephone conversations seemed to disappear into the plug-hole with the foam. I dressed, and on my way out I kissed Joan and my daughters and they all looked at me and then went about their business. The girls did not cling to me or try to prolong the parting the way they did whenever I brought them home again after spending a rare day with them. They raced back to their television and Joan went back to her ironing as though I had never been away.

I got into my car and started it. My mother and the long night I had spent with her had vanished from my mind. All I was thinking about was how I was going to rehabilitate Alex and teach him to become part of me and our family. Take away the disappointments he had known and help him learn the language and get to know the country and bring him into the business as soon as possible. All those sweet plans I had made the day I saw him last, when he came to the airport and then to the office and we sat together and talked. I drove slowly, and for the first time in many months I was happy. I was home again and soon the office would become a home too, with Alex there with me.

The office was unusually quiet. My secretary greeted me from her desk and I walked into my room and sat down. There was a large envelope on the table. On it, in Alex's neat writing, was my name. Nothing else. I tore it open. There it was, all of it. The land documents and maps and the signed request for building permission and Abraham Moreno's death certificate and, on its own, wrapped in newspaper, his will.

There was a two-page handwritten letter from Alex. I tossed the thick pack of documents aside and settled back to read it.

My dear little brother,

Here you have it, hermanito, the legacy, that part of our

father you so wanted. I have told you before, money and possessions hold no fascination for me. And wouldn't even if they had come from another source. I hope you will not think me cruel for having made you work so hard for it. There were many times – to be precise – whenever you heard me shut you out with something like 'I don't want to discuss it now' – when I did want to tell you everything. Keeping you in the dark for so long was, I now know, as hard for me as it was for you, but I also know, little brother, that you are an intelligent man. You will work it all out for yourself. You will know, if you don't know already, why I had to take the road I took.

I have told you I am bad with family. That ballet of emotions other people perform with loved ones is alien to me. I do not think I can live in this country because it has become like most others. It does nothing for me, maybe because it was Abraham's…not the one from the Bible, but our Abraham's, our father's country. I do not want to be a successful lawyer or sit by the seashore and live on interest. I have got things to accomplish first, and if I fail I won't be the first man who has failed to convert an idea into a way of life.

I have taken five thousand dollars from your friend, my lawyer. The rest is my parting gift. I have given him a signed document leaving all Abraham's property to you alone. Would you kindly pay him back? It may sound corny, but by the time you read this, as they say, I will have left, and I suppose we shall not meet again.

Had I been born with a different character and nature I might have been able to stay and share the rest of time with you. I am happy you are back with Joan.

You want to know about the end. Well, you are entitled to it now that you know Abraham's beginning. He died in jail and, yes, in my arms.

Was it a moment of tenderness or did he try to atone?

Atonement only helps the sinner, not the victim.

Whichever it was, it came too late for me. It would only confuse the complicated life of an already complicated man. Make of it what you will.

In my way I love you more than I ever loved anyone or anything, except the liberation movement. Remember always to be considerate of others and nothing bad will happen to you.

Alex

His name was all alone at the bottom of the second page. It was separated from the rest as though mirroring his loneliness. It was simply scribbled there, in pencil, as if it were an afterthought, but then my brother Alex never did anything without meaning to do it. Maybe he wanted me to think of him as unimportant. I shall have to give this more thought.

* * *

I don't know how long I sat there. Of course I understood why he did what he did. All he wanted was for me to find out who my father was. That was why he came here. That was why he did not try to hide his identity from the Americans. They made him leave because he wanted them to make him leave. And me? My brother Alex wanted me to find out who Abraham was and what sort of man he was and then make my own mind up, without the shadow of his own hate for our father. I would have listened to everything he said and accepted his verdict without question, but that was not what he wanted. He wanted me to have the freedom to choose my feelings for Abraham by myself and for myself.

It takes a great and generous man to do that.

My secretary came in and I told her she could go home. I would lock up, I said. I lingered there for a little while longer and then I picked up the phone and called Joan. I said she could choose what she wanted us to do that evening, that I would be home soon.

* * *

The streets are full of people and cars and buses and taxis but this does not concern me. It will take me a long time to get home, but I am in no hurry. Many questions remain unanswered, many roads remain unmarked, but I shall have to look for the answers and for the route maps inside myself. Besides, some questions are never answered; and some things once started are never completed. I must not feel sorry for myself. The end often comes abruptly when you least expect it, and you are never ready.

I know I am never going to see my brother Alex again. He came for me and we were together and now he is away but not gone. He is with me most of my waking hours and sometimes in my dreams. I hear his footsteps in the corridor and I listen to his voice and see his sad eyes and his pale skin. In time, I know, all of it will join together and enter my soul and mingle with the rest of me and remain part of me until we find the answers when we all meet in the wilderness at the end of the road